To the elders and their wives at
Curtiss Street Bible Fellowship.
This dedication comes with my love,
thanks, and deepest admiration.

Acknowledgments

I so enjoy this page. It always gives me great joy to thank the people I love.

- Abby, for the covered bridge. It's extremely fun to have it in each book. Also, thanks for all your help with the names.

- Phil, for the seven Rs and all the hours spent on theocentricity.

- Jane, you ought to be on the payroll. Your generosity and encouragement are a blessing. Harvest House doesn't know it, but you might be their best salesperson.

- If I have my way, Mary, this will be the last time we have to rush. As always, you hung in there with me. All your perseverance does not go unnoticed.

- My Bob, for hanging in there throughout the process. This is book number 33! How did we do it? I know only this: God has used you in the most amazing way. Do you remember what you said that day long ago? *This is good—keep writing.* You know better than anyone that I did exactly that. It would never have happened without you.

LORI WICK

Just Above
a Whisper

HARVEST HOUSE PUBLISHERS
EUGENE, OREGON

All Scripture quotations are taken from the King James Version of the Bible.

Cover photo © Allison Miksch/Brand X Pictures/Getty Images

Cover by Terry Dugan Design, Minneapolis, Minnesota

JUST ABOVE A WHISPER
Copyright © 2005 by Lori Wick
Published by Harvest House Publishers
Eugene, Oregon 97402
www.harvesthousepublishers.com

Library of Congress Cataloging-in-Publication Data
Wick, Lori.
Just above a whisper / Lori Wick.
    p. cm.—(Tucker Mills trilogy ; bk. 2)
ISBN-13: 978-0-7369-1159-7 (pbk.)
ISBN-10: 0-7369-1159-6
1. Indentured servants—Fiction. 2. Women domestics—Fiction. 3. Housekeepers—Fiction. 4. New England—Fiction. 5. Bankers—Fiction. I. Title. II. Series.
PS3573.I237J87 2005
813'.54—dc22   2005009573

Printed in the United States of America

05 06 07 08 09 10 11 12 / BP-CF / 10 9 8 7 6 5 4 3 2 1

↭ Characters ↫

Maddie Randall — pregnant since the end of May
Jace Randall — her husband
Clara — works for Jace and Maddie
Doyle Shephard — Maddie's uncle, who owns the general store
Cathy Shephard — Maddie's aunt

Reese Thackery — an indentured servant
Mr. Zantow — the man who owns Reese's papers

Pastor Douglas Muldoon — pastor at one of the meetinghouses in town
Alison Muldoon — his wife
Their children: Hillary, Joshua, Peter, Martin, and Jeffrey

Conner Kingsley — owner of the Tucker Mills Bank
Troy Thaden — Conner's business partner
Dalton Kingsley — Conner's brother
Jamie Kingsley — Dalton's sick daughter

Some of the townsfolk:
Doc MacKay — the town doctor
Mrs. Greenlowe — Mr. Zantow builds a porch for her
Mr. Jenness — the bank manager
Mrs. Lillie Jenness — his wife
Gerald Jenness — their son
Mr. Leffler — the bank teller
Mr. Hank Somer — the town complainer
The Reverend Mr. Sullins — pastor at Commons Meetinghouse

Prologue

The coach had been built for comfort. It was plush and large and moved easily as the horses pulled it clear of the town limits and onto the road beyond. The two inside were comfortable as well, not only with the seats, but with each other.

"I'll miss Grandmother," the young man said, his voice changing often these days.

"We'll see her at Christmas," his sister reminded him, thinking that they'd not gotten out of town as soon as they'd planned. She was regretting there would be no daylight to travel in at all.

"Yes, but she looked so sad."

"She did, didn't she?"

"I think she has been since Grandfather died."

"He was her favorite person," the young woman said, her romantic heart sighing a little.

The 12-year-old wasn't willing to keep his seat any longer. He shifted over to sit next to his sister, never enjoying the dark rides home from Tucker Mills.

For a few miles they talked of nothing in particular. They knew their own mother would be looking for them in several hours and would begin to pace when the coach was late getting in.

The young man suddenly heard his sister chuckle.

7

"What are you laughing at?" he asked.

"I was remembering the other night when Grandmother began—" she started to tell him when she suddenly felt the coach begin to slow.

"Are you going to tell me?" he asked.

"Shh," his sister warned, her hand going to his arm with more strength than he expected. "Be quiet," she said. "Not a word."

By then the coach had stopped. Brother and sister sat very close, holding hands, listening to the conversation outside.

"Throw down your gold!" a voice snarled.

"We haven't any," one of the coachmen called back.

"Check inside," the voice commanded, and the two in the interior cowered in fear. By the time the door was wrenched open, they were terrified.

The highwaymen were not long in their work. Within ten minutes, it had started to rain. By then they had taken the goods they sought and left all four people dead or dying.

One

Tucker Mills, Massachusetts, 1839

Maddie Randall, working on a baby's quilt, happened to look out the window in time to see her husband heading toward the house. It was too early for their noon dinner, and there was plenty of weeding to be done in the fields at this time of the year. For a moment she wondered if he might be hurt. He was inside their farmhouse kitchen and calling for her before she had time to worry.

"Maddie?"

"Right here," she answered from the small room off the parlor, the room where she kept her sewing and needlework. Jace appeared in the doorway as she came to her feet.

"Is everything all right?" Maddie asked.

"Yes, sit back down," Jace directed. Knowing that the summer heat was causing swelling in her ankles, he realized that having her feet up was the best thing she could do. "Where's Clara?" he asked after kissing her, checking on the woman who came a few days a week to help Maddie in the house.

"Upstairs, I think."

Jace took the room's only other chair.

"Is something wrong?" Maddie asked, showing her tendency to be a worrier.

"No, I just came from town, and I wanted to talk to you."

Maddie knew a moment of dread but still calmly asked, "Did you stop and see Mr. Muldoon?"

"No," Jace replied, looking surprised. "I told you I wouldn't do that again without telling you first."

"Oh, that's right. I forgot."

"Have you figured it out yet, Maddie?" Jace asked patiently. "Do you know yet why my seeing Pastor Muldoon bothers you?"

"I think I finally do have it figured out. For a long time I was so fearful and upset that I was missing something God had for me, but then you convinced me that all was well. Now, you're not sure. You're asking questions about death and eternity, and I don't know what to think. You were the stable one, and I made you my rock."

"And now I've crumbled," Jace said quietly.

"That's just it!" Maddie exclaimed. "You haven't crumbled! You're not a crying, fearful mess like I was. You're confident that you'll gain answers, and you're willing to search until you do, not caring what anyone says or thinks."

"I care what *you* think. And I'll just keep apologizing for not listening to you sooner. You knew something wasn't right, Maddie, but I didn't see it."

Maddie sighed. They had had this conversation at least six times since she'd told him they were expecting and he'd announced his need to see Mr. Muldoon. Mr. Muldoon was one of the pastors in town, but he wasn't their pastor. At least, not yet. Maddie could tell even that was going to change. Her aunt and uncle attended services at the meetinghouse on the green, and she often went with them. But Mr. Muldoon's congregation was building their own meetinghouse. They had been worshiping together in the Muldoons' parlor and kitchen for years.

"I don't want you to be upset with me," Jace cut into her thoughts. "Or feeling like I've betrayed you."

"I don't feel that way," Maddie said, even as she remembered that a few weeks ago she did. "I just fear that you're going to go someplace and not take me along."

Jace took her hand. He held it tenderly, as tenderly as his eyes held hers.

"What kind of husband would I be to do that?" he asked, his fingers gently stroking hers. "We're going to stick together, the three of us."

"I know you won't leave me," Maddie cut in.

"I'm not talking about that, Maddie. I'm talking about all of us understanding what God wants and what is required of us."

"How can you be so sure?"

Jace didn't have an answer, but he did feel certain of one thing: After all of Maddie's searching, God would not turn her away. Jace's search for truth was relatively new, but he also believed that God would not reject him.

Maddie's hand slipped from his. She had wanted an answer, and the disappointment on her face told Jace he'd failed. Jace's mind searched for something to say, but he was out of words. He *did* want to go see Mr. Muldoon again but wasn't sure how to broach the idea with his wife. When she picked up her handwork again, he knew that now was not the time.

"Why did you go to town?" Maddie finally asked, her eyes on the tiny squares of fabric in her lap, her voice a bit tight.

Jace smiled very gently before admitting, "I had to see a man about a cradle."

Completely sorry for the things she'd been thinking, Maddie looked up. "Oh, Jace," was all she could manage.

"Don't give up, Maddie," Jace urged. "We can figure this out together."

Not sure if she believed this or not, Maddie didn't say anything, but when Jace reached for her hand again, she did not pull away.

Reese Thackery opened her bedroom door very slowly. She didn't have a large room, or a fancy one, but the door had a lock—something that was important to her. She moved as slowly as she could manage this day because the room had something else: a door that tended to squeak, sounding very loud in the early morning hours.

Mr. Zantow had not had a good night. He was never at his best when drinking, and last night had been worse than usual. Reese always thought about living and working elsewhere at these times, but it wasn't that simple. Reese Thackery was an indentured servant and had been for more than four years. It wasn't slavery, but in a very real sense, Mr. Zantow owned her.

From her small room that sat to the rear of the house, Reese made her way quietly into the kitchen, only to be startled by the sight of Mr. Zantow by the fire.

"Good morning," the servant said when she found her voice, wanting to laugh at how quiet she'd been, thinking him still asleep.

"Good morning, Reese," he said tiredly. His eyes closed as he balanced himself with a hand to the mantel. "Is there coffee?"

"I'll put it on right now."

Reese glanced his way when he moved slowly to the table and took a seat. It wasn't a large kitchen, so for her it was an invasion of space, but she kept to her task, casting occasional glances in his direction. Clearly he had a headache, and that seemed to be all that was on his mind.

Breakfast preparations began as soon as the coffee was on, and twice Reese forgot herself and began to hum. Humming was something she did as she worked. It was a natural part of her, but she knew that now was not the time. Even without looking behind her, she was certain that Mr. Zantow was not feeling better.

When the coffee was ready, she took him a cup and asked if he wanted cream.

"I want you to run an errand," he said, not having heard her question. "Go see Mrs. Greenlowe. Tell her I'll be late today."

"All right," she agreed with quiet relief. "Do you need anything else?"

"No, and don't hurry," he told her, thinking she was much too cheerful this morning.

Forgetting about breakfast for the moment and going down the back hall in order to leave by that door, Reese exited without further word. She walked past the fenced-in kitchen garden, overflowing with fruits and vegetables, and made her way onto the street.

Mr. Zantow worked with wood. He could turn his hand to any task that dealt with wood and end up with perfection. Right now he was repairing a porch for Mrs. Greenlowe. Reese knew it would last for at least 50 years when he was done. He never went to a job intoxicated, and his work was known around town as the best. He didn't work steadily in the winter, but come spring and summer, he was never without a task. He had a small workshop at the back of his property where he made furniture, but that work was sporadic, and he usually only turned out a few pieces each winter.

This past winter had been the exception. He'd had steady work making pews for the new meetinghouse in town. They weren't quite finished, but it wouldn't take long if he could keep his head. He also had a recent request for a cradle, all of which pleased Reese. She found that when Mr. Zantow was busy, he did less drinking. In fact, he was an easy man to work for until he got a little too deep into his cups. Unfortunately that happened every weekend and now some weeknights.

"Hello, Reese," Alison Muldoon called as Reese passed her house.

"Hello, Alison," she called in return, heading that way.

"Are you shopping this morning?" Alison asked. She was married to Reese's pastor, Douglas Muldoon.

"No, just running an errand and taking my time about it."

"How is Mr. Zantow this morning?"

"Not at his best." Reese's expression, which was almost

comical, said more than her words. "He sent me to tell Mrs. Greenlowe that he'll be late, and he doesn't want me to hurry back."

Alison's head tipped with interest. "How will you know when to return?"

Reese smiled. "I'll just force these long legs to walk slowly. If he's still not feeling well when I return, I'll find something quiet to do."

Alison returned the smile and invited her to stop and talk if she found herself at loose ends. She watched Reese go on her way, utterly captivated with the tall redhead.

Reese had come to them only six months past, having had a close call with Mr. Zantow and wanting to speak about it. Douglas had talked to her for more than three hours. Alison had joined them as much as time allowed. After hearing all that Douglas had to say about Jesus Christ, Reese confessed Him as her Savior. The months that followed had proved beyond a shadow of a doubt that her heart had been real.

Reese Thackery was remarkably humble and thirsty for knowledge of the Scriptures. She came with questions every week, never arguing but listening to each answer with a keen intelligence. And she never seemed to run out of energy. Joining the Muldoons for Sunday dinner when she was able, she never tired of the discussions they had or the concepts Douglas introduced to her. Alison thought she was one of the best things to happen to their small church family in a long time.

And to their own family. Reese was always swift to lend a hand with a meal or cleanup, and the Muldoon children adored her. She was good with the baby too, and he was less than six months old.

Alison shook herself from these mental wanderings and went back indoors. Her husband and five children would be looking for breakfast.

"Mrs. Greenlowe," Reese called out as she knocked, not sure if she would hear. "Mrs. Greenlowe, it's Reese."

The door took some time in opening.

"Come in, Reese," Mrs. Greenlowe invited when she saw the younger woman's face. "I want you to do something for me."

Not surprised by this request, Reese entered. She had learned never to be surprised by Mrs. Greenlowe, who was always busy with a project of some type.

"Do you see that tin on the top shelf?" The woman had taken her to the kitchen and now pointed to a high shelf.

"Yes, do you want it?"

"Please."

Without having to fully extend her arm, Reese retrieved the tin and handed it to Mrs. Greenlowe. As Reese stood there, the other woman opened the tin. Reese thought she was beyond surprise, but when the open tin revealed a pile of bank notes, her brows went up. Mrs. Greenlowe looked up and smiled, her eyes glinting with mischief.

"You won't tell anyone about my stash, will you, Reese?"

"No, ma'am." Reese grinned in return.

"You're a good girl, Reese." Having stuffed two notes into the pocket of her apron, Mrs. Greenlowe handed the tin back so Reese could replace it. "I don't trust banks, you know. Now, where's Zantow this morning?"

"He sent me to tell you he'd be a bit late."

"I don't trust men either," she proclaimed. "But Zantow does good work, and I'm willing to wait." She began to turn away but whipped back around. "Don't you tell him I said that!"

"I won't," Reese agreed, a small laugh escaping her.

"Come on," she turned once again. "Have some breakfast with me."

Reese fell to helping in the kitchen, laying the table, and putting the tea on. She did these things to the sound of Mrs. Greenlowe's voice. That lady had opinions on many issues, and Reese quietly heard her out.

"Your father didn't do right by you." This was the issue on Mrs. Greenlowe's mind as they finally sat at the table. "He had no business including you in the deal when he indentured himself."

Reese silently agreed but knew there was no point in commenting.

"Would you like me to pray?" Reese spoke for the first time in several minutes.

"Go ahead, Reese," Mrs. Greenlowe agreed quietly, respectfully bowing her head.

"Heavenly Father, I thank You for this food and for this day. Please bless Mrs. Greenlowe, and help Mr. Zantow to feel better. I pray in the name of Your Son. Amen."

"You didn't ask for a blessing on yourself," Mrs. Greenlowe commented immediately.

"I did earlier today," Reese replied cheerfully.

"You can't do it more than once?"

"I can," Reese clarified. "I just didn't this time."

"You're a good girl, Reese," her hostess commented again, bending over her plate to eat. Mrs. Greenlowe had always believed Reese to be a good girl for not rebelling against her circumstances. Reese didn't agree with her but knew that an explanation right now would fall on deaf ears. Reese hadn't rebelled, but neither did she think the label "good" fit her very well.

"What will keep you busy today?" Mrs. Greenlowe asked.

"I've got to get out into the garden. I'll be picking and putting up all week."

"Well, don't feel like you have to linger, but tell Zantow I want him here."

Reese was almost done, so there was no need to rush. She thanked Mrs. Greenlowe for breakfast and made her way back to the house. She knew a moment of relief to see that Mr. Zantow was just getting ready to head out.

He had no instructions for her, so Reese went about her business, more than happy to have the house and yard to herself.

Without further delay, she put on an old apron and went to work.

∞

About 24 hours later, Douglas Muldoon exited the new meeting-house, his son Martin beside him, and shut the door in their wake. They were still short two pews, but that didn't matter. They had met using chairs for a long time, and even though the room didn't look done without that last row, the pews they had would hold them.

His 17-year-old daughter Hillary had volunteered to clean the new building, along with a few of the other young ladies from the church family, and all was looking to be in order for their first Sunday.

Douglas was pleased, but he knew he would also miss the meetings they had held at the house for so many years. It had been a good time of hospitality, with great growth and fellowship.

"You look sad," Martin said.

"I'm not, Marty. I was just thinking about some things."

"Was it what we had for dinner? 'Cause I didn't like it either."

Douglas wanted to scold him for not being thankful, but all he could do was laugh.

"What didn't you like exactly?" he finally managed.

"Tomato pie. I thought it was going to be pumpkin or apple."

"Pumpkins and apples are not in season right now," Douglas said reasonably. "And you saw the cake your sister Hillary made. Did you really think your mother was going to serve a dessert in the middle of the meal?"

"Well, I hoped she would."

Douglas laughed again. Martin was six and as honest as the day was long. At times he needed to be reminded to be thankful, but he was refreshingly forthcoming, and right now Douglas didn't have the heart to get after him.

"Did you eat some of the tomato pie?"

"Yes, a small piece."

"And once you realized it wasn't dessert, did you enjoy it?"

The face he gave Douglas told he wanted to say yes but couldn't manage.

Douglas fought the laughter this time, but he did smile. With a gentle hand to his son's small shoulder, he simply steered him in the direction of home.

∞

Jace had let a few days pass. In fact, it was already Saturday evening. His questions were almost constantly on his mind, but he didn't allow his wife to know this. He wanted to make sure she felt comfortable and cared for right now. That concerned him more than his questions for Douglas Muldoon, but if he wasn't careful, Maddie would never believe that.

"How are you feeling?" Jace asked after evening tea, having noticed that Maddie had not been very hungry.

She frowned a little. "Why do you ask?"

"You just didn't eat much. I hoped you weren't feeling sick."

Maddie hesitated. Jace watched her, wondering what he'd missed.

"I had a craving," she quietly admitted.

Not knowing what to say, Jace didn't comment.

"I was very hungry for pie."

"Well, we had that pie you served after dinner. Did you have some of that?"

"I ate the rest of it," she confessed. "Almost a whole pie. That's why I didn't want tea."

Jace's hand had come up to cover his upper lip, but that didn't hide the laughter in his eyes. Maddie glanced his way, but she didn't want to smile, so she looked swiftly away.

"You think I'm a pig, don't you?"

"No, I'm just glad you're not sick. I did wonder, however, why you didn't offer me anything sweet with tea. You always do."

"I have some cookies."

"It's all right. I'm fine."

Maddie heard the amusement in his voice but still wouldn't look at him. She knew that he watched her, but she couldn't stand to return his gaze.

"Maddie," Jace called to her and was ignored. "Madalyn," he tried, but she would have none of it.

She heard him move and knew that he would be beside her in a moment. She was on the sofa in the parlor, and he sat down, his arm sliding along the back until it brought him very close.

"Mrs. Randall," he whispered coaxingly.

This time she smiled and let him pull her head to his shoulder.

"I love you," he said.

"I love you too," Maddie replied, never tired of saying it or hearing it.

Jace held her close, truly glad she wasn't sick but also debating the question in his mind about services in the morning. He forced himself to push it aside. He wanted to attend where Mr. Muldoon taught, but something stopped him from mentioning it to his wife. He held her as well as his tongue, hoping there would be an opportunity the following week.

❧

Reese sat on the floor of her dark bedroom, her back against the door, and listened to Mr. Zantow bang around in the kitchen. It was late, and he'd just arrived back from the tavern. She knew the lock on her door worked, but when he was especially loud, she felt better blocking the door with her body as well.

She didn't want Sunday to end this way. Mr. Zantow usually

did most of his drinking on Saturday nights, but lately he'd added Sunday as well. Reese gave her head a little shake and remembered the nice time they'd had in the new meetinghouse that morning. Douglas had taught about faithfulness, and Reese had learned some surprising truths. She was glad no one made a big deal of the new building. It had been fun to see it done and to smell the freshly cut wood, but for the most part it was business as usual.

"Reese!" Mr. Zantow suddenly shouted, but Reese knew enough not to come out.

Mr. Zantow shouted one more time, but this time with less volume. Reese thought he might be wandering away, and she relaxed some. Debating whether she wanted to go to bed or sleep right where she was, Reese deliberately shifted her mind back to the sermon and what Douglas might tell them next week.

⚬⚬⚬

Maddie could hardly believe she was there, and with her husband beside her. She had watched this meetinghouse being built but had made herself not think about the pastor and the conversations they'd shared in the past. Now her own spouse had an interest that made hers look tame. He had questions and was determined to find answers.

Jace had asked Maddie midweek to think about going to the new meetinghouse with him and she'd agreed, but not until last night had she finally asked him why he was so urgent. His face and voice a mixture of humility and excitement, Jace had revealed everything.

"It's the baby," he had said softly. "I've never felt so excited and frightened at the same time. This is what I've dreamed. Almost from the moment I met you, I wanted this: a life with you, in our own home, and with children. Now that it's happening, I find I don't have all the answers. I can see this little person looking up to us and asking questions, and we can't tell him a thing."

"Do you remember when you asked me about what our children might believe?"

"I remember."

"I said that they would believe what we believe."

Maddie watched her husband grow speechless. She waited, but he was still quiet.

"Jace, what is it?"

"I don't know what I believe, Maddie. I'm not sure of anything. I can hardly think of anything else, it has me so bothered."

Maddie could have chosen to be angry, but she remembered how patient he'd been with her in the past. And in truth, she still had her own unanswered questions. They weren't made more urgent by the baby's arrival, but at night she was still inclined to fall asleep with her mind unsettled and confused. It wasn't at all restful.

"Are you all right?" Jace suddenly took her hand and bent toward her.

Maddie nodded, glad they were in one of the back pews. She felt as though everyone had stared at them, and many people had looked when they came in, but the faces had been smiling, and Maddie remembered the one other time she'd met with this church family. Her sister-in-law had been with her, and everyone had been extremely kind and welcoming.

A moment later, Douglas Muldoon was up front, smiling and welcoming the congregation. Maddie's apprehension melted away in the next few minutes. Indeed she might have been alone in the room. She hung on every word spoken and listened carefully to the verses read and songs sung.

She didn't want to talk right now—she might miss something—but just as soon as the service was over, she would thank her husband for bringing her along.

"We've been invited to the Muldoons' for dinner," Jace told Maddie as they exited the meetinghouse.

"Who invited us?" Maddie asked quietly, her eyes huge.

"Mr. Muldoon."

Maddie's mouth opened, but no words came out. Jace watched her.

"We don't have to go," he started, but Maddie had taken his arm.

"Please, Jace, don't go without me."

He knew she wasn't talking about dinner. Not caring if anyone noticed, Jace put his arms around her.

"Remember what I said about giving up?"

"Yes."

"We won't do that. Not on our questions, and not on each other."

"What if he can't answer our questions?"

"I don't think that's our problem, Maddie. I think we're in greater danger of not wanting the answers."

Maddie looked up at him, knowing how true it was.

"Maddie?" Jace asked quietly, calling her name and leaving it up to her.

"Let's go to the Muldoons'," Maddie answered, not sure if the fluttering under her ribs was about the decision she'd just made or the dinner to follow.

Two

"You mentioned a verse about creation," Jace mentioned over dinner in the Muldoons' parlor.

Douglas nodded, and Jace took that as permission to continue.

"If the gospel is the news that Jesus Christ died for the sins of man, I don't understand how you tied that verse into the gospel."

"Did you catch my use of the word 'theocentricity' this morning?" Douglas asked.

"I think so."

"Are you familiar with that word?"

"No, but I know it's talking about something being in the center."

"That's right. *Theo* is the Greek word for God. *God*-centered. God in the center."

"The center of what?"

"Of everything: creation, Scripture, our lives. There is no better place to start to get a grip on that truth than Genesis, because it shows God's authority over His creation. And that tells us that He's to be the center of our lives."

Jace nodded, taking it in, not aware of what was going on with his wife.

"Mother," Hillary said quietly from the other end of the table. Alison leaned toward her daughter.

"Is Maddie all right?"

Alison looked toward Maddie to see what her daughter was talking about and found their guest very pale. The men were still talking, and Maddie was listening, but Alison stretched her hand over and touched her arm.

"Are you feeling all right?" she asked quietly.

Maddie felt a little light-headed but didn't want to interrupt the conversation. She gave Alison a smile and a nod, but the older woman was not convinced. She was still watching her when Jace looked Maddie's way.

"Maddie?" he began.

"I'm all right," she said, not sure what everyone was seeing but not feeling all that bad. "May I ask a question?"

"Certainly," her husband agreed, his eyes still watchful.

"Is there a verse that talks about this theocentricity?"

"All of Scripture is theocentric," Douglas explained. "But one of my favorite verses on that subject is John 1:3, which says, 'All things were made by him; and without him was not anything made that was made.' And also the first chapter of Colossians, which says in part, 'For by him were all things created, that are in heaven, and that are in earth, visible and invisible, whether they be thrones, or dominions, or principalities, or powers—all things were created by him, and for him; and he is before all things, and by him all things consist. And he is the head of the body, the church; who is the beginning, the firstborn from the dead, that in all things he might have the preeminence. For it pleased the Father that in him should all fullness dwell.'"

"Do you have the whole Bible memorized?" Maddie had to ask.

"I wish I did, Maddie. I can recite those verses for you because our church family has been studying that subject for a long time."

Douglas glanced at his wife and found her hiding a smile. Douglas had to do the same. Alison often said he had every verse of Scripture memorized. It was a common teasing point between them.

It was not long, however, before they turned their attention back to their guests: Douglas to the questions Jace and Maddie had, and Alison with a "mother's" eye on Maddie's pallor.

∞

"Reese," Mr. Zantow called from the table in the parlor during his Sunday dinner. Reese left her dinner at the kitchen table and went to him.

"Do we have any more of that berry preserve you put up last summer?"

"I think so," Reese answered, turning back to the kitchen to look.

Had someone been watching them—someone who didn't know the details—they would have been amazed at the transformation. Reese found the jam, gave it to Mr. Zantow, and was thanked for her efforts.

When Mr. Zantow was not drunk, he was not an unkind individual, and he treated Reese with a detached level of courtesy. They were not friends; she was very clearly his servant. It was only when he was drunk that he frightened her.

Reese's papers bound her for two more years, but she had thought a number of times that if she didn't have to live in the same house with Mr. Zantow, she could easily go on working for him.

Looking for dessert, he came into the kitchen when he was done with the meal she had fixed. Sometimes he called for it, and sometimes he came seeking.

"Is there dessert?" he asked, knowing there would be.

Reese stood up again, having grown used to the fact that she towered over him. He was a small man, slimly built and not even of an average height. Standing almost a foot above him,

Reese thought she could pick out the top of his balding head in a snowstorm.

"Whortleberry pudding," she said, plucking the pan from the shelf by the hearth, knowing it would still be warm. "Do you want me to serve it up, or do you want the whole pan?"

"You can serve it," he told her, taking the coffeepot with him and returning to the parlor. "With cream," he called back to her, and Reese served a generous portion for him and covered it with cream.

She prepared her own dessert when she got back, wishing he'd not taken the coffee but content to sit and eat her own dessert before she was called again.

❦

"How are you feeling?" Cathy Shephard asked of her niece, Maddie.

"I feel fine, a little odd at times but no complaints."

The women had shared a warm hug before sitting down in the parlor. Cathy had been working in the kitchen, but she wanted a break.

"I worried a bit when you didn't come for services yesterday."

"We went to the other meetinghouse."

"Did you?" Cathy asked in a voice Maddie couldn't label. "Is the new building all done?"

"All but the last two pews. Mr. Zantow is still working on those."

"He does fine work."

The conversation came to a comfortable halt at that point, which gave Maddie a chance to think. For the first time, it occurred to her that her aunt knew nothing of the conversations she'd shared with Jace in the last few months, and she certainly didn't know about dinner yesterday. Jace had wanted to talk about theocentricity the rest of the day. Maddie had never considered how much God was in the center of everything, and she could feel her own excitement mounting.

"Do you have a long list today for the store?" Cathy asked. Cathy and her husband, Doyle Shephard, owned Tucker Mills' general store.

"No, Clara's over there now. I'll check on her later."

"You look a little tired."

"I am."

"Everything all right with you and Jace?"

"Yes," Maddie answered with a smile, thinking of how solicitous he'd been with her the whole day. Even amid his excitement about their dinner conversation, he had checked with her almost constantly.

"Put your feet up." Cathy suddenly stood and moved the footstool. Maddie took the offer and even fell asleep for a few minutes. Clara came looking for her not long afterward, and as soon as Cathy had put together a basket of baked goods for them, they returned to the Randall farm to work the rest of the day out.

୬୬

"Well, Reese," Mrs. Greenlowe popped her head out the front door to the almost-finished porch, a surprised look on her face. "Zantow is done for the day."

"Yes, but he forgot a tool, and I need to look for it."

"Well, come in when you're done and sit for a bit."

Reese's mouth was opening when the door shut. Reese would have to explain that Mr. Zantow was waiting. She began to look around the porch, spotting various tools but not seeing the one he had described. She didn't want to carry the entire lot back to the house, but it was looking as though she had no choice.

A little more searching ensued before she began to move boards. Finally she spotted it: a chisel. Reese took long enough to explain to Mrs. Greenlowe that she couldn't stay and started home.

A certain level of frustration filled her when it seemed that everyone she passed wanted to talk. On a day when Mr. Zantow told her to take her time, it was hard to find a soul who wanted to visit. He would never understand that the last person to stop her had been Mr. Somer, the town's complainer. He had decided to tell her all about his back and the remedy he was trying to alleviate the ache. Still shaking her head with the irony of it all, she sped up her pace, not wanting Mr. Zantow to be impatient with her.

"Maddie and I talked for a long time after we left here on Sunday," Jace told Douglas on Tuesday afternoon while sitting in the pastor's study. He hadn't planned to stop but had found himself with a little extra time. "She said I can come and see you whenever I like."

"You couldn't before?" Douglas clarified.

"Not without warning her that I was coming, and that's my own fault. Twice I came home and told her I'd been here, and she got upset. She had so many questions before we were married, but I told her everything was fine. Now I'm the one looking for answers."

"And it upsets her."

"Very much. I had convinced her that all was well, and by my asking questions, it's confused things in her mind all over again."

"Aren't you thankful?" Douglas suddenly asked, and Jace looked surprised.

"Yes," he agreed softly. "I guess I am. If Maddie hadn't been asking those questions all along, I don't know if my mind would have been so troubled."

"How is she feeling, by the way?"

"She's all right. She was so pale at the table on Sunday that it scared me a little. And she did admit to me later that she felt dizzy, but she didn't want to interrupt or miss anything."

"You both have good questions, Jace," Douglas said.

Jace shook his head a little, having a hard time believing that, but he was too desperate to argue the point.

"I have to get back to the farm, but I do have one final question."

"Let's have it."

"I want to believe that God would forgive me, but I've been smug and sure of myself. Now I want some part of Him, and what makes me think I have anything to bring or offer?"

"You don't, Jace," Douglas put it bluntly. "Well, you come with your sin, but nothing else. It's all on God's part, the grace and the saving. And the reason we can be certain of His love is because He tells us in His Word."

"It's always back to the Bible, isn't it?"

"Thankfully, yes. Nothing else stays the same. The Bible is consistent, understandable for all who believe. I stake my very existence on it."

"And you think that if I believe, God will accept me?"

"Yes. He's looking for humble hearts who know they need a Savior. He's waiting to be that Savior. He's the only one who qualifies."

"Because He was sinless."

Douglas was able to answer with a pleased nod, glad to know this man had been listening.

❧

While Jace sat in the study working to take this in, Alison answered the knock she heard on the front door. She found Reese on the porch.

"I'm sorry to bother you, Alison, but could I possibly speak with Douglas?"

"He's with someone, Reese. Can I help you?" she asked when she noticed Reese was trembling.

"I don't know."

"Come in," Alison offered kindly. Reese Thackery had the most amazing effect on the pastor's wife. She never saw her without wanting to say a kind word or do something for her.

"I didn't know who else to tell," Reese said when Alison followed her into the parlor. "Mr. Zantow is dead."

Alison's face filled with compassion. Just then a dish was dropped in the kitchen. It sounded as though something broke.

"Give me just a moment, Reese." Alison went swiftly that way and gave orders to her oldest son, Joshua, who was watching baby Jeffrey. When she returned to the parlor, shutting the door for privacy, it was only to pass through on the way to Douglas' study. Both Douglas and Jace joined Reese in the parlor.

"Reese," Douglas began. "How did it happen?"

"I don't know. He wanted me to run an errand, and when I got back, he was slumped over his worktable."

"Sit down, Reese," Douglas urged.

"I don't want to," she stated plainly.

No one debated the point, but neither could they miss the way she shook.

"I wished him dead before I came to Christ," she told Douglas, "but not anymore. I pray for him every day. He wasn't an easy man to live with, but I didn't hate him. I didn't know who else to tell."

"I'll tell you what we will do," Douglas said, taking charge. "We'll get Doc MacKay to check on him to be sure. All right?"

"I'll go get him," Jace offered, "and meet you there."

"Thank you," Douglas said, not even turning when Jace exited.

"Would you like something, Reese?" Alison spoke up. "Water or tea?"

"Maybe some water."

"Are you sure you don't wish to sit down?" Douglas asked as soon as his wife exited.

"I don't think so," Reese answered, but the hand she put to her face shook.

The next few minutes passed in something of a haze for Reese. She didn't remember drinking the water Alison handed her or accompanying Douglas out the door, but five minutes later they were at the workshop, entering to find Doc MacKay and Jace.

"You were right, Reese," the doctor said, coming directly to her. "He's dead."

Reese nodded, comforted by his calm presence.

"Did you touch anything or move him?"

"No, but he didn't answer, and I thought his eyes looked strange. I didn't think to find you; I just went to the Muldoons'."

"You did fine. Why don't you go to the house and make a fire. You look chilled."

"Would you like tea?" she offered automatically.

"Yes. I'll come and drink some with you."

Jace waited only until Reese had left—and they'd moved Mr. Zantow's body onto the floor—to speak.

"What will happen to Reese?"

"I don't know," the doctor answered. "I'm not sure she knows."

"Will she have to lay out Mr. Zantow on her own?"

"I'll come and help her with that," Doc MacKay confirmed. He turned away from the men, heading toward the door.

"I'll come in with you," Douglas said before turning to Jace. "Thanks for getting Doc. Can we talk later, Jace?"

Jace was swift to agree, exiting the workshop behind Douglas. He wanted to get home. He wanted it in the worst way. It was getting dark, and Maddie would be worrying, but it was bigger than that. He had things he had to speak to her about, things that wouldn't last another day.

❧

The doctor found Reese by the fire, her arms wrapped tightly about her body. She didn't turn but spoke when she heard the door.

"What killed him?"

"Probably his heart. Had he been sick or complaining of anything?"

"No, nothing like that. He had more work than he had time for. That was the only thing troubling him."

The kind doctor began to make the tea. Reese had put the kettle on but done nothing else. A widower for more than ten years, he was adept at taking care of such things and was laying the table when Douglas entered.

"Does the preparation work have to be done this evening?" Douglas asked of Doc MacKay.

"There's no need to rush. We'll see to it in the morning."

"Why don't you come and stay with us tonight, Reese?" Douglas offered. "We have plenty of room."

Reese turned from the fireplace for the first time but only stared at him.

"Reese," Doc MacKay tried. "Do you feel safe staying here tonight?"

"I never felt safe staying here," she said quietly. "Not since my father died. Tonight would be the first time."

"Maybe you should go to Muldoons anyway," the doctor pressed.

"I won't sleep much, Doc, and that will only disturb them. I'll be all right."

At last her voice sounded normal. The doctor looked to his pastor and nodded, telling Douglas he could take his leave.

"We'll check on you in the morning, Reese," Douglas told her.

"Thank you."

Reese finally sat down. She pulled a teacup close to her and wrapped her slim fingers around it. She was quiet, but the distant stare was gone.

"Are you going to eat something? Is there enough food in the house?"

"There's enough food to feed the church family," Reese said, her tone and words sounding the way they always did. "I'll fix us something."

The town doctor settled back and carried on a light conversation while Reese worked. They ate companionably, like old friends, which in fact they were. And not until the meal was over did Doc MacKay mention what must be done in the morning. Reese was pragmatic about it; after all, she'd laid out her father. As the doctor left, they established a time for him to return the next day. Upon his exit, Reese didn't wait long to turn in, not sleepy, but lying in her bed not having to listen for noises for the first time in many years.

∞

"I was starting to worry," Maddie said to Jace as he came in the kitchen door. She'd heard him come into the yard but waited while he fed the stock.

"I thought you might be. Mr. Zantow died, and I couldn't get away."

"I didn't hear the bells," Maddie said in confusion.

"Clara and I have never heard the bells out here. We're just a little too far away. And besides, they probably won't ring them until morning."

"Was he sick?" she asked.

"I don't think so. Reese looked too shocked for it to have been expected."

"I forgot about Reese. What happens to indenture papers when the holder dies?"

"I don't know," Jace answered, thinking about how lost she'd looked. "I was talking to Mr. Muldoon when I found out," he added, sounding as shaken as he felt.

Maddie put her arms around him, wanting to be close.

"Listen to me, Maddie," Jace spoke from above her head. "We have to do this together."

Maddie didn't need an explanation. She knew exactly what her husband was talking about. At the same time, she remembered she'd wanted this for a very long time.

I'll go with you, Jace," she told him, a peace stealing over her. "I'll go see Mr. Muldoon whenever you want to."

"Mr. Zantow was gone without warning. Do any of us really know how long we have?" Jace moved enough to see her face. "We have to take care of this, Maddie, and soon. I'm not ready for eternity, and you're not either."

Maddie looked into Jace's face and thought she could easily cry. He was scared. He was excited, but fear was evident as well.

"I ordered a cradle, assuming he would complete it in plenty of time." Jace's voice was thoughtful with wonder. "And now he's gone."

Maddie didn't reply to this—there was no need. It was very sobering news. Death was a part of life, but also a sad part.

"Do you want anything to eat?" Maddie asked after a long time. "I've got tea ready."

"Tea sounds fine. How are you feeling?"

"Good," she told him truthfully, and for the next few hours, they went about their normal routine. Not until it was time to turn in did the discussion return to their eternity again. The timing couldn't have been worse. It didn't let either of them sleep until late in the night.

∞

Alison sat in the dark of the bedroom, five-month-old Jeffrey at her breast, her heart praying for Reese Thackery. If she looked out the window and peeked around the tree, she could just make out the Zantow house. There were no lights burning, and Alison hoped that meant Reese was sleeping soundly.

Jeffrey fell sound asleep when Alison wasn't paying attention, and she bounced him a little to see if he wanted more, but he was completely relaxed, boneless as a cat, and ready to go back to bed.

Alison tucked him into his cradle and slipped back into bed with Douglas, who had learned to sleep through the night feedings. Alison fell back to sleep too, but not before she had time to talk to God about trusting Him. Douglas had been talking about trust in his sermons. Trust was always the issue when she prayed. Did she pray believing God had a plan and she wasn't the center of the universe? Or was she more willing to lie in her bed and tell God what to do with Reese Thackery's life?

Sleep came swiftly, but only because on this night Alison chose to pray in belief, knowing that God's love for Reese laughingly outweighed her own.

ꝏ

The bells rang early. First nine times, and then 48 times for Mr. Zantow's age. Reese and Doc MacKay certainly heard them, but it didn't deter the work. They had moved the body into the parlor, where the coffin and a piece of hastily prepared white sheeting were ready for the body.

Doc MacKay sent Reese from the room just one time. Other than that, they worked side by side, doing what had to be done for the funeral the next day. While they worked, they talked. Doc MacKay, a fellow believer, wanted to know how Reese was really doing.

"Are you afraid for the future, Reese?"

"Not afraid, but certainly not sure of anything."

"Have you ever seen your papers? Do you know what to expect?"

"I did see them one time, but not to read." She made a face. "By the time I realized I should know what they said, my father was gone. I shouldn't have been such a chicken."

"What do you mean by that?"

"I never asked to see them because I feared angering Mr. Zantow."

The doctor nodded in understanding and asked, "Do you own anything in this house?"

"A few items in my room, but nothing of value."

"Will you try to find work and stay in Tucker Mills?"

"That's exactly what I'll do. I don't know if anyone will hire me, or if I will be able to make enough to live on. I just know that I don't wish to be indentured any more."

"I don't think it will come to that," Doc MacKay reassured her. "Don't forget, you have the church family."

Reese smiled at him, her heart taking comfort in the reminder. She didn't know what the future would bring, but she could trust that God had a plan. She could also thank Him for saving her and putting her with a church family that loved her unconditionally.

Three

The viewing was not largely attended. Mr. Zantow did work for many people, but he did not have a great many friends. Reese had sat by her father's casket in this same living room, but she did not sit next to Mr. Zantow's coffin. He was not family, and she felt to do so would give a false impression of their relationship. She had discussed her decision with Doc MacKay and Douglas, and they both agreed that it was a wise one.

But Reese was in the house. She greeted people who came in the door and thanked them when they spoke kind words. What she hadn't expected was the outpouring of good wishes directed toward herself.

You've deserved better all these years, Reese.

He didn't know how good he had it.

You're a good girl, Reese.

I hope whatever you do now, you'll be happy.

And on it went for more than an hour. The townsfolk came, said very little about Mr. Zantow, save how good he was at his craft, and then turned their attention to Reese, whom they thought so much of.

When it was time for the coffin—one that Mr. Zantow himself had made—to be loaded onto the wagon that would go to the cemetery, Reese found herself mostly surrounded by her church family. Mrs. Greenlowe was also in attendance, as were Jace and Maddie Randall.

The Reverend Mr. Sullins, who held Sunday services in the Commons Meetinghouse, had come to read a passage of Scripture. He talked about Mr. Zantow a little, even mentioning some things that Reese did not know.

No one lingered at the gravesite. When the reading was done, Reese threw a handful of dirt on top of the coffin, her heart sad that his life had ended so abruptly and with little interest in godly things.

The Peternell family was waiting nearby. They asked Reese to join them for dinner. Reese was all too glad to accept. She walked back to town with them, glad that for the moment she didn't have to return to the house.

❧

"Can we set up an appointment with you?" Jace asked of Douglas. They had left the cemetery and were headed for town. Jace and Maddie had brought a buggy into town, but they'd left it at the Zantow house.

"Certainly," Douglas replied. "What time is good for you?"

"We wanted you to tell us that. I've been stopping by with little regard for your schedule and family. Even talking to you today, when a man's just been buried . . ." Jace halted, clearly uncomfortable to go on.

"You haven't been disruptive at all," Douglas reassured him. "I can meet with you right now if you like."

"Join us for dinner," Alison put in, walking beside her spouse, his hand holding hers.

"Are you sure?" Maddie checked.

"Yes, please come."

Jace looked down into his wife's face. He didn't want to go another day with questions burning through him, and from what he knew of the Muldoons, they wouldn't mind having them again. The Randalls thanked them for the offer and returned to the Zantow house only to move their buggy to the Muldoons. They ended up staying for several hours.

∞

Mr. Victor Jenness had seen better times. He was not an old man, but neither was he young or in the best of health. And since he managed the bank and was not at the counter daily dealing with bank patrons, he was often able to hide this.

However, he did know what went on all over town, and news of Mr. Zantow's demise reached his ears even before the bells rang. It was for this reason that he sent for Reese the very day after Mr. Zantow was interred.

Reese was at home when a young man came with a missive for her, a small bit of paper folded in half, asking her to present herself to Mr. Jenness, the bank manager, as soon as she could arrange it.

Reese had no reason to delay. She had assumed the house would be sold and had been doing some extra cleaning, but as soon as she brushed her hair and washed her face and hands, she left for the bank. She wasn't nervous, but curiosity propelled her straight to the building, where she stepped inside and found Mr. Leffler, the bank teller. He smiled at Reese and greeted her by name. Reese had no money in the bank, but errands she had run for Mr. Zantow over the years had brought her to this building on many occasions, where she always found Mr. Leffler extremely kind.

"Mr. Jenness sent for me, Mr. Leffler. Is he in?"

"In his office, Reese. You can go right ahead."

The office was not a separate room, but a large space off the main floor. The furniture was set up in such a way that privacy could be had. Reese stepped around a tall bookshelf to find Mr. Jenness at his desk.

"Mr. Jenness?"

"Ah, yes," he greeted. "Sit down, Miss Thackery."

Reese began to relax. Few people addressed her as Miss Thackery, but he sounded as though he was pleased. She hoped he could direct her concerning Mr. Zantow's goods and took one of the wooden chairs, sure she was there for that very reason.

"It has come to my attention that Mr. Zantow has passed away."

"Yes, sir. Just this week."

Mr. Jenness, feeling very good about his decision, nodded complacently.

"It has also come to my attention that he has a large out-standing debt with this bank."

This was a surprise to Reese, but she didn't comment. He had lived very well, and she had assumed he was more than comfortable.

"It is the decision of this bank to sell his home and all his possessions."

Reese nodded, assuming this was the best course of action.

"Unfortunately this will not cover his debt. So it is also the decision of this bank to retain your indenture contract until such time as you would have ceased to work for Mr. Zantow."

Reese stared at the man, wishing he would repeat his last sentence.

"Is that clear to you, Miss Thackery?"

"The bank will own my papers? I'm indentured to the Tucker Mills Bank?"

"Yes," he replied, actually smiling. "I'm glad we understand each other."

"I have no money, Mr. Jenness."

"Of course you don't." He frowned. "Otherwise you wouldn't be an indentured servant."

"Where will I live?"

"Where will you live?"

"Yes. You said Mr. Zantow's home is to be sold."

The frown deepened. Mr. Jenness had not thought of this.

"Well," he improvised swiftly, his voice sharpening a bit. "You'll be given a small stipend for rent. I'm sure you can find a place."

"And food?"

"Yes, and food." Sharper still. "You shouldn't need much!"

Reese's disappointment was so keen that for a moment she couldn't move or speak. She had thought she was free, and now it would be two more years. Or would it?

"I wish for you to tell me exactly what my papers say. I wish to know how long the bank will own my contract."

Mr. Jenness did not look pleased about it, but he rustled through a few sheets on his desk and came up with the right document.

"Let's see," he peered at the paper. "The original contract with your father is for February 29, 1834, and you became the primary concern in May of 1835. That means you have 19 months to go. This is July, so you will be released in February of 1841."

Wanting to check the dates for herself, Reese put out her hand and the papers were given to her. She tried to find some comfort in what she saw, but at the moment she was at a loss. Mr. Jenness was staring at her oddly, and she wondered what her face looked like.

"What exactly will I do?" she remembered to ask.

"For starters, you'll ready all of Mr. Zantow's belongings for auction or sale. After that is taken care of, you'll report here each morning for a list of jobs. Cleaning this office twice a week will be on that list."

Reese nodded, wondering at the feeling of numbness that was stealing over her. She'd received bad news in the past, but none that seemed to affect her like this.

"Do I live at the house until it sells?"

"Of course not! It must be in a salable condition! I'll expect it to be cleaned, and I'll be checking the job myself. You must move out today."

Reese didn't know what she looked like when he said this, but her expression must have registered alarm, since he began to recant.

"Well, actually," he said as he cleared his throat and began to stack papers, "I guess you can have the weekend. I'll expect you out by Monday morning."

Reese nodded and stood. Shock was setting in, but a woman in the other room speaking to Mr. Leffler and asking about money in her account stopped her.

"How much will I be getting to live on each month, and when will I get it?"

Mr. Jenness looked irritated all over again, but Reese was knowing some irritation of her own. She had never heard of a bank holding someone's papers.

"Mr. Jenness?" Reese pressed, deciding not to leave until she had an answer.

"At the end of each month," he said, thinking this was the end of it until Reese sat back down. He stared at her in surprise until she spoke.

"I've been an indentured servant for more than four years, Mr. Jenness. I do what I'm told with only a roof over my head, two dresses, and food to show for it. I have nothing, and you are telling me I must leave my home. The end of the month is days away. What exactly am I to live on until you decide to pay me?"

The bank manager had not expected her calm logic. She had seemed so compliant when she first came in. He had not expected her to stand up for herself.

"Yes, well," he said quietly, seeing that he might have been a bit overzealous. "I can give you money today, it's the twenty-sixth, and I'll do so on this day each month."

"How much am I to receive?"

His mind scrambling, Mr. Jenness listed a number that was

quite low, but Reese didn't argue. She knew it wasn't enough to
live on but thought she might have said enough at the moment.
However, she had another thought that had to be expressed.

"And where are the papers I am to sign concerning this agreement between the bank and myself?"

Mr. Jenness sat up as though he'd been stung. "I see no need
for such papers."

"No?" Reese asked, almost gently. "Mr. Zantow just dropped
dead over his worktable, leaving me at the mercy of this bank. I
want some documentation stating the terms we've agreed upon
today.

"And," Reese went on, not caring anymore if she said too
much, "I want Mr. Leffler to witness it."

Mr. Jenness' face flushed with anger, but Reese didn't back
down. Not even when he stood and stomped his way to the
teller's counter and had a few words with Mr. Leffler.

That Mr. Leffler was uncomfortable with the whole situation, entering the office and casting stunned glances at his boss,
was lost on Reese. It was finally hitting her like a blow to the
heart: She was where she'd always been.

ᘓ

"Doc," Reese called as she opened his door. "Are you home?"

"In the back, Reese."

Reese went to the small room where he prepared poultices
and remedies and found him on a stool up close to the table, his
head bent over a clear glass bowl.

"How are you?" he asked when she walked in.

"I've been better," she said quietly.

"What's going on?"

Reese explained what had just happened, her voice calmer
than her heart.

"The bank retained your papers," Doc MacKay said in wonder. "I've never heard of such a thing."

"That makes two us. Unfortunately Mr. Jenness would not agree, and he's the man in charge. He seemed completely delighted with the idea."

"And what exactly will you be doing for the bank?"

"Well, I'll clean the bank twice a week and go every day for a list."

"Reese," the doctor replied, working to stay calm, "that makes no sense. A bank has no need for a woman to be on staff to clean."

Reese shrugged, not able to explain.

"I did stand up to him," she finally put in.

"How so?"

"I made him put in writing that I would get money to live on. And he paid me for the first time today." She banged her hand against the table for emphasis. "And Mr. Leffler witnessed it!"

Doc MacKay laughed until he asked how much she was being paid. The amount Reese named tested the doctor's emotions all over again. He kept his mouth shut, however, and simply asked Reese if she had told Douglas and Alison. When Reese said she'd come directly to him, the helpful doctor told her he'd go with her to the Muldoons.

⬡

"How do I tell Cathy what happened to us yesterday?" Maddie asked Jace over dinner the next day, glad that Clara was at her own home for the day.

"Maybe you don't right now."

"You think it might be best to stay quiet?"

"It's all so new, Maddie. I know what I said in my heart to God was real. I confessed my need for a Savior and my belief in His Son, but I'm just starting to understand what it all means."

Maddie nodded but didn't comment.

"Remember how changed Eden was?" Jace spoke of his sister. "She changed so much that we couldn't help but notice. Now I know you're not an abrasive person like Eden was, and your aunt and uncle might not notice a huge change, but I'd still rather we give this some time and not talk about it until we're a little more sure of what we're going to say."

This made sense to Maddie. Could she even explain what had gone on yesterday? She had never done a good job of telling people why she'd been so uncertain and unsettled. The first person to ever understand was Mr. Muldoon. Not even Jace had seen the situation clearly until quite recently.

But Jace was right. She needed to stay quiet right now. It didn't diminish the quiet peace she felt inside or that she knew in her heart and from a verse that Douglas had shared with them that God was willing to wait. Always a little troubled with worry, Maddie wondered what would happen if she was never able to tell her aunt and uncle about her belief in the Lord Jesus Christ but then realized how foolish that was. If God would wait for her, He would also wait for Doyle and Cathy Shephard.

৵৹

"I'm sick of talking about myself, Doc. I'll let you tell Douglas and Alison what happened at the bank. I'm going to go play with the kids."

That said, Reese had exited the Muldoons' parlor moments after they arrived, gone to the kitchen, and shut the door behind her. She found Joshua, Peter, and Martin at the kitchen work-table. Reese joined them and picked up a piece of string she found there.

"Hi, Reese," Peter opened.

"Hey, Pete. What are you guys doing?"

"Having a quiet time," Joshua explained.

"Are you in trouble?"

"No, just helping Marty," Joshua matter-of-factly reported, working not to be bored. "He doesn't sit so well these days."

Reese looked to Martin. "During services?" she asked. "Is that the problem?"

Martin nodded. "I wiggle and itch."

Reese had all she could do not to laugh.

"The time's almost up," Joshua informed them, and at the moment they heard someone on the small back stairway that led into the kitchen. It was Hillary, Jeffrey in her arms. Reese wordlessly held her hands out, and Hillary surrendered the littlest Muldoon with a smile.

"Still sitting?" their sister asked.

"We're done now."

"How'd it go, Marty?"

"I only itched a little."

Reese finally felt free to laugh at this, and the Muldoon children joined her. The baby still in her arms, she suggested a game. The family was all for that, and Reese couldn't have been more thankful. She didn't want to think about what was being discussed in the other room.

❦

Alison's elbows were propped up in her lap, her hands covering her face. She'd been in this position for a full two minutes. She wanted to sob her eyes out but knew it would do no good. She listened to the men in quiet discussion, trying to take in their words when all she really wanted was for Reese Thackery's circumstances to change.

"*How much* is she getting?" Douglas asked, sure he'd heard wrong.

"You heard correctly," Doc MacKay told him. "But that's not my big worry. There are enough of us in the church family to aid her. My fear is that she'll be vulnerable to someone again. Whose houses will she be cleaning? Will Jenness expect his house cleaned and try to take advantage of her physically—the same way Zantow tried?"

A shudder ran over Alison's frame. Douglas noticed it but didn't say anything. He was asking God for a rescue in this situation. He didn't want to go and argue with the bank manager. He didn't want to challenge his authority in the matter. But neither did he trust him to have Reese's best interest in mind.

"She can live here," Douglas finally said. "If she does that, maybe we'll be able to keep an eye on her. She can tell us how long a job should take, and if she's not back, we can check on her."

"That's perfect," Alison said, so desperate to help this younger woman. "Do you think she'll agree, Doc?"

"I don't know. She's weary of taking people's time with her problems. She won't want to be a burden."

A squeal and laughter floated in from the other room, and Douglas spoke.

"If she only knew what a wonderful addition she would be."

The doctor and pastor's wife both nodded. All three were ready to head to the kitchen and tell her she had a home, but before they could do that, there was a knock on the front door.

∞

Reese Thackery could be formidable when she chose to be. She was much too thin, but her height—inches that totaled six feet—was hard to ignore. Doc MacKay was an inch taller, but she looked Douglas directly in the eye. She towered over Alison and Mrs. Greenlowe, the woman who had come to the door.

"How did you learn about the bank and my papers?" Reese asked of Mrs. Greenlowe, looking none too happy.

"This is Tucker Mills, Reese! What did you expect?"

"I didn't expect word to be out this fast," she told her.

"Well, it is, and my offer is an honest one."

Reese's eyes narrowed. "I can't even pay you a normal room and board. How is your offer an honest one?"

"I know you, Reese. Even if I told you to sit around and do nothing, you would still work around my house."

"I don't even know how much I'll be home, Mrs. Greenlowe. For all I know, Mr. Jenness plans to work my fingers to the bone."

"Don't you mention that man's name to me!" Mrs. Greenlowe was instantly upset. "What could he be thinking? And Zantow! Owing money like that."

Reese had to smile. Mrs. Greenlowe could be so feisty. Seeing the smile, that lady calmed almost immediately and smiled back at Reese. The younger woman shook her head, glancing at the three other occupants of the room.

"I don't know why we're having this discussion in your parlor, Alison. You have better things to do."

"Nothing that I can think of. And besides, I wouldn't want to miss this."

Reese sighed quietly, more shaken by all of this than she wanted the others to know.

"I have until Monday to be out of Mr. Zantow's house. I think I'll take the weekend to decide what I should do."

Doc MacKay wanted it settled immediately, but Douglas spoke first.

"That's fine, Reese. Remember that you have at least two options, and if you want to bounce ideas off of us, you know you can."

Reese nodded and said she had best get home and back to work. Alison gave her a hug, and Mrs. Greenlowe reiterated her offer before leaving. Douglas saw Reese and the doctor out the door soon after.

"Are you all right?" Doc MacKay checked on the walk back.

"I think so. It's all such a surprise. With so little warning, my world has been turned on its head."

The doctor agreed, still wishing he could do more for Reese, and Reese herself wishing she wasn't so helpless in the situation.

Had they but known it, Douglas was in the same boat. He returned to his office, his heart in turmoil, and then decided some air might help. After telling Alison he was headed out, he took a walk toward the woods, thinking and praying.

He wanted to trust God for this, but it was testing him. He feared for Reese's safety if the bank manager sent her all over town on her own. Douglas couldn't picture why a bank would do this, and that made him even more uneasy.

Walking swiftly, Douglas prayed and asked God to protect Reese and put His saving hand on Mr. Jenness. He was confident that God had a plan and knew that his job was to trust and keep obeying.

A face and a name popped into Douglas' mind so fast that he stopped walking. He'd been so taken with Mr. Zantow's death, Jace's and Maddie's conversions, and Reese's problems, that he had forgotten there was something he could do.

Douglas made a beeline for home. He had a letter to write, and the sooner he sent it, the better.

Four

"Jace," Reese called, approaching him on Sunday morning when she saw him arriving for services.

"Hi, Reese. How are you?"

"I'm doing all right. I wanted to ask you something and hope you won't find me intrusive."

Maddie came up at that point, and Reese greeted her.

"Go ahead," Jace said.

Reese's voice lowered. "Did you by any chance order a cradle from Mr. Zantow when you came that day?"

"Yes, I did," Jace admitted; they were still not telling people their news, although they knew it was spreading fast.

"He finished it," Reese told the couple. "I was cleaning in the workshop, and I found a cradle."

Jace and Maddie smiled at each other.

"What exactly will happen to it?" Maddie asked.

"All of Mr. Zantow's belongings will be auctioned, so watch for the notice. I assume the cradle will go too."

"Thanks, Reese," Jace told her sincerely before asking about her future plans.

And he was just the first. Nearly everyone in the church family asked after her, brought her something, or invited her to eat or stay with them. As she knew it would, news about the bank holding her papers had spread swiftly, and people asked after her needs.

By the time the sermon began, Reese couldn't think of a person in the room who hadn't checked with her. She didn't hear Douglas' opening remarks. She was too busy praying for this small church family, so thankful to be a part of it.

∞

"How is it going?" Douglas asked when both Jace and Maddie headed his way after the sermon.

"It's going well, but we were wondering about the seven Rs," Jace admitted, referring to something Douglas had mentioned in the sermon.

"I wondered if that might not be confusing for you. We've been talking about the seven Rs off and on for years now. It's just a little formula I made up to help us keep short accounts with God. By short accounts, I mean confessing sin regularly, and not repeating it."

"What are they again?" Jace asked.

"Recognize, Repent, Rethrone, Replace, Rejoice, Remember, Repeat," Douglas said, working not to rattle them off too swiftly. "*Recognize* is the step where we see that we've sinned and we're out of fellowship with God. *Repent* is the next step, when we agree with God about our sin and confess to Him. *Rethrone* is the mental action of putting Christ back in the center of our lives, because sinning pushes Him out.

"*Replace* is understanding that we've got to put something else there or the sin comes right back. Working on a memory verse that deals with the sin, or even getting your mind busy with prayer and good works helps. *Rejoice* is my favorite. We need to stop and realize that our fellowship with God is unbelievably sweet and not forgot to rejoice in that fact. *Remember* might be the hardest of all. Keeping these good thoughts in mind as we move through each day. *Repeat* is simply that, repeating the process again and again, as often as necessary."

"It's so much," Maddie couldn't help but say.

"And I probably rattled them off too fast. I'm sorry." Douglas was compassionate. "If you only remember one thing this week, Maddie, let it be the *R* that stands for repentance. God loves a repentant heart. You'll be learning for years about all the ways we push God out of the center of our lives, but if you can first of all learn to be a woman of repentance, God can change and work in your heart in a mighty way."

Both Jace and Maddie couldn't help but smile at him. He was always so encouraging, and they were helped every time they talked. When the couple finally left the meetinghouse, the seven *R*s were all they could talk about.

⚭

While Jace and Maddie discussed their questions with Douglas, Reese and Alison sat in the rear pew and discussed her decision.

"Have you told Mrs. Greenlowe?"

"Yes. She's expecting me this afternoon."

"Are you sure, Reese?" Alison had to check. "We still wish you'd come and stay with us."

"Why, Alison? You have five children. Why would you want an extra person under foot?"

Reese watched as Alison laughed. "Do you remember when we met?"

"Sure." Reese smiled as well, thinking back to that day almost three years ago. "I had just run an errand for Mr. Zantow and had had a run-in with a pig at the Eppling farm."

"You were so angry and so funny," Alison said, still laughing at the things Reese had said about mud, pigs, and farms in general.

"Is that why you and Marty walked me to the pond?" Reese asked. "Because I made you laugh?"

"That and the color of your hair."

Reese's mouth opened in surprise. "The color of my hair?"

"Yes." Alison couldn't stop smiling. "My sister's hair is the same red as yours. She's nowhere near as tall as you are, but that was the first reason I was drawn to you."

Reese laughed but still said, "You didn't really answer my question."

Alison put a hand on the younger woman's arm, her face now serious.

"I want to take care of you. I want to know you're safe. But even more than that, I love having you around. I love your hardworking attitude, your hunger for God's truth, and your marvelous sense of humor."

Reese was very touched. She did not regret her decision to live with Mrs. Greenlowe—somehow she thought they would do very well together—but it was good to know that she was welcome at the Muldoon home.

∞

"Are you willing to feed us on short notice?" Maddie asked when she opened her uncle's front door and put her head in.

"Come in," Doyle Shephard called from the parlor, managing at the same time to let his wife know that Jace and Maddie had arrived.

"Where are you coming from?" Cathy asked, carrying a bowl from the kitchen to the table in the parlor.

"The new meetinghouse," Jace answered.

Maddie watched the faces of her aunt and uncle, wondering how this news would be received, but she saw nothing out of the ordinary. They both looked interested and not the least bit upset.

Maddie felt herself relaxing. Her faith in Christ still so new, she prayed, trying to remember the things she'd been taught in just a few weeks.

Please forgive Doyle and Cathy, Lord. Show them the truth. Help Jace and me to always have this good relationship with them. And please show them what You've shown me.

∞

Linden Heights, Massachusetts

Dalton Kingsley's brow lowered in concentration and very real concern as he read the letter in his hand. He hadn't heard from Dooner—Douglas Muldoon—in many years, but that didn't change his opinion of this old friend. He knew Dooner to be a man of great faith and integrity, which made it easy to believe every word of the missive he'd sent.

Much as he hated to do it, Dalton wasted no time in sending for his brother. This was not a situation that could be ignored.

∞

When silence fell on their conversation, Dalton stared across the small parlor at his youngest sibling, Conner Kingsley, thinking the younger man still looked tired. Their mother had died just two months earlier, and for the last six months of her life, her mind had slipped. She had wanted Conner with her constantly, becoming frightened and tearful if she couldn't see him.

Conner had done everything in his power to be with her, even giving up his job at the bank, but it had taken its toll. The fact that she was like a small child when she died had hurt all of her children, but especially Conner, since he had been with her so much at the end.

"I hate to ask this of you, Conner," Dalton added, "but I feel this has to be handled by a family member. I would go if Jamie's condition hadn't just worsened."

Jamie, Dalton's youngest daughter, was very ill.

"I understand, Dalton," Conner said softly, which was his way. "Don't worry about it."

"I'll get a letter off to the bank manager tomorrow. When do you wish to leave?"

Conner thought about it, named a date he thought he could manage, and fell silent.

"How will you do in Tucker Mills, Conner?" Dalton asked when the silence lengthened. "It's been a long time."

Conner smiled a little. "I guess I'll find out."

"Thank you, Conner," his brother told him sincerely, the two men embracing when Conner stood to leave.

The younger man climbed into the waiting coach, thinking about what needed to be done to leave Linden Heights and trying not to think about how draining the last months had been. His brother needed him to do this, and he would. He'd take Troy Thaden—a friend and coworker—with him, and that would make a huge difference.

For a moment his mind was assailed with memories from the past, but he pushed those thoughts away. It was not time to think about them. He would be forced to deal with his past in Tucker Mills soon enough, but not today.

꒰∞꒱

Tucker Mills

"It's a hot day," Mrs. Greenlowe told Reese about a week after she moved in. "I'm going to check on you at Zantow's."

"I'm done at Mr. Zantow's. I'm headed to the bank to see what needs to be done."

Mrs. Greenlowe frowned. She wanted to tell Reese to check in with her but knew that wasn't practical.

"Well, drink plenty of water" were her only words.

Reese thanked her with an amused smile and headed out. The walk to the bank didn't take long, Reese's long legs eating the distance, and before she was ready, she was giving a small wave to Mr. Leffler behind the counter and heading toward the alcove that was Mr. Jenness' office.

"Come in," Mr. Jenness commanded as soon as he spotted her. No greeting, no invitation to sit down, no attempt at formality—just an order. "Is the house complete?"

"Yes, Mr. Jenness."

"Very well," that man said, standing and going to the coat rack for his hat. "I shall go directly there. You will accompany me," he stopped long enough to say, and then finished pompously, "*I* will be the one to judge if you are finished."

Reese did not follow Mr. Jenness around the house. He had an adverse effect on her emotions. She stayed in the kitchen, not because she'd been told to, but because she hadn't been told to follow. She had no desire to trail after Mr. Jenness, whose mere presence made her tense and irritated.

Hearing him on the stairs, Reese tensed all over again and waited for him to enter.

"This will do," he condescendingly announced as he stepped across the threshold, and Reese knew that it pained him not to find something to criticize. "You may go to my home now and help my wife. Return to the bank promptly at 4:00. I will give you one hour to clean there."

Reese didn't comment but nodded silently and headed for the door. It occurred to her as she exited that, negative or not, this had been her home for more than five years. Memories of the early days, days when her father was still alive, came rushing to her, swiftly followed by the days and years after his death.

"Reese!"

In her preoccupation with leaving Mr. Zantow's house, she forgot that reporting to the Jenness home would take her directly past Mrs. Greenlowe's.

"Where are you headed?" that lady demanded. Reese moved closer so as not to shout her answer.

"You don't want to know," Reese surprised her by saying.

Mrs. Greenlowe's eyes narrowed. "You're going to his house!" she hissed.

Reese only smiled at her, waiting for the tirade to begin.

"Who does he think he is? How is that helping the bank? He's got no right, I tell you. And that Lillie Jenness! She's a cold one. You mark my words. All she does is work."

When the words seemed to run out, Reese calmly said, "Then I'm headed to clean the bank at 4:00. I'll be back as soon as I'm done."

Reese turned away, but Mrs. Greenlowe's voice, calmer now, stopped her.

"You might be an indentured servant, Reese, but you're still a person. Make sure they treat you like one."

By way of a reply, Reese waved but didn't say what she was thinking. Being an indentured servant meant they could treat her any way they liked.

∞

He had said he was going to do something. He had said that he had a surprise for her. But even though Reese Thackery was standing in her parlor, Mrs. Lillie Jenness could hardly believe her eyes.

Lillie found her voice after a few pained moments of silence. "What did he tell you to do?"

"He didn't, Mrs. Jenness. He said to come here and be a help to you."

Lillie's eyes all but closed in frustration. She was a woman who prided herself on a spotless home and a perfect table. She didn't need help. What could Victor be thinking?

"All right, Reese." Lillie stayed calm, willing to take this matter up with her husband. "Come into the kitchen. I'll have you work on some candlesticks that need polishing."

Reese didn't comment, but she was surprised. She expected to be given the most difficult, arduous job in the house. Polishing at the table was not it. Nevertheless, Reese didn't complain. She took the apron that was handed to her—it was spotlessly clean— and sat down to work.

Reese didn't look up while Mrs. Jenness moved around the room a bit. She didn't look up until the lady of the house exited and the door to the next room closed rather hard.

∞∞

Reese had been working along for the better part of an hour when Gerald, the Jenness' teen son, came into the room.

"Who are you?" were the first words out of his mouth.

"I'm Reese," she stopped humming and replied, barely glancing up from her work.

"What are you doing?"

Reese spoke before she thought. "I'm swimming in the pond. What does it look like?"

Not until the sarcastic words were out of her mouth did Reese look up, her eyes a bit wide until she saw that Gerald was laughing. She relaxed a bit but still kept her eyes on him, watching as he sat down, still chuckling.

"Where's my mother?"

"I don't know," Reese answered, going back to the candlesticks.

"Why are you here?" Gerald tried.

"Because I was told to come."

"Do you always do as you're told?" Gerald asked, and Reese heard a tone she didn't like. She looked up into his eyes and saw something she dreaded: interest.

Reese's gaze returned to the work at hand, even as she wished she had a reason to stand up. If Gerald was no taller than his father, he would find himself looking up to Reese. She'd yet to meet a young man who could overlook this fact and believed it to be the quickest way to cool any ardor he might be feeling.

"Well, do you?"

"It depends on who's doing the telling," Reese responded, trying to keep her voice light.

"You're different," Gerald said, lounging back in the opposite chair as if he had all day.

"Am I?"

"That's what I mean." Gerald came forward in his excitement, as though she'd made his point. "Just by the way you said that! I can tell you don't let folks boss you around. You're your own person."

Reese glanced up at him and then back down before he could read the unbelief in her eyes. He clearly had no idea to whom he was talking. It was true that the Jenness house was not situated on the green, but it was still in town. Reese wondered if Gerald Jenness got out of the house much. Every other person she knew, and many she didn't, had heard about her situation with the bank.

"Gerald?" Mrs. Jenness called from the other room. "Gerald? Where are you?"

Reese listened to Gerald's impatient sigh, but he still pushed to his feet and exited by way of the door his mother had used. Reese heard their low voices from her place at the kitchen table but didn't try to listen. She went back to polishing, humming once again and wondering what she would be asked to do for the rest of the day.

"So tell me," Mrs. Greenlowe waited only until they'd sat down for tea to question Reese. "How did it go at the Jenness house?"

"It went fine," she said, surprised even now.

"What did Lillie Jenness have you do?"

"Not much. A bit of silver polishing and trimming the frayed edges of an old rug. I did a lot of sitting around, waiting for her to come back to tell me what to do. I don't think she wanted me to help with the cooking."

"She does nothing but clean," Mrs. Greenlowe muttered, pushing more food in Reese's direction. She still served her main meal at noon, but now that Reese lived with her, she made sure she always had plenty to offer with the evening tea; the girl was too thin for her liking.

"Did she give you a proper dinner?"

Reese had to think about that and then admitted to herself that it hadn't been that great. Mrs. Jenness clearly hadn't wanted to waste a bit of meat on her. Reese's piece was so small she finished it in three bites. Mrs. Jenness had prepared Reese's plate and told her to stay in the kitchen to eat. She was used to that, but not used to having little more than bread and vegetables with not even a dessert to take her through until tea. At least Mr. Zantow had let her eat what he enjoyed.

Mr. Jenness had not come home for dinner, and Reese had been surprised by that. But she'd been pleased that Gerald had spent most of the day out of the house. She sensed that his mother might have sent him on an errand.

"And at the bank?" Mrs. Greenlowe asked before Reese could gather her thoughts to answer the other question; she thought it might be just as well.

"There isn't much to do," Reese explained. "I dusted and swept some. I'll mop the floor next time, but today there were folks inside, so I couldn't. I'll probably have to wash the windows at some point."

Mrs. Greenlowe allowed Reese to eat in peace for a short

time and didn't have anything to complain about until Reese began to help with the cleanup.

"You work all day," that lady muttered darkly, but Reese wasn't tired and knew that she was years younger than her landlady. And although Reese wasn't weary, it didn't hurt her feelings at all when Mrs. Greenlowe said she was ready to turn in, freeing Reese to seek the privacy of her own room.

She had washed in the kitchen after tea, stripping down and scrubbing every inch of her, and now it felt wonderful to slip her nightdress over her head and crawl onto the middle of the mattress. Here she knelt, as she had every night since her conversion, and prayed. Her knees were too bony to manage the floor, and she was certain God understood.

For long moments she didn't pray. The candle flickering more noticeably as the light faded from the windows, Reese looked around at the most wonderful bedroom she could ever remember having.

It was done in greens and pinks, soft and inviting. The wallpaper was subtle and blended nicely with the quilt Mrs. Greenlowe had made for the bed. All the drawers in the dresser worked properly, and Reese's bed was soft and comfortable.

"Thank You, Lord," Reese finally began to whisper to her heavenly Father. "You have given me so much. I still wish to be released from my papers, but if that is not to happen, please help me to be safe where I work. Help my actions and words to be honoring to You.

"Help me to be careful around Gerald. I don't want his attentions. Help me not be amusing or too fun. He seems to be drawn to that. I think he's lonely and needs You, Lord. Help him search in the right places."

Reese went on to pray for the church family and the people of Tucker Mills, especially folks she knew personally, like Mrs. Greenlowe and the Jenness family. She confessed the irritation she felt with Mr. Jenness, but that did not come easily. Just the thought of him made her tense and upset.

Reese sat very still, working to control her emotions, but she was having little success. She finally climbed into bed, using just a sheet on this warm night, and planned to speak to Douglas or Alison about the Jenness family. Mr. Jenness reminded her of her powerlessness with Mr. Zantow, and right now Reese's heart couldn't take it. With both men on her mind, she fell asleep in agitation.

∞

"Return to my house" were the only words Mr. Jenness said the next morning. Reese assumed her days would look like this for a time and hoped Mrs. Jenness would not be quite so surprised.

She wasn't surprised, but neither did she look happy. Reese was shown through the kitchen and into the buttery where she was asked to churn butter. Everything was prepared; she was not to touch more than the handle and to call for Mrs. Jenness when the butter was ready. Reese was working steadily along until she was joined by Gerald.

"I thought I heard you humming," he began, and Reese wished she'd kept quiet. "Swimming in the pond again today?"

"Something like that," Reese said, working to be careful with her words.

"How long will this take?"

"I wouldn't think very long."

Gerald fell silent, but Reese knew she was being watched. She would have asked Gerald to leave the room had she known that his mother was standing outside the door in the kitchen, listening to every word.

"You got a boyfriend?" Gerald tried.

"That's none of your business," Reese said firmly.

"You can tell me."

"I'm sorry, Gerald, but I don't wish to discuss private matters."

"Is your hair soft?"

"That's another private matter, Gerald."

Reese had kept her eyes on her work, but she was aware when Gerald moved toward her.

"Don't touch me, Gerald." She held his eyes and slanted away from him. "I don't want you to."

Her eyes and tone were just stern enough that Gerald stopped, looking uncertain and frustrated all at the same time. At the same moment, they both heard a noise in the other room, where Lillie, shaking like a leaf, pretended she'd just come into the kitchen.

"Where is that boy?" she muttered a bit loudly, going to the door that led outside and opening it a bit. "Gerald, are you out here?"

Reese didn't begin breathing again until Gerald sighed in annoyance and walked from the buttery.

Five

"Go ahead and mix that dough, Reese," Lillie made herself say. She hated having this woman working with their food, but she was desperate. She would keep Reese busy in the kitchen until Gerald was close enough to hear their conversation.

It took longer than she had hoped. Gerald clearly wanted to be alone in the kitchen with Reese. Lillie saw him come into view several times, but when he spotted his mother, he would go swiftly on his way.

For many reasons, Lillie did not want this woman in the house, but in all fairness, Reese knew how to behave. Her manner was docile, and she had said nothing in the buttery to encourage Gerald. Lillie had even given her a little more dinner today, thinking about how thin she was and wondering whether Mr. Zantow had fed the woman properly.

"I've been meaning to ask you, Reese," Lillie said as soon as she realized Gerald had parked himself in the small sitting room off the kitchen, giving him a view of Reese. "How old are you?"

"I'm 22."

"And you've been an indentured servant for how long?"

"More than four years."

"And how long do you have to go?"

"Almost two years."

"What did your father do to indenture himself to Mr. Zantow?"

"I'm not sure."

This stopped Lillie. She thought Reese would know all about it. Her mind scrambled for a new topic.

"Where is your mother?"

"She's dead."

"That's too bad," Lillie said, trying to sound compassionate. "Two more years before you can have any kind of life to call your own. What an awful thing."

Reese didn't comment. She had heard a noise in the other room and assumed it to be Gerald. She thought she understood why Mrs. Jenness would do this, but she was tired of being used. Why didn't Mrs. Jenness simply speak to her son about this issue?

Both women heard a chair move in the next room, and then all was quiet. Reese kept on with the chore she'd been given. Lillie did the same with her own work, not knowing if her little plan had done the trick or not. Nevertheless, she would tell Victor that if this woman was at her door in the morning, she would personally bring her back to the bank and do her best to embarrass him in front of anyone who happened to be watching.

❧

"What do you think this verse means?" Jace asked Maddie, leaning close to her over the parlor table.

"The first verse?"

"Yes, in chapter 3. Have you read that one yet?"

"I'm still in chapter 2."

The two of them were reading in Genesis. They did at least a few verses each night, working their way through those chapters at Douglas' suggestion and feeling amazed over all they had learned in a short time.

"How is an animal subtle? I'm not sure I get this."

Maddie studied that verse as well.

"And he talks," Maddie finally commented. "I've never been amazed by that, but I think I should have been."

Jace's head hurt a little. He was learning so much and was very excited, but it was all a lot of hard work too.

"Let's just remember to ask Mr. Muldoon about these and not get bogged down."

"Okay."

"Or," Jace amended, "we could stop and think about what we've already read."

"And not just rush on," Maddie confirmed, both remembering some tips Douglas had given them.

And so for the next 30 minutes they only talked about what they'd already read, planning to go to Douglas not just with questions but also with some ideas they both had as to what the text might be saying. And as always, they finished their study time with prayer.

∞

"You're to stay here at the bank and clean today," Mr. Jenness said sternly to Reese, his wife's words still ringing in his ears. "You'll not disturb customers in any way. You'll wash windows and be absolutely invisible. Do not talk to anyone or be in anyone's way. Do I make myself clear?"

"Yes, Mr. Jenness," Reese answered readily enough, but her heart was sinking with dread. Not talking to the townsfolk was going to be tricky. She knew that even if she kept her eyes down, the people who knew her—and quite possibly even the ones who didn't—would still call a hello to her or speak to her.

"Well, Reese."

Already humming, she heard her name just moments after she began on the side windows of the building. She knew it was Doc MacKay, but all she did was glance at him.

"Hi, Doc."

There was a moment of silence before the doctor said, "Does he want you busy?" He could not have missed the fact that she had not stopped working or even had eye contact with him for more than a moment.

"Yes. I can't talk; will you spread the word?"

"I'll do that, Reese," he said, even as he struggled with what felt like an injustice. He'd been planning on stopping at the bank but changed his mind. He needed to have a word with Alison Muldoon first.

"What are you looking at?" Cathy asked of Doyle when she came to the store and found him at the front windows looking down the green.

"It's Reese. She's washing windows, but we're not supposed to talk to her."

"What's that all about?"

"Oh, probably that Jenness. He has no control at home, so he wants to control things from the bank."

"How did you hear about it?"

"Doc came by and told me she asked him to spread the word."

"And just what is that girl supposed to do for dinner?" Cathy suddenly demanded.

"I had the same question, but I think Doc took care of that too."

"Well, you just keep an eye out, Doyle," Cathy warned. "If she doesn't go somewhere, I'll march a meal over there myself."

"Switch to the front windows," Mr. Jenness hissed at Reese just before dinner. "And get a move on it!"

Reese swiftly finished with the window she was on and climbed down from the ladder. She moved it to the front of the building, wondering what was suddenly so urgent.

Had she been given a moment's reprieve, she would have noticed that Mr. Jenness sat very still at his desk. He had a letter in front of him that he'd read twice and was now reading again.

> Mr. Jenness:
>
> This letter is to inform you that my brother, Conner Kingsley, and his partner, Troy Thaden, will be coming to Tucker Mills on 16 August. They will arrive by train and wish to take up residency in the Kingsley house. If my memory serves, the bank has a key. Please make arrangements to have the house cleaned. Hire as much help as you need to get the job done before he arrives.
>
> It's been some time since anyone has visited the bank there, and Mr. Kingsley and Mr. Thaden are planning to stay for several months. A thorough look at the books can be expected, as well as a general measurement of the needs of the residents of Tucker Mills. In other words, we wish to assess all aspects of the Tucker Mills bank and see that needs are being met.
>
> Please send word that you have received this letter. If you have questions, plan on discussing them with my brother. Thank you for seeing to this matter.
>
> Dalton Kingsley

Mr. Jenness sat back, his heart beating painfully in his chest. He sent his flawlessly written reports to Linden Heights each month. There was never a hint of a problem. Why would they come after all these years? He ran this bank to perfection. Why would they come now?

Mr. Jenness felt his heart speed up a little more. He told himself to calm down and breathe slowly, but it was proving to be impossible. He knew he'd done nothing wrong, but that wasn't the point.

"Are you ready to go?" Mr. Leffler called, suddenly putting his head around the corner, ready to close the bank and have dinner at the tavern.

"Yes," Mr. Jenness answered, trying not to sound breathless as he pushed himself out of the desk chair. He could feel himself sweating as he joined his teller at the door. He hoped others who noticed would blame it on the warm day.

"Why am I here for lunch?" Reese asked of Alison the moment that lady opened the door.

Alison couldn't stop her smile.

"Don't you know?"

"No." Reese was grinning now too. "Mr. Jenness suddenly came out and told me to come here and eat."

Alison laughed and pulled Reese inside.

"It was Doc's doing. He knew Mr. Jenness wouldn't think to send you to dinner, so he came here and checked with me and then told Mr. Jenness what he needed to do. Doc is respected enough in town to get away with it."

"I could have gone home. Mrs. Greenlowe will hear of this and wonder why I didn't."

"Won't you have fun explaining," Alison teased.

Reese knew she'd been plotted against and laughed. She followed Alison into the kitchen to find the family gathered, waiting only on Douglas. He wasn't long in joining them, declaring that he could smell the stew and fresh bread all the way from his office. He took his seat and smiled as they all bowed their heads.

"Not today," he stated and waited for everyone to look up. "Today, *all* our conversation is going to be about things we're thankful for. It's too easy to bow our heads and recite words we say without thinking."

"We're not going to pray?" Peter double-checked with a perplexed furrow of his brow.

"We might at the end of the meal, but not right now. Will you please pass me the bread plate, Hillary?"

Reese wanted to laugh. She wasn't all that accustomed to praying before a meal, so the shock for her was mild. The Muldoon children, however, looked as though their father had suggested something criminal.

"Who wants to be first?" Douglas asked as he buttered the bread in his hand.

"I'm thankful that Reese could join us," Alison said, breaking the silence and smiling down the table at her spouse.

Douglas grinned back before looking to his children. They were still taking it in when Douglas said, "A verse on thankfulness works too."

This got things moving. One by one the children chimed in with a verse or a word of thanks until they were interrupting each other. It made for a delightful meal. And Douglas remembered what he had said. When the meal was over, he asked everyone to bow their heads so he could pray.

❦

"This is the key to the Kingsley house," Mr. Jenness said the following morning, dangling the key but not handing it to her. "The house is to be cleaned from top to bottom. I want it spotless. You have a week."

The irritation had returned the moment she stepped into the bank—it was swiftly followed by shock. He was holding the key out to Reese now, but she didn't reach for it.

"What's the matter?"

"A week?" she asked softly, her tone belying her severe gaze. "It's the largest house on the green. It's the largest house in town!" she amended. "And it hasn't been occupied in all the years I've lived here."

"I am well aware of the status of the Kingsley house, Miss Thackery," Mr. Jenness began pompously but tempered his tone when he noticed Reese's eyes. She was, for the most part, a willing worker. But he was learning that she had her limits. He was tempted to bring up the subject of her papers, but in truth the house had to be done. He had also learned that although Reese was a hard worker, she was just one woman.

"What about the stable and the outbuildings?" Reese asked. "Am I cleaning those as well?"

"No. I'll have someone else see to that. Just come back before we close today," Mr. Jenness commanded, amending the original order, "and give me a report on what you accomplished."

Reese finally took the key, reminding herself she was supposed to be praying for this man and that he had retracted his original order.

"I'll be going to Mrs. Greenlowe's for dinner today," she felt a need to tell him. "Is that a problem?"

He opened his mouth to tell her not to take much time, but his wife's observation came back to him. He also wondered if she'd been fed enough over the years. Not even he could be so cruel.

"No," he said shortly and turned to sit behind the desk, effectively putting an end to the conversation.

Reese didn't linger. Sitting halfway down the green, the largest house in town awaited her. She knew she had not a moment to spare.

᧣᧣᧣

"You're filthy," Mrs. Greenlowe observed when noon rolled around and Reese stepped into her kitchen from the porch. "What does he have you doing today?"

"I'll tell you all about it during dinner, if you'll allow me into the house looking like this."

"Of course I will," she returned, becoming all at once brisk. "Get yourself in here."

"I'm starving," Reese said as she sat down, trying not to move too much.

"Well, go ahead and pray!" Mrs. Greenlowe said with excitement. "I've got to know where you've been."

Reese had to control her laughter first. She had never met anyone like her landlady. She was unfailingly harsh to the unjust, but to the hard-working she was completely accepting.

"Heavenly Father," Reese began. "Thank You for this wonderful food and for all of Mrs. Greenlowe's hard work. Thank You for strong bodies and capable minds. You've blessed us this day, Lord. Amen."

Food was being pushed in Reese's direction when she said, "I'm at the Kingsley house."

Mrs. Greenlowe actually gasped, "No one's lived there for years!"

"That's why I'm covered in webs and dust."

"Why are you there?"

"I was told I had a week to clean it."

"A week?" Mrs. Greenlowe nearly came out of her chair, but a look from Reese stopped her. "All right, I won't start on that bank manager, but only because I want to know what it's like in that house."

Reese actually whispered, "It's beautiful. I've never seen such high ceilings, and the main stairway," Reese paused to smile, "is curved and open and wide. Even the portraits are still hanging on the walls.

"And in the dining room, the dish cupboards are built directly into the walls. That room is so spacious that it holds a table with ten chairs and still has room for the fireplace and fabric-covered chairs in three of the corners."

"How many fireplaces did you see?"

"I counted six, but I just did a swift walk through the down-stairs."

"So you started upstairs?"

"Yes. I didn't want to track that dirt through a clean house."

"Good idea," Mrs. Greenlowe complimented her. "What of the kitchen and buttery?"

"The kitchen is on the main level, and it's large.

"And the buttery?"

"It's below."

"Three stories?" The older woman was astonished and stopped. "The property drops away to the barn and outbuildings on that side, doesn't it?"

"Yes, and the buttery's huge! Two rooms to work in, plus extra storage, and so many built-in shelves and cupboards . . ."

Just then Reese remembered she had no time to linger and tucked into her food. Mrs. Greenlowe opened her mouth to ask another question and knew it would have to wait. While Reese finished, Mrs. Greenlowe had an idea.

"You might get hungry and thirsty this afternoon." Mrs. Greenlowe's attempt to sound casual failed miserably. "I might need to bring you something."

Reese's shoulder shook with laughter as she said, "Don't let Mr. Jenness see you."

❧

"How far did you get?" Mr. Jenness asked of Reese, and she wondered whether he talked to everyone as he talked to her: never a greeting, just demands and commands.

"Two rooms are completely clean. I've started on a third, and I think the rest is manageable. Are there certain rooms you want me to concentrate on in case I don't get done?"

"No, if you're not going to finish, let me know with enough

time to hire more help. I'll come after dinner tomorrow to check your progress."

Reese nodded.

"Are the windows getting done?" he suddenly asked.

"I do them as I do each room."

"Are you finding mice or other vermin?"

"No, nothing like that."

"Very well. Keep the key with you and go directly there in the morning."

Considering how stingy Mr. Jenness had been in the past, Reese took this as a compliment. She half-expected him to demand that she check in each morning. This was to her advantage. If she was up and around before the bank opened, she could get right to work.

❧

"Who's moving into the Kingsley house?" Cathy asked of Maddie, who'd stopped in after she finished her errands in town.

"I don't know. I just learned that Reese is cleaning there."

"Do you think Reese knows the details?"

Maddie looked as doubtful as she felt. She wasn't privy to all the dealings in Reese's life, but she somehow doubted that Mr. Jenness had confided anything.

"Probably not," Cathy complained, looking put out. Her voice was that of a spoiled child, and Maddie smiled.

Cathy saw the look. "What?" she asked.

"You have the greatest source of information about 30 feet away, but you ask me, and I live outside of town."

Cathy's look was comical.

"I assumed you'd been to the store," her aunt said.

"I came straight here today."

The older woman was instantly on her feet.

"Come on, Maddie. We need to pay a visit to your uncle."

∽

"Reese?" Doc MacKay called as he stepped inside the front door of the Kingsley house. "Are you here?"

"Hey, Doc," Reese called, poking her head around the door frame of a small room at the back of the house before dropping her cloth into a bucket and going into the wide downstairs hallway to meet him.

"How are you doing?" Doc MacKay questioned her, studying her face carefully.

"I'm doing well." Reese smiled. "It's a wonderful house."

The doctor nodded in agreement, his head going back. He'd not been in here in years, but he remembered the layout well.

"Things look great," he complimented Reese.

"Thank you. Do you think it's to be sold?" she asked him.

"You don't know?"

Reese's mouth turned up at the corner. "Mr. Jenness doesn't exactly confide in me."

Doc smiled back at her.

"So who lived here?" Reese asked.

"George and Nettie Kingsley. George came to open a bank, and they ended up liking the area so much they built this house and stayed."

"Did they move away or die?"

"Both are dead. Nettie probably more than ten years ago by now, and George about five years before her."

"The family might be ready to sell," Reese suggested.

"I don't know," the doctor said thoughtfully, but in his heart he was doubtful. The Kingsley family was a large one. He could see someone from that family coming here to live someday.

"Well, I'd better get back to work," Reese finally observed.

"Okay," Doc agreed with a gentle touch to her arm. "I'll see you tomorrow."

"Sunday," Reese said with a smile. "I can hardly wait."

⚮

"What type of voice can God hear in prayer?" Douglas asked the group gathered on Sunday morning. "Does He simply wait in heaven to hear the prayers of any man? And before we look at the answer to that, let me remind you what prayer is. It's agreeing with God. For those of you who would have said it's talking to God, that's not enough of the picture.

"Look at our verse in Proverbs 28. I'll read it to you. 'He that turneth away his ear from hearing the law, even his prayer shall be an abomination.'" Douglas read this from his Bible and then looked at the folks gathered before him. "That's pretty serious, isn't it? But we need to hear those serious words to remind us how dire it is when we have unrepentant hearts toward God.

"You might be tempted to say you've heard enough on repentance, that I preach about it too much, but think about your life this week. How did you do with keeping God in the center of your life? Or did you push Him out of the center for sinful, selfish pursuits?"

Douglas smiled at the people before him, the folks he loved so well. He wanted nothing more than to see them be strong in Christ, repentant and changing. He kept his closing remarks brief.

"Let me just read the verse for you one more time. God says it so much better than I do. 'He that turneth away his ear from hearing the law, even his prayer shall be an abomination.'

"Let's work on memorizing that this week, shall we? Let's remember how delighted God is with ears, and ultimately hearts, that are attuned to hearing the law."

⚮

The cleaning was done. Reese had not needed help, but in the last day and half, her muscles had begun to ache. She felt she knew every inch of the Kingsley home and couldn't think of a room, closet, or hallway that she didn't like. It was the most wonderful house she'd ever seen. A small part of her hoped that a family would be coming, one that would be looking for help in a few years' time, and she could come back each week and work here.

Reese shook her fanciful head a little and stood closer to the kettle she was trying to boil in the preparation room off the buttery. She had lit a small fire so she could wash herself before going home. For some reason, what she was working on today had been especially dirty, and after dinner she'd brought her clean dress with plans to wash and change.

A lone candle burned on the mantel above. Reese didn't need a lot of light to get the job done, and when she had warm water, she took delight in scrubbing herself. Her hair needed washing too—she would see to it tomorrow—but for now, a bath over the basin would have to do.

She didn't dawdle. She'd already missed tea with Mrs. Greenlowe. In her efficient way, she was soon climbing into her clean dress. She was starting to pin her dress when the door suddenly opened. Reese's heart lurched, but she kept her head, reaching for the fireplace shovel with its long handle.

"You can't come in here," she said to the man who had started to come through the door. "This is a private home. If you're looking for lodgings, you'll have to try the tavern farther down on the green."

For a moment the man didn't react. Reese squared her shoulders since her dress was not fully pinned at the back and made ready to raise the shovel, but the man simply thanked her, and backed out the door.

Reese wasted not a second after the door closed. She blew out the candle, rushing to the window to see if he had lingered, pinning the dress as she went. Trembling that she might actually be forced to use her makeshift weapon, Reese stepped outside a moment but found all quiet in the moonlight.

Reese relaxed. He'd moved on his way. She went calmly back inside and finished cleaning up behind herself, gathered her things, and exited through the very door the man had tried to use. Starting the walk home, Reese smiled at the job she'd done, thankful and a little sad that it was over.

Not until she was well past the edge of the house and down the green did the man emerge, another man with him. They had been standing in one of the sheds by the barn. They stood together, not speaking, and watched her walk out of sight. Only then did they head back to the house and slip quietly inside.

Six

Reese woke up sore but with a fine sense of contentment filling her. Last night Mrs. Greenlowe had been pacing on the porch by the time she arrived, but Reese had warned her that she planned to work until the job was done. Reese smiled when she thought of Mr. Jenness checking on her in the morning—he had formed the recent habit of coming by before the bank opened—and finding the house locked and her not in attendance.

Reese was just about to crawl from bed when the door opened slowly. Mrs. Greenlowe's face peeked in, and she met Reese's eyes.

"Are you still alive?" that lady asked.

"What time is it?"

"Nearly 7:00!" Mrs. Greenlowe announced this fact as if a crime had been committed.

"You're not going to let me be lazy, are you?"

"You've never been lazy a day in your life! I've got a great big breakfast ready to go on the table, and you need to come and eat."

"I'm coming," Reese responded obediently and told God, much as she did every day, that He'd certainly been looking out for her the day He sent Mrs. Greenlowe into her life.

"With the house done, where will he send you?" the landlady asked as soon as Reese prayed.

"I'll find out, I guess."

Eggs, ham, corn muffins, and skillet potatoes were pushed her way. Her coffee cup was refilled before it was half empty, but Reese did not hurry. She had until the bank opened today and wasn't going to rush; it would be the first time since Sunday she didn't feel the pressure of hurrying to work.

"Did you hear about the kitchen fire at Berglunds'?" Mrs. Greenlowe asked.

"I heard the commotion in the middle of the day yesterday but didn't know whose house it was."

"Well, that's Lillie Jenness' aunt, you know—her great aunt. Don't be too surprised if you find yourself over there helping out and getting covered with soot."

"You might be right. Was anyone hurt?"

"Not that I know of," Mrs. Greenlowe said, no compassion or concern in her voice. "Where Lillie got her clean streak, I don't know. Opal Berglund couldn't be a worse housekeeper. I think she burns her kitchen down at least three times a year. If she would keep it neater, she wouldn't be setting towels and whatnot on fire."

It wasn't a nice thing to say, but Reese felt herself laughing. Mrs. Greenlowe had that effect on her. In fact, she was still chuckling a little when she started for the bank building.

❧

Conner Kingsley woke slowly, not disoriented about where he was but still surprised that he was actually here. It had been a long time. His eyes roamed the room, taking in the familiar sights even as he felt his mind rushing backward in time.

Pushing the covers off, Conner sat up on the edge of the bed. He didn't have the time or the energy to deal with those thoughts right now. He was weary from the trip that ended up being by coach and not train, and he had other things to think about. He was certain that Troy was up, so he dressed and went in search of him. Taking the back stairway that led directly to the kitchen, Conner found him there.

"Do I smell coffee?" he asked, his voice its usual whisper.

"You certainly do, and if I can find a bowl to mix them, I'll start the eggs."

"Where did you find eggs?"

"Unlike some people who slept until after 7:00, I've been all over town already this morning."

"Good for you," Conner said dryly. "Did you hit several chicken coops or just one?"

"No, I came across a woman who was headed toward her chicken pen with a basket over one arm. I offered her honest coin for a dozen, and she was delighted."

Conner smiled at Troy's smug look and peeked into the pan.

"This won't work without butter."

Troy handed him a small crock.

"I'm not even going to ask," Conner said, staring down at the butter and knowing he would have gone hungry this morning if it hadn't been for Troy.

"You didn't shave," Troy suddenly noticed.

"I'm not going to the bank today," Conner explained. "I realized last night before I fell asleep that it might be best to let you go on your own."

"Why is that?"

"I just think I should lie low for a time. The Kingsley name always has an effect on people, and even though Dalton said I was coming, you can explain to Mr. Jenness that I'm seeing to other things right now."

Troy's look was skeptical. "It's not as though you can walk around town and not be noticed, Conner."

"True." Conner was too large a man not to agree. "I might ask you to deliver a letter later today and have someone come to me."

"I can do that."

The men went to work in earnest on the breakfast, and in a short time they'd eaten their fill. Troy had been truly resourceful in the time he'd spent.

"The house is impressively clean," Conner noted before Troy could exit for the bank.

"Do you suppose that was her last night?"

"Our indentured servant? Probably."

For a moment, the two men looked at each other in silence.

"I'll see to it, Conner," Troy assured him before exiting by way of the front door. Conner quietly thanked him, praying that today would be a success in more than one way.

❦

"I went to the house!" Mr. Jenness exclaimed, wasting no time before attacking. "Where were you?"

"The house is clean," Reese stated. "I simply waited for the bank to open."

"But you must have known that I wanted to check it."

Reese said she was sorry, but in truth he had been checking in every day. He had never criticized her work the way she had expected, so she assumed it had been to his standard. And only just in time. He had said it needed to be done by today.

"Go to the Berglund home," Mr. Jenness ordered. "There's been a fire, and they can use your help."

Reese nodded in agreement and went on her way, knowing that Mrs. Greenlowe would gloat over being right but not over Reese having to work there. She didn't remember until she was far down the green that she still had the Kingsley house key in her pocket. She didn't go back right then but planned to return some time later.

"Mr. Jenness?" Troy asked of the man behind the counter.

"Mr. Jenness is in the office," Mr. Leffler explained. "May I tell him who wishes to see him?"

"The name is Troy Thaden. I'm with Conner Kingsley."

"Very well, sir," Mr. Leffler said graciously, not needing any information beyond the man's name. Troy Thaden's name was as well known in the world of banking as the Kingsley name. "If you'll give me a moment."

Troy nodded, his eyes not missing a thing.

"Mr. Thaden," Mr. Jenness said as he came rushing from his desk, his heart beating painfully. "I didn't expect you, sir."

"We were ready a number of days early and realized we wanted a coach in town with us, so we didn't take the train," Troy said kindly, willing to give this man the benefit of the doubt. "We arrived late last evening."

"Were you able to get into the house?"

"Yes, Mr. Kingsley has a key."

"Please come in." Mr. Jenness led the way and waited for his guest to take a seat. "Is Mr. Kingsley not with you this morning?"

"He asked me to begin on my own," Troy explained.

"Well, yes, all right then." Mr. Jenness stumbled a bit and then lied outright, "I'm happy to help in any way I can."

"Excellent," Troy said, opening the small satchel he held on his lap. "I have a few questions here. I'll just get my papers."

Sweat seemed to be pouring from every part of Mr. Jenness' body. He didn't know when he'd felt so nervous. He tried to tell himself he had nothing to fear, but the argument was falling flat in his mind.

"I think I'd like to ask you about this woman, the indentured servant," Troy began, and Mr. Jenness relaxed. He had thought this one of his more brilliant ideas.

"Certainly, sir. Reese Thackery was indentured to a man who

owed us a good deal of money. When his holdings did not cover the debt, I kept her papers in an effort to earn some of the bank's money back."

"I see," Troy responded, able to keep a look of interest and not judgment on his face. "And how is Miss Thackery earning money for the bank?"

"Well, she readied Mr. Zantow's house and property for auction."

"Mr. Zantow?"

"He owned her papers."

Troy nodded, unwilling to admit that this was all familiar to him. He'd read the bank report, but he wanted to hear it from Mr. Jenness' own lips.

"Go on."

"She cleans the bank building, and when word came that Mr. Kingsley's house needed to be readied for your arrival, she also took care of that."

Again Troy nodded before asking, "Anything else?"

"Well, she's at the Berglund home right now. They had a fire in their kitchen."

"And is the Berglund home owned by the bank? Is it being readied for sale?"

"Well, no, but you see, Opal is a relative of my wife, and," Mr. Jenness stopped. He hadn't meant to admit that.

"And what of your home?" Troy was astute enough to ask. "How often does Miss Thackery clean there?"

"It was only a few days." Again Mr. Jenness answered when he hadn't intended to.

"And how is she living, Mr. Jenness?" was Troy's next question.

"How's that?" The banker was turning more pale with every breath.

"I assume she lived with Mr. Zantow, but the bank has no facility to house someone. How is she living?"

"She boards with Mrs. Greenlowe."

"How does Miss Thackery pay Mrs. Greenlowe?"

"I give her a stipend."

"How much?"

"Four dollars."

"A day, a week, a month?"

Mr. Jenness could hardly breathe. He had thought that this news would be so well received, but even though Mr. Thaden didn't look upset, the line of questioning was making him look like a complete fool. How *did* he think that this would make money for the bank? Right now Mr. Jenness could not recall.

"Mr. Jenness?" Troy pressed him. "How often do you give Reese Thackery her stipend?"

"Monthly."

"And she's able to live on that?"

"She's found room and board."

"That's good to hear," Troy commented. "I shall need to see the books next," he went on, "and I want to get into the safe as well."

"The safe?" Mr. Jenness asked, panic clawing at his throat.

"Yes," Troy replied as though nothing was amiss. "Strictly routine."

"I have to go home," Mr. Jenness suddenly blurted out; he even went so far as to stand.

"Are you all right, Mr. Jenness?" Troy asked in all sincerity. "Maybe you should sit down."

"No, I have to go home. I'm sorry, Mr. Thaden. I don't feel well."

"It's all right. I can see you there."

"No!" Mr. Jenness' voice came out rather sharp. "I'll just go."

The bank manager stumbled away from Troy and across the bank to the front door. No one was around save Mr. Leffler, who watched the scene in surprise.

"I'm sorry, I didn't get your name," Troy began.

"Leffler, sir."

"Tell me, Mr. Leffler, does Mr. Jenness suffer from ill health?"

"At times he does, sir. Was he ill just now?"

"Yes, it seemed to come on suddenly."

Both men stood looking toward the front windows of the bank, even though Mr. Jenness was far from view.

"Were you aware of this situation with the indenture papers, Mr. Leffler?"

"I was, sir." That man's voice dropped with disapproval. "I witnessed them."

"And what did you think of the whole affair?"

Before he could answer, a customer came in. Troy knew there was something to be learned here. He asked the bank teller to come to the alcove office when he was free.

❧

Reese didn't mind working at the Berglund house. Opal Berglund could be scattered-brained, but she was kind, and she seemed to genuinely appreciate Reese's help. They talked of various things as they worked side by side, and not once did Reese have the impression that Opal thought her position better than Reese's. In fact, she seemed to be interested in Reese's life and asked her a number of questions.

"Is it easier working for the bank or Mr. Zantow?"

"It was predictable with Mr. Zantow, and sometimes that can be nice," Reese answered tactfully, fully aware that this woman was some sort of relation to Mr. Jenness' wife.

"And what of the Kingsley house? Was that interesting to clean?"

"It was. I've never seen a house like it."

"I knew Nettie Kingsley," Opal confessed and then began to reminisce. "She didn't get out much in her later days. She certainly loved her grandchildren."

Reese listened with only half an ear. The smell of the smoke-charred kitchen was a little strong at times. It helped to have all the windows and door open, but Reese was beginning to see that this might become a long day.

᠅

Even at the risk of losing his job, Mr. Leffler was honest with Troy. He did not speak out of turn, but when asked a question he was direct with his response.

"You didn't have a chance to give me your view, Mr. Leffler."

"Holding the papers was not something I understood, sir. I would have liked to have seen Reese gain her freedom. She's a good girl."

"How old is she?"

"I'm not sure, maybe 20."

"And did she fight Mr. Jenness at all? Did she argue her case?"

"She insisted that she have something to live on. That was the only struggle I knew about."

Mr. Leffler had no more answered when he was needed at the counter. He had taken a seat in the alcove that allowed him to see the door and excused himself as soon as someone came in.

Troy looked through the papers that were still on the desk. Everything looked in order, but this was a fraction of the documents that needed to be inspected. By the time Mr. Leffler returned to him, Troy had decided, at least for the moment, what he wanted to do.

"If you could give me directions to Mr. Jenness' house, I'm going to check on him. I'll be going to dinner after that and checking back here later."

"Very well, Mr. Thaden."

"One last thing, Mr. Leffler. Can you get me into the safe at some point today?"

"Certainly, sir. Anytime you wish."

Troy thanked him, his face showing nothing, but inside he was pleased.

❧

"You can say I told you so," Reese began when she found Mrs. Greenlowe in the garden.

"Look at the soot on you!"

"We worked past dinner. Would you mind fixing me a plate?"

"Didn't Opal offer you something?"

"Yes, but I wanted to get away from the smell for a little while, so I told her you had food for me here."

"Well, of course I do!"

Mrs. Greenlowe having gone into the kitchen, Reese sat down on the ground, her back against the fence, and waited for her food. It had not been a bad morning, and she liked to stay busy, but she only had two dresses and was concerned that at this rate they would not hold up.

It had not been much of an issue at Mr. Zantow's. She had done all aspects of housework and not simply cleaning. Cleaning was tough on fabric, especially when things were so dirty.

"Here you go." Mrs. Greenlowe talked all the way down the porch. "You eat all of that now."

"Yes, ma'am." Reese took the plate before bowing her head. She kept her prayer brief, knowing she had to get back to the Berglunds'.

Mrs. Greenlowe had grabbed the old wooden stool she kept outside and sat nearby. Reese could see she was ready with questions, and it occurred to her in that moment that she was this woman's window to the world. Mrs. Greenlowe didn't leave her house or yard much but depended mostly on word from other people to tell her what was going on in town.

Reese ate swiftly and answered questions just as fast. Unfortunately for Mrs. Greenlowe, she didn't know much. She had to remind her landlady that she was not allowed to ask how the fire had started. Her job was to work.

"Thank you," Reese said as she stood and gave her the plate.

"You're welcome. That bank manager doesn't have another job for you this afternoon, does he?"

"I don't think so. I'm sure I'll be at Berglunds' the rest of the day."

"Take care now" were Mrs. Greenlowe's final words. Reese only waved, planning to do just that.

∞∞

"Hello," Lillie said, greeting the man at the door rather coldly.

"Excuse me," Troy offered, his hat in hand and his tone kind. "I'm looking for Mr. Jenness."

"Well, he won't be here," she replied, frowning. "He's at the bank at this time of the day."

"Actually, he said he wasn't feeling well and was coming home."

Lillie blinked and stared at him.

"I'm sorry to have disturbed you," Troy said as he read her look over his news and began to back away. Lillie's voice stopped him.

"Who are you?"

"I'm sorry I didn't introduce myself. I'm Troy Thaden. Are you Mrs. Jenness?"

"I am, yes. Who are you exactly?"

"I'm here with Mr. Kingsley. I'm his business partner."

"Mr. Kingsley's here?"

"Yes, ma'am."

"So the bank is being audited."

"Not exactly. It's just been a long time since anyone has visited."

For a moment she stood in silence and then asked, "Why did my husband leave the bank?"

"He said he wasn't well. Has he not been here?"

She shook her head, her face pale. "I've been home all morning. Maybe he went to dinner early. He eats at the tavern."

Troy wasn't going to look all over town for this man. It was not his job. However, he wanted to be gentle in the way he handled this.

"When you see your husband, Mrs. Jenness, will you please ask him to come to the bank or send word to me as to when he'll be returning?"

Mrs. Jenness could only nod. Troy thanked her and went on his way. He wasn't aware of the way she moved to the window and watched him, hoping beyond hope that history wasn't about to repeat itself.

❦

"How did it go?" Conner asked as soon as Troy returned to the house.

"You won't believe it. The man looked like his heart was going to stop in his chest, and then he left."

"Left for where?"

"He said home, but when I went there, his wife said she hadn't seen him."

"What did you talk about that got him so upset?"

"We started on Reese Thackery's situation. At first he seemed pleased with his decision to retain her papers, but the more I questioned him, the more strained he became. When I mentioned seeing the books and the safe, he said he was ill and had to leave."

"But he didn't go home?"

Troy's brows rose as he wondered whether Mr. Jenness realized how bad this looked for him.

"I didn't get a chance to buy anything for lunch. Let's go to the tavern and eat."

"I'll get my coat," Conner agreed.

Not until they were almost to the tavern did Troy remember that Mr. Jenness might be there. Part of him hoped they would not see him. Right now he just wanted to eat dinner in peace.

∞

The morning had not been easy for Conner. He had walked around the house, unable to fend off the memories of the place. He could still see his grandmother sitting in her favorite chair but couldn't hear her voice anymore.

He could envision his parents, Dalton, and his sisters around the dining room table when all of them would visit Tucker Mills. In the later years of visiting the family home, Conner would come with just one of his sisters, usually Maggie. They were the youngest, and their lives hadn't taken the busy tone of his older siblings' lives yet. They still had time to come and see Grandma, especially after Grandpa had died.

With the memories and feelings that surrounded him, Conner wanted out of the house for a while. He'd forgotten how beautiful the area was. It was a warm day—a little too warm, actually—but he didn't plan to be out long or overwork his mount. He escaped to the barn and saddled one of the horses they'd brought, planning to head toward the outskirts of town for a long, leisurely ride.

∞

"Has there been word from Mr. Jenness?" Troy asked Mr. Leffler when he returned to the bank.

"No, sir."

"Did I see you at the tavern for dinner?"

"Yes, I was there."

"Did anyone mention seeing Mr. Jenness?"

"I was asked about him, but no one had seen him."

"Is this normal behavior for Mr. Jenness?"

"Not at all, sir. He's very punctual and conscientious."

Troy stood for a moment in indecision.

"And what of Miss Thackery? Will she be in today?"

"She was in this morning and was given her job for the day."

"Cleaning a house, wasn't it?"

"Yes, the Berglund home—a kitchen fire."

"When does she come back again, in the morning?"

"Exactly."

"Mr. Leffler, thank you. I'm going to start on the files. Tell me if Mr. Jenness or Miss Thackery arrives back."

"Did you want into the safe, sir?"

"Probably not today."

Mr. Leffler went back to work behind the counter, thinking of the times he'd wondered how he would do as the bank manager. At the moment, he couldn't have been happier that the position was filled by another man.

Seven

Reese got to the bank at the normal time on Saturday morning, the key in her hand so she would not forget. Preparing to smile and greet Mr. Leffler, she stepped inside as she always did but found him coming around the counter to meet her.

"There's someone here to see you, Reese."

Reese stared at him, trying to gauge the serious look on his face. Mr. Leffler was usually so cheerful.

"His name is Mr. Thaden, and he's using Mr. Jenness' office."

"Where is Mr. Jenness?"

"Feel free to ask Mr. Thaden," Mr. Leffler said, following his instructions.

"Have I done something wrong?"

"Not at all. You'll like Mr. Thaden."

Reese nodded and looked toward the alcove. As usual, the bookshelves kept her from seeing anything, so she went that way.

Troy, who had heard every word of the conversation, was looking up when she came into view.

"Miss Thackery?"

"Everyone calls me Reese."

Troy came to his feet. "I'm Troy Thaden." He held out his hand, and Reese shook it. "Please sit down."

"Thank you."

Reese took a seat and looked at this well-dressed businessman. He seemed kind, but Reese was still under the impression that she might have committed some infraction. Not until she felt the key biting into her hand did she realize how tense she was.

"Mr. Thaden," Reese began. "I have the key to the Kingsley house. Should I leave it with you or Mr. Leffler?"

"Actually, why don't you hold onto it for the moment. There's some business I need to discuss with you."

"Did Mr. Jenness ask you to?"

"Not exactly." Troy worked to be gracious, already impressed with this young woman. She was not unlike his own two girls. "Are you aware that the Kingsley family owns the bank here in Tucker Mills?"

"Yes."

"Well, I work with Conner Kingsley, and the two of us have come to check on this bank and assess how business is progressing. Some changes will be made, and some things will stay the same."

Reese nodded again, not sure what any of this had to do with her.

"Mr. Jenness was under the impression that having an indentured servant would be to the bank's advantage. On the other hand, Mr. Kingsley and I do not think it the best idea, so we'll be turning your papers over to you. You are no longer an indentured servant."

Reese looked for a moment at the contract he held out to her and then took it. The silence hung over them like a blanket. Reese stared down at the document, saw that it was in fact her papers, and returned her gaze to him.

"What about Mr. Zantow's debt?"

"That is not your problem. The bank will have to take a loss on anything outstanding."

Reese was not taking this in. The news was so very unexpected. She looked down at her papers and back at the banker.

"So what happens to me?"

"You're free."

Reese's face cleared. "So I should get work and continue to pay the bank that way?"

"No," Troy adamantly shook his head. "You don't owe anyone. You are certainly free to get a job, but the money is your own. In fact," Troy continued, picking up a small stack of bank notes, "this bank never should have owned your papers, so these notes are to cover the hours you worked while we held your papers."

Reese reached out mechanically to take the money but was utterly speechless. It was becoming clear to her now. She was free. She wasn't owned by the bank or anyone else. She was free!

"I should tell you," Reese remembered, "that Mr. Jenness gave me a stipend. Has that amount been deducted from these notes?"

"No, and it won't be. You'll keep the stipend and the notes I just gave you."

Reese nodded slowly and then bit her lip.

"Are you sure Mr. Jenness approves?"

"You're free, Reese," Troy repeated quietly. "You are no longer an indentured servant."

Reese glanced down at the paper and notes again. She was beginning to grasp the news, and when she looked up again, Troy saw that her eyes had widened.

"I could buy shoes," she said in wonder. "And put money in the offering plate at the meetinghouse."

Troy had to suddenly clear his throat and remind himself that he still had business with this woman.

"You certainly could do those things, and you could also consider an offer I have for you," Troy began, finding it easier at that moment to look down at the desk than at Reese. He moved a few papers and then looked up. "Mr. Kingsley and I will be in Tucker Mills for an indefinite period of time, but no less than three months. We would like to hire you to cook and clean house for us."

"You're offering me a job?"

"Yes."

"At the Kingsley house?"

"That's right. We'd like you to keep the house up, look after our clothing needs, and prepare breakfast each morning and dinner for us each noon. You will have Sundays off."

Reese suddenly stood up, and Troy smiled at how tall she was. He didn't know why he had missed that when she came in. He watched her walk out of the alcove and heard her speak to Mr. Leffler, who was behind the counter.

"He set me free and then offered me a job."

"You should take it," Mr. Leffler said, his own emotions giving him trouble.

"It's at the Kingsley house."

"You love that house," the teller reminded her.

"Oh, no," Reese turned. "I walked out of the office!"

She rushed back, a hand over her mouth, but Mr. Thaden was smiling.

"I'm sorry. I had to tell Mr. Leffler."

"It's wise of you to check with someone. Do you want the job?"

"Yes." Reese made herself sit down and told herself to breathe. "Do you want me to start today?"

"In a way, I do. We have very little food in the house. Do you suppose you could shop or arrange to have some things delivered on Monday? You wouldn't have to come to the house until then, but that would give you something to work with."

"Do you have an account with Doyle Shephard?"

"I don't think I know Doyle Shephard."

"He owns Shephard Store."

"That would be a good account to have. Do I need to set that up, or can you?"

"I can do it," Reese said simply, and Troy found himself relaxing. She was going to be perfect. Clearly she knew her way around a house and this town, and right now that couldn't have been a better combination.

"I think you'll also want an account with Mr. Veland. He'll sell meat he's butchered, and Sammy Fletcher has a dairy herd, so they always have extra cheese and cream," she said, thinking back to life at Mr. Zantow's.

"Can you take care of those?"

"Certainly," Reese said, feeling so excited that she could hardly sit still. "Mr. Thaden, is it all right if I take about an hour and see some people? Then I can work on those accounts."

"I want you to handle this however you like, Reese. You don't need to limit yourself to an hour. If there's dinner on the table at noon on Monday, and you're looking after the house by that day, then we won't worry about the details for today."

"All right," Reese agreed, but for a moment she couldn't move. It was so wonderful, and she had to take a moment to pray and thank God.

"Are you all right?" Troy asked, watching her face closely.

"Yes. I'll get out of your way now."

"I'll see you Monday morning?"

"Yes. Thank you," Reese said softly, her voice telling Troy that she was overwhelmed by it all. Reese left the office alcove and almost headed to the door. At the last moment, she realized what she must do. Approaching the empty counter, she spoke to Mr. Leffler.

"Mr. Leffler, can you help me open a bank account?"

"It would be my pleasure, Reese," he told her, his smile as wide as his face.

Behind the bookshelves, still at the desk, Troy let his head fall back, hearing Reese's voice at the counter as she asked questions and opened her own account. Troy thought that giving Reese Thackery her freedom might have been the sweetest moment he'd ever known. Coming from a man with two grown daughters and two grandchildren, this was a pretty significant emotion.

⬦

"Doc?" Reese called from inside his front door, but there was no answer. She stood and called for about a minute, but he didn't seem to be around. Reese was disappointed not to share her news with him, but she realized she had two more stops to make.

Her walk was a little slower than it had been. She certainly wanted to tell the Muldoons and Mrs. Greenlowe, but Doc had been first on her list. Reese made herself shake off the sadness and went ahead to Mrs. Greenlowe's.

To Reese's utter astonishment, that lady was not around. She was always at home! Reese looked all over the house and yard but came up empty. The Muldoons lived closest to the bank, and Reese was beginning to wish she'd started there. At the same moment that she came to this conclusion, she decided to let the Tucker Mills grapevine spread the word about her freedom and new job. She would simply wait for people to ask her about it, confident that it would happen sooner than later.

⬦

Troy went back to the house about midmorning. He had a stack of papers in his satchel and had told Mr. Leffler that he would be at home if needed. Troy found Conner in the study working over the desk, but the younger man seemed pale and quieter then usual.

"Any word from Mr. Jenness?" Conner asked, making room on the desk for Troy to work and spread out the papers.

"No."

"I hope he didn't wander off and collapse somewhere. Even if he's guilty of something, we don't want that."

"Mr. Leffler had not heard or seen a thing. I did get to speak to Reese, however."

"What did she say?"

"At first she didn't understand, and then when it sank in, she was overwhelmed."

"I can imagine. Did she accept your offer to work here?"

"In a heartbeat. She's already planning to set up accounts around town today."

Conner's brows rose in admiration. "You certainly picked the right person, Troy."

"According to Leffler, she had no help on this house. And she did it in just over a week. Now, we might find that she can't cook a thing, but we'll take that as it comes."

"What's she like?"

"Early twenties, I would guess. She's tall and redheaded. Too thin. Quiet and unassuming. I can tell she's used to being invisible."

Conner nodded, and Troy finally asked about him.

"I have a headache," Conner admitted. "I suspect it's tied to being here again. I'm experiencing more emotions than I'd planned."

"Are you sleeping?"

"I did the first night, but not last night."

"Did you go see Douglas Muldoon this morning?"

"No, I changed my mind about that. I know he has children, and this head pain could mean something else. I decided not to risk spreading a possible illness."

These details out of the way, the men went to work. Conner had a mind for numbers that was astounding, whereas Troy liked words. Reports were read, numbers were checked, and a good bit of ground was covered before the two decided it was time to break for dinner.

Troy had something on his mind while they worked but couldn't quite recall it. Not until he glanced around the room and noticed the bookshelves did he think to explain to Conner the way Mr. Jenness had set up the alcove.

"He had the bookshelves blocking the view of the desk, like a wall?" Conner clarified.

"That's right."

"Did he say why?"

"We never got to that."

Conner only shook his head. If Mr. Jenness was in fact an innocent man, he was going about showing it in all the wrong ways.

Jace came in from evening chores, his mind distracted with his thoughts. Not until he'd washed up did he realize that tea was ready to go on the table but the house was quiet. Jace thought he would find his wife upstairs, but as soon as he started that way, he spotted her bent over the desk in the corner of the parlor.

"There you are," Jace commented.

Maddie turned to receive his kiss.

"I'm just finishing a letter to your sister and was absorbed."

"Did you seal it?"

"Not yet."

"I'll add a bit," Jace offered and took Maddie's place at the desk. He wrote and told her he wished it was the time of year he could be away from the farm but a visit would have to wait. In the midst of this, he stopped and looked at his wife.

"Did you tell her about the baby?"

"No. Why don't you?"

While Maddie put their meal on, Jace added more to the letter. He smiled as he wrote the good news to his sister, and watching him from the table in the parlor, Maddie smiled at the sight. She hoped that Jace's sister would come after the baby was born, but mostly she wanted to see her husband's face when they finally met this little person.

"Where have you been today?" Mrs. Greenlowe asked Reese when she came in close to teatime. Reese had been at the Shephard Store around dinner time, and Cathy had insisted on feeding her.

"I was here earlier and missed you," Reese began.

"Well, you'll never believe what I heard around town," Mrs. Greenlowe said, clearly in her element. "Seems you've been released from your papers and hired at the big house. I told folks it was nonsense. I said I would have known."

When Reese didn't say anything, Mrs. Greenlowe's eyes got big.

"Reese Thackery, you tell me right now."

"I tried earlier. I stopped by, but you weren't here."

Not even upset that she didn't know, Mrs. Greenlowe demanded to hear the whole story. Reese was in the midst of it when there was a knock at the door. Reese was closer and went to open it.

"Is it true?" Doc was standing there, wanting to know.

"It's true," Reese confirmed with a smile.

The doctor's heart felt as though it would burst in his chest. He put his arms out, and Reese welcomed his hug.

"Oh, Reese," he murmured quietly. "You can't know how I've prayed, how I've begged God to rescue you."

"Well, He did," Reese said, looking to find tears in the doctor's eyes.

"Get in here and have tea with us," Mrs. Greenlowe suddenly ordered, and the doctor did not argue.

"All right, Reese," Doc MacKay began once the dishes had been passed. "Who did this exactly?"

"A Mr. Troy Thaden. He works for the Kingsley family, or with them, or something like that."

"Where is Mr. Jenness?"

"I don't know. Mr. Leffler suggested that I ask Mr. Thaden, but I forgot to do that."

"And how did it come about that Mr. Thaden hired you?"

"I don't know, but I assume he knows I cleaned the house. I think he and Mr. Leffler have talked some."

"You got your orders from Leffler?" Mrs. Greenlowe asked in confusion.

"No, but he always knew where I was headed for the day."

"And what will be your jobs at the big house?" Mrs. Green-lowe needed to know.

"Dinner every noon, the house, and their clothing. Sundays off."

"Do they plan to work you like a dog?"

"I don't know," Reese had to answer honestly, "but at least I'll be paid for my efforts."

"And if she doesn't like it," the doc put in gently, "she has a choice about leaving."

Mrs. Greenlowe and the doctor fell to talking about something else happening in town, but Reese didn't join in. She took a long drink of tea, still trying to take in the morning's news and hoping that the wonder of this time would not wear off very swiftly.

❧❧

Troy stood over the boiling kettle in the kitchen early Sunday morning. Not expecting to hear Conner come in behind him, he turned to find the younger man very sober and knew in an instant that his head still hurt.

"Why don't you go back to bed? I'll bring you some tea."

"Since when are you stuck with the job of nursemaid?"

"Whenever needed."

Conner stood still, keen disappointment knifing through him. He'd planned to attend services that morning at the meet-inghouse. He knew now he would not hear a word of the sermon, and trying to meet people and interact when he felt so lousy would not have been a good idea.

Conner did take the cup of tea offered to him, but he drank it by the stove, hoping the heat would drive the ache from his head and neck. Troy offered him some breakfast, but he declined. One more cup of tea later, Conner returned to bed.

∞

Is it true? was the question on everyone's lips at the meeting-house. The folks were so happy for Reese that Douglas asked her to come to the front so he could ask some questions of her.

Alison did very well until Reese smiled at the congregation and admitted to opening her first bank account. The pastor's wife buried her face in Jeffrey's little neck and cried. Her husband couldn't help but notice that many folks were in this condition, and he called for a time of silent prayer in an effort to give everyone some time to regroup.

When a few minutes had passed, Douglas prayed out loud, thanking God for always taking care of His loved ones. He also asked God to bless and keep Reese as she entered this new phase of her life. The wise pastor asked God to give Reese greater knowledge of His saving love and understanding that no matter what her situation looked like, free or not, her goal was godliness as His child.

∞

Troy checked on Conner in his bedroom a few hours later. "How are you?"

"Didn't you go to services?"

"No, I didn't feel comfortable leaving you."

"I'm sorry, Troy. I wish I had realized."

"So how are you?"

Conner thought about this. "Hungry, I think. That must be a good sign."

"I asked the tavern to bring us something about noon. Will you be all right until then?"

Before Conner could say that he needed food immediately, both men thought they heard someone knocking on the door. Troy went downstairs to check and found a man he didn't know.

"I'm sorry to bother you," Douglas Muldoon began and then introduced himself. "I'm looking for Dalton Kingsley. Does he happen to be here?"

"Please come in, Mr. Muldoon," Troy invited. "Or should I say Dooner?"

Douglas laughed. "I can see the family has been talking."

"Actually, Conner is here," Troy explained as they moved further into the hall. "Dalton wanted to come, but his daughter is quite ill right now."

"I'm sorry to hear that."

"Dooner?" Conner spoke from behind the men as he came down the stairs and into the wide hallway.

Douglas did not hear Conner's voice, only the floor creaking behind him. He turned and smiled at the youngest member of the Kingsley family.

"Hello, Conner," Douglas greeted, putting his hand out. "How are you?"

"I think I'll live."

"Are you not well?"

"Just a headache. I didn't come to visit in case it's more than that."

Douglas smiled suddenly, his eyes full of fond memories.

"I had forgotten that you were even bigger than Dalton."

Conner's eyes twinkled as well. "You mean my little, big brother."

Douglas laughed. "Something like that. Oh," he said, suddenly remembering the basket in his hand. "My wife has been baking and sent some things with me."

"Thank you," Troy acknowledged when the basket was handed to him.

Conner said, "Just in time. I'm starving."

"Please don't tell me you men don't have food here."

"We're doing fine," Troy spoke up, wanting this kind pastor to believe him.

"And besides," Conner got in when it was quiet enough to be heard, "Reese Thackery comes tomorrow."

"About that," Douglas tried to begin but couldn't manage the words. In the wake of this humble man, the younger brother to an old friend of his, he felt overwhelmed.

"I think before it's over with, Mr. Muldoon," Troy spoke up, "we'll be the ones thanking you."

Nothing more was said about the matter as the men visited for a time. They learned that Douglas had come straight from the meetinghouse and was missing his dinner, but even when theirs arrived, he would not stay.

Conner told Douglas he would visit soon, and before they began to eat their dinner, he'd found the cookies in the basket. He made a mental note to thank Mrs. Muldoon when he met her, and he also hoped Reese's baked goods would be half as tasty.

Eight

Reese felt her heart pound a little as she opened the side door and let herself inside the big house. She had woken early that morning and memorized a verse from Psalm 18. Two large baskets that had not been fun to carry from Shephard Store were now able to go on the worktable, and Reese realized she'd recited the verse all the way to the house.

With the merciful thou wilt show thyself merciful; with an upright man thou wilt show thyself upright. Reese repeated the verse one more time before she started to carry items up the small staircase that led directly to the kitchen overhead.

It was a lot of extra steps on this first day. She had not been told to use the side door that led out to the barn and other buildings, but she felt better doing that. The front door did not seem to be the right place for her. Not at this house.

Reese stood for a moment, not sure if anyone was about, and then realized she had no time to spare. She wanted to see to the house and have dinner on the table in less than three hours. It was time to get to work.

⚭

"What was he thinking, Troy?" Conner, who was feeling like himself again, asked about Mr. Jenness as he looked at the office setup in the alcove at the bank. Conner, having nothing to hide and enjoying customers, found the arrangement rather cramped and confining.

"Let's rearrange," Troy suggested, having wanted to do that on the first day.

"All right."

"I'll move the desk; you do the shelves."

Conner told himself not to laugh, but it didn't work. This belief that Conner could lift anything was Troy's continuing joke. And he was a strong man, but bookshelves almost as tall as he was and full of books were certainly beyond his reach.

"Why don't I move the desk, and you start unloading the books?"

"Always the lackey," Troy teased, making Conner laugh again.

"Just a minute," Conner said, suddenly stopping him. "I'm going to check with Mr. Leffler about this."

"All right."

"Mr. Leffler," Conner began when he got to the counter. "We want to rearrange the furniture in the alcove. Is that going to disrupt business for you?"

He was so soft-spoken that Mr. Leffler had to strain upward to hear him. He hoped he caught all the words and said, "Not unless I need to get into the vault and my way is blocked."

"Are you certain? We can leave it until after hours this evening."

"It should be fine, Mr. Kingsley. The customers won't mind."

"Tell me, Mr. Leffler. Are you free for dinner this noon?"

"I am, sir."

"Good. You'll come home with us."

Troy had come around the bookshelves to hear all of this and immediately offered to head home and tell Reese.

"Or I can go," Conner realized.

"No, I'll do it."

Conner smiled slowly. "You're getting out of moving things, aren't you?"

"Not at all," Troy said, but he wasn't convincing. He exited while the youngest Kingsley was still laughing.

               ∽◯◯

A pork roast stew was bubbling on the stove, rolls were rising nearby, and the pie she'd made the night before at Mrs. Greenlowe's was ready to be cut. She still had a cheese soufflé to bake, vegetables to cut and add to the meat, and butter to dish out, but the meal was shaping up nicely.

Reese had taken out the most lovely dishes to place on the table. She wasted several minutes admiring them before she remembered that the clock was ticking. She'd put the dining room to rights and then started on the rest of the house. The bedrooms were in good order, but the downstairs parlors needed dusting already. It hadn't rained for more than a week, and the layer of dust on the fine, dark furniture could certainly attest to that.

Things still looked a bit sparse, but Reese had not felt it was her job to decorate. Other than the various Argand lamps, the shelves and tables were still basically bare, and Reese simply hummed along, dusting cloth in hand, her hair pulled back at the nape of her neck so she could bend without getting it in her face. This was how Troy found her.

"How is it going?" he asked when she heard steps and looked to find him in the doorway of the small family parlor at the rear of the house.

"I think it's going fine. Is there something special you wish me to concentrate on?"

"If that's dinner I smell cooking in the kitchen, I don't care about anything else."

Reese couldn't help but smile.

"Will it be a problem if there are three of us for dinner?" Troy asked, remembering why he had come.

"Not at all, Mr. Thaden. I'll set another place. Will you be coming directly at noon?"

"Yes, as soon as we close the bank."

"I'll have it on the table."

"Are you finding everything?" Troy questioned, some urge inside of him wanting to make life a little easier for this woman.

"I think so. If I've missed something, I hope you'll tell me. I didn't find any clothing to wash."

"We'll let you know, all right?"

"Certainly."

"You can call me Troy," that man suddenly added, not liking it when she addressed him as Mr. Thaden.

"All right," Reese agreed, but she looked a bit surprised.

"'Mister' makes me feel old," Troy explained, which was only partly true.

"You don't look old," Reese told him, her face relaxing.

"I'm a grandfather."

Reese's look turned comical.

"You can't be!"

"Twice over," Troy added with plenty of grandfatherly pride.

Reese was still looking surprised when Troy smiled at her one more time, waved, and went on his way. Reese went out into the hallway to see him exit through the front door, and in doing so realized the stairs were quite dusty. Not wanting that to be the first thing the men saw when they came home, Reese went to work on those.

She worked along steadily until she came to a portrait on the wall. She thought this might be Nettie Kingsley and wondered exactly how she was related to the Kingsleys who were here in Tucker Mills. When she'd talked to Douglas before services the day before, he'd said that Dalton Kingsley was here. Reese didn't think that was the name Troy Thaden had used but admitted to being rather unsettled by everything Mr. Thaden had said.

For a moment Reese stood and wondered about it. She thought it uncanny that Douglas knew this family from another town and had ended up living in Tucker Mills. Going back to her humming and dusting, Reese decided to ask Douglas more about it. The story was probably worth hearing.

∞

Reese put the last of the serving dishes on the dining room table and slipped out of sight into the kitchen. Telling herself to relax and breathe normally, she stood and hoped they would come soon. For some reason, she didn't want to be around when they ate. She thought her cooking would be fine, but for some reason, she felt awkward. A desire to please Mr. Kingsley, a man she hadn't even met, as well as Troy Thaden, was strong within her.

In the midst of these thoughts, she heard the front door open. She quietly glanced around the kitchen to see if she'd forgotten anything and then slipped down the narrow stairs to the workroom and out the side door. She didn't want to be in the way right now and had already told Mrs. Greenlowe she would be home for dinner.

She walked away from the house with a sense of accomplishment and excitement. She only hoped they would enjoy the meal.

∞

"Oh, my," Troy said when he saw the dining room. Reese had not answered his call, but clearly she expected them to eat. The men took seats, all thinking that Reese had outdone herself. Three places were set on one end of the table, and all the dishes were in reach. If the aromas could be trusted, they were in for a treat.

"Will you please pray?" Conner asked Troy when the men had gotten comfortable. Troy obliged.

Mr. Leffler hadn't expected this, but he didn't comment or do anything more than bow his head. He didn't even hear the prayer. He was too busy thinking about Mr. Jenness. Wherever that man had gone, he was certainly missing out. He'd not been a kind employer or a personable banker, but a small portion of Mr. Leffler's heart was sorry for him.

"I think I want you to check on Mr. Jenness again," Conner said when they began to eat. "Maybe his wife has heard from him."

"I'll go after dinner," Troy replied but then turned to Mr. Leffler. "Would she hear from him and not tell us?"

"What do you mean?"

"I asked her to inform me if he was in touch. Would she do that?"

"I think so," Mr. Leffler said, not wanting to ask what he was thinking. Would Mrs. Jenness protect her husband and help hide him if he'd somehow cheated the bank? Mr. Leffler had not had that many dealings with Mrs. Jenness, but she didn't seem the type to stick up for her husband. Indeed, they seemed cross with each other every time Mr. Leffler had seen them interact.

Mr. Leffler need not have worried about sharing any more. The other two men had no intention of putting him on the spot, at least not more than they already had. They asked Mr. Leffler to tell them about his family and how he'd come to live in Tucker Mills. The subject of the bank and banking did not come up again.

∞

"How did it go?" Mrs. Greenlowe was ready with questions as well as the meal.

"I think all right. The meal smelled good."

"Did they say if they liked it?"

"I didn't stay to find out."

This gave Mrs. Greenlowe pause.

"Why was that?" she asked quietly this time, not usually her way.

"I don't know. I just didn't want to be in the way, and I felt a little embarrassed."

Mrs. Greenlowe's heart turned with compassion. If there had been someone in this girl's life to give her confidence and deserved praise, it had been more years ago than anyone could remember.

"You're a good girl, Reese," was all the landlady would say.

Trying to eat her own food, Reese smiled at her and hoped that the men were enjoying what she made.

⧓

When Mr. Leffler did not have a customer, he helped Conner with the office. The books had to be returned to their rightful place, and some were quite dusty. The men worked side by side, not talking a lot, but as the afternoon wore on, Mr. Leffler was better able to catch Conner's soft tones. He was greatly curious to know why this man whispered but would not have asked under any circumstances.

"I think we need a railing along this area," Conner pointed to the place where the bookshelves had been used as a wall. "Something about so high," he used a hand to indicate some three feet off the floor. "And with a small swinging gate. It will keep an air of professionalism and still be welcoming to the public."

"It seems to me that there used to be one," Mr. Leffler looked at the walls for marks and found some under the paint. "Yes. It was right where you're suggesting."

"It must be in my memory then," Conner surmised. "Now who would we ask to make this?"

"Mr. Zantow was the best, but he died recently."

"Was that the man who had Reese Thackery's papers?"

"The very one."

"And he was a woodworker?" Conner clarified.

"Yes, you look surprised."

"I am. I pictured the owner of a larger business, since Mr. Thackery was the first indentured servant. What did Reese's father do for Mr. Zantow?"

Mr. Leffler looked surprised before admitting, "I don't recall."

Conner nodded, but his mind had gone to the fact that Reese had never made an appearance. The men had gone so far as to clear their own dishes back to the kitchen, but they never saw Reese to thank her for the wonderful meal.

He thought he might ask Troy to check on her when he returned, even then wondering how Troy might be faring at the Jenness home.

❦

"Hello," said the young man who answered the door this time. Troy guessed him to be about 16.

"Excuse me, I'm looking for Mr. or Mrs. Jenness."

"My mother is here," the young man confirmed and stepped back, allowing Troy's entrance.

Troy watched the youth walk away and heard voices before Mrs. Jenness returned on her own.

"I'm sorry to bother you again," Troy began, thinking she looked even more severe than before. "I just wanted to check on Mr. Jenness. Is he all right?"

"I don't know," Lillie admitted. For all her severe looks, her tone was humble and subdued. "I haven't heard from him at all."

"I'm sorry. If I'd known that discussing bank business would have been so upsetting, I would have handled it differently."

Lillie looked him in the eye, realizing she could not let this opportunity pass.

"Can you come in?" she asked, wanting to add his name, but she'd forgotten. "I'd like to know what happened."

"Certainly, Mrs. Jenness," Troy agreed, seeing no reason to hide anything from this woman.

"What did you talk about exactly?"

"We started with the subject of Reese Thackery. I needed him to explain his reasons for retaining her papers."

"I don't know what he was thinking," Lillie put in, her voice filled with confusion. "He even had her come here." Lillie shook her head a little. "I didn't need her help. I didn't want her here, but he seemed so excited."

Troy nodded, not sure what to say next.

"Was that all?" Lillie pressed.

"Well, almost all. I then asked about the account books and the safe. He became very distressed at that point and said he must leave."

Lillie put a hand to her face before whispering, "Victor, what have you done?"

"You need to know, Mrs. Jenness," Troy spoke right up, "that as questionable as your husband's behavior may seem, we've found nothing out of order. We're still going over things, but so far there are no issues."

Lillie nodded, looking hopeful for the first time. Troy, however, knew he had to say the rest.

"Should we find something, Mrs. Jenness, I will certainly come and inform you, but you need to understand that I'd also be going to the authorities. I really would have no choice."

"Yes, of course." Lillie uttered the words automatically, even as her heart cried for it not to be true. Her marriage was not at all what she had hoped it would be, but Victor was a good provider, and she knew Gerald needed a father.

"I won't keep you any longer," Troy said, standing, his hat in hand. "Thank you for seeing me, Mrs. Jenness, and I hope you learn very soon that your husband is well."

"Thank you," Lillie returned, coming out of her misery long

enough to remember her manners and realizing as he left that he had been kind. She had no more shut the door when she saw that Gerald had come in behind her.

His questions about his father and what he'd done only served to make Lillie's head hurt. She had no answers. It hurt even worse when Gerald thought she was hiding something from him and left the house in anger.

"Are you leaving, Reese?" Troy asked when he gained the kitchen and found her headed for the stairs, basket in hand.

"Yes, I'm done for the day. I left everything ready for your tea," Reese said, nodding her head in the direction of the table in the kitchen.

"We couldn't find you at dinner," Troy said, going right to the point.

"Oh, I'm sorry. Did you want me to serve you?"

"That's not it. We weren't able to thank you, and I was concerned that you hadn't eaten."

"I went home for dinner. Thank you for asking."

"Was there a reason you did that? Did you think that's what we wanted?"

"I wasn't sure, and I didn't want to presume."

"Starting tomorrow, we'll expect you to eat the same food you've made for us. You don't need to serve us, or eat when we do, but we expect you to partake of our food for dinner."

"Thank you," Reese said, unable to avoid a smile; he had sounded so severe.

"Am I being laughed at?" Troy's face told her she could joke with him.

Reese couldn't stop smiling. "You were a little serious just now."

"Are you going to stay and eat here?"

"Yes."

"Then it worked, didn't it?"

Reese laughed. "As long as you're here," she changed directions, "is there anything you need me to do before I go?"

"I'm sure not. If I spot something, I can tell you in the morning. Breakfast, right?"

"I'm planning on it."

"That's a relief. I'm tired of my own eggs."

Wanting to laugh all over again, Reese only smiled and went on her way. They hadn't said when she would be paid or how much, but never having been so appreciated in her life, she almost thought she could work there for free.

∞

"Is he ever going to go to sleep?" Alison asked of Douglas, who was sitting on the edge of their bed long after the rest of the children were down for the night, still holding six-month-old Jeffrey.

"I don't know," Douglas answered, still smiling at his little son.

"It might help if you stop playing with him."

"What fun is that?" Douglas teased her.

"I think it's fun to sleep." Alison rolled over and got comfortable. "Goodnight, you two."

"Can you tell Mama goodnight?" Douglas whispered to Jeffrey, who smiled in delight. "We're going to pray for Mama now," Douglas added, and _very_ softly he thanked God for the wonderful wife He'd given to him and also asked for His blessing, his voice lulling both his wife and son to sleep.

∞

On Tuesday morning the breakfast aromas wafted up to him

as Conner descended the stairs. Troy's efforts in the kitchen had been fine, but they hadn't smelled as enticing as this. Cutting through the dining room to get there faster, Conner came to a complete halt on the threshold of the kitchen. There he was greeted by a sight that brought him to a standstill. Reese faced away from him, her hair hanging straight down her back, thick and dark red, and the top of her head not many inches below his own. Conner backed out before he could be spotted. He went in search of Troy, who was in the study.

"What's the matter?" Troy asked when he saw Conner's face.

"Reese is in the kitchen."

"Yes, I just spoke to her."

"She's tall."

"I told you that," Troy reminded him.

"She's taller than my sisters."

"Yes," Troy smiled, wondering what the younger man had been expecting. "Did you meet her?"

"No, she seemed busy."

"Well, come on, I'll introduce you."

Conner trailed along, suddenly feeling much younger than his years. He didn't know exactly why he'd not gone in and introduced himself. She had just been such a surprise.

"Reese," Troy began congenially, "I want you to meet Conner Kingsley. Conner, this is Reese."

"Hello," Conner said in a way that Reese could not hear. Her own greeting was equally soft, her eyes watchful.

"We won't stay in your way," Troy said, not sure what he was seeing between the couple. "About ten minutes until breakfast did you say?"

"Yes," Reese replied, finding her voice by looking at Troy. She glanced back at Conner, but he didn't try to speak again.

Conner exited the kitchen and decided to wait in the dining room. That only worked, however, until Reese came in, was startled by his presence, and nearly dropped a dishful of food. Conner decided to wait in the hall until Troy joined him.

"Did Reese seem all right to you?" Conner asked, not having to be worried about being heard.

"I think so. You might have been a surprise to her."

"Why is that?"

"Well, you were surprised by her height. She's probably not accustomed to many folks in Tucker Mills being taller than she is. And if she does know some, she's used to them by now."

"But you think she'll be all right?"

"Certainly," Troy said dismissively. "She's a very capable young woman. And from what I can see, nothing much discourages her."

Conner chose to take Troy's word for the matter. After all, he'd had several days of dealing with her, and Troy's character judgments were exceptional.

What the men did not know was that Reese wasn't all right. She nearly set her apron on fire before finishing the final touches on breakfast, and just as soon as she was able, she went down to the buttery to stand alone and gain control of herself. She even heard Troy calling for her, probably to say thank you, but she couldn't make herself move.

When she did move, it was after she'd heard the front door open and close, and the house became silent. Waiting a bit longer to be sure, she scooted back up to the kitchen, checked to make sure she'd not left a fire unattended, and then headed out the front door.

Panic of the most severe type rode hard on her heels. She had to speak to Douglas, and it had to be now.

Nine

"I've got to see Douglas!" Reese shouted breathlessly into Alison's surprised face.

"He's in his study," Alison said, stepping back when Reese rushed in.

"Douglas!" Reese began calling, going toward the study door.

Douglas had heard the commotion and was headed that way. He opened the door only to have Reese step quickly inside. Alison stopped at the threshold, but Douglas approached their guest.

"Reese, what is it?"

"Have you seen Mr. Kingsley?" Before Douglas could answer, Reese exclaimed, "He's huge, Douglas! He's gigantic! What am I going to do?"

Douglas started to speak, but Reese was too distraught to notice.

"What am I going to do?" she repeated, wringing her hands.

"Reese, why don't you sit down," Douglas suggested, only to have Reese's agitation grow.

"Douglas, you don't seem to understand. He's huge! I won't be able to do a thing. I always felt I could stop Mr. Zantow, but it's not going to work this time.

"And what do you really know, Douglas? What do you truly know about this man? What if he gets to drinking?"

"Reese, I want you to sit down," Douglas commanded firmly, and Reese had enough presence of mind to obey. She sat in the chair as directed and visibly trembled.

Looking at her, both Douglas and Alison were reminded of the morning she'd come to them, terrified of something that had happened and desperate for answers.

"He's huge," she whispered now. "It seemed like the perfect job, but I don't know if I can stay. He's so large."

"Did something happen? Did he speak to you in a belligerent way or act threatening?"

"No, he just stood there. So tall!" Reese could have gone on, but Douglas put a hand on her shoulder.

"You need to trust me on this, Reese," Douglas began before she could grow more upset. "Conner Kingsley is a fellow believer in Christ and is not going to harm you. It's the very last thing he would do."

Reese looked up at Douglas, not really seeing him.

"Why would God do this, Douglas? Why would He ask me to work for a man who scares me?"

"I can tell you something wonderful about that, Reese," Douglas began gently. "God's plan for you is perfect, and right now, His plan is that you took that job, or it wouldn't have happened. You feel fear right now because you don't know Conner, but you can trust me, Reese. He's never going to hurt you. So you can keep your job, and you'll have to begin working on your fears of him."

Douglas found his arm gripped with a nearly bruising hold.

"So you think I should go back?" Reese looked as panicked as she felt.

"Yes. I wouldn't send you if there was danger, but I know these men won't harm you."

"You would send Alison or Hillary?" Reese felt desperate enough to ask.

"Absolutely," Douglas told her, and Reese saw the peaceful truth in his eyes.

For a moment silence fell on the room, leaving each with his own thoughts. Reese was the first one to speak, her voice resigned.

"I might as well go. When Mr. Kingsley sees the way I act around him, he'll only fire me."

"That's his choice. That's not the type of man I know him to be, but if he wants to do that, then we'll ask God to find more work for you."

Reese finally noticed Alison at the door. Tears were standing in the older woman's eyes.

"I'm sorry I made you cry, Alison."

"Don't worry about me. I'm just hurting for you."

"I didn't mean to rush in like that."

"Come on," Alison said. "I'll walk you back."

"And I'll pray before you go," Douglas offered. "Father in heaven, we thank You for Your plan and Your perfect and holy ways. You know all about Reese's fears, Lord, and You understand because she has been hurt. Protect her now from the temptation to let her fears take over. Help her to give Conner a chance. Help her to see that he's a godly man and a fair employer.

"Thank You, Lord, for this wonderful job You provided. Help Reese's mind to be full of good works and not her fears. Help her to know she can turn to You at all times and come to us whenever needed. Thank You for this opportunity to turn to You in need. In Your Son's name I pray. Amen."

Reese was still trembling when she left, Alison at her side, but that wiser woman simply talked to Reese all the way back to the house, asking her about what she would prepare for dinner and what cleaning she had to do.

Alison didn't press Reese to take her indoors to see the house, although she was curious, but gave her a hug to send her on her way.

Reese remembered everything Douglas had prayed for and prayed the prayer again. Then she made herself go back to work.

∞

"Is that Reese?" Conner asked of Troy from the desk chair. Troy turned to the window to see two women walking past; one was indeed Reese.

"Yes, it is. Does she look upset to you?"

Conner didn't comment. Reese was upset, and Conner did not have a good feeling about this. She could certainly come and go as she liked, as long as the agreed-upon work was getting finished, but for some reason this scene, coming on the heels of their introduction, was out of the ordinary.

"Did you want me to check with her?" Troy offered.

"No, but I need to warn you about what I'm thinking: She's more afraid of me than you first thought."

Not about to argue, Troy nodded and then watched Conner go back to work on the papers they had found in the vault. The older man hoped he was wrong, but either way, Conner clearly didn't wish to speak of it anymore.

∞

Lillie's hands shook as she opened the letter that Doyle had handed her that morning. She had more shopping to do but cut it short to go home and read her husband's handwriting.

Lillie, it began simply.

> *I'm sorry to have left town so suddenly, but I was called away on business. I hope you were not unduly distressed. Please inform Mr. Leffler that I shall be in touch soon, and please give Gerald my regards.*
>
>

Take care of yourself,
Victor

Lillie's hands continued to shake as she read the brief missive two more times. It didn't say why he left or when he would return, but it meant that as of at least a few days ago, he was safe. Lillie sank into a chair in the parlor and tried to find comfort in the only news she had.

She had been so torn between fear and anger; fear that she would never see him again and Gerald would be utterly lost for answers, and anger that he would leave without telling them.

Lillie knew in an instant what she must do. She must head to the bank. It would be best to tell Gerald right away, but if he wasn't home, she would go directly to the green and see the man who had visited her twice.

It might not take all suspicion of her husband away, but it certainly meant something that he planned to be in touch. Lillie would be making a request of them this time. She would ask to be informed as soon as they'd heard.

᠀᠀᠀

"Hello, Mrs. Jenness," Mr. Leffler greeted her from behind the counter as soon as she walked into the bank. "May I help you?"

"Hello, Mr. Leffler," Lillie began, sounding slightly more cordial than she had in the past. She stepped closer to the counter, dropped her voice, and did not take her eyes from the teller. "I'm here to see that gentleman over there, the smaller man, but I can't remember his name."

"Mr. Thaden?"

"Yes. I need to tell him something."

"I'll tell him you're here."

Mr. Leffler slipped over to the alcove and had a word with Troy. He was swift to come toward Mrs. Jenness, a smile on his face.

"Hello, Mrs. Jenness. How are you today?"

"I'm well, thank you."

"Please come over and meet Mr. Kingsley, my business partner."

Troy took care of the introduction and then asked the lady to be seated. Troy took the chair next to Lillie, and Conner took the seat behind the desk. Nevertheless, Troy handled the questions.

"What can we do for you?"

"I've had a letter." Lillie reached into the small bag she carried, took the paper out, but didn't hand it to either man. "It's from my husband, and he says he'll be in touch with Mr. Leffler soon."

"Does it say he's all right?" Troy checked right away.

"It would seem that he is. He said he was called away on business and that he hoped we hadn't worried."

"I'm glad to hear he's well, but I was wondering about Mr. Jenness' other business. Where might he have gone on such short notice?"

"He's not in another business, and in truth, I don't know where he might have gone," Lillie told him. She hadn't expected this question but wasn't overly surprised that he'd asked it. She'd been asking the same question herself.

"Might he have gone to see a relative?" Conner inserted, hoping he could be heard.

"They all live far away," Mrs. Jenness answered, appearing as uninformed in all of this as she truly was.

A moment of uncomfortable silence fell among the three, all of them aware that customers had come in, some looking their way.

Troy stayed focused on Mrs. Jenness, and she eventually spoke again.

"I would ask a favor of you," she began, her eyes darting back and forth to each man. "As you asked of me, I would like to know when my husband is in touch. Would you allow Mr. Leffler to do this?"

"Certainly. We'll inform him of what your letter says as soon as he's free, and I'm sure he won't have any objections to easing your mind."

"Thank you for coming in, Mrs. Jenness," Conner told her sincerely.

Troy saw her to the door, still ignoring looks that came their way. When she was gone, he waited only for the customers to exit to speak with Mr. Leffler about the nature of her visit.

∞

Reese asked herself what she'd been thinking when she told Troy that she would stay for dinner. She warned Mrs. Greenlowe that she might not see her most days, and now she stood, waiting for the sound of the front door, hoping not to die of fright.

She stood by one of the kitchen windows as the men came in and went right to the table. She thought one of them might have prayed but couldn't be sure. She was just beginning to relax when she heard her name called. Reese forced herself to move.

"Yes?" she asked at the door, hoping to control her emotions.

"May we have some butter, Reese?" Troy asked.

"Yes," Reese agreed, turning to see where she'd left it and taking it to the table.

"Did you eat, Miss Thackery?" Conner tried but didn't think he was heard. In fact, Reese was headed out of the room when Troy's voice stopped her.

"Reese, did you eat yet?"

"No," she answered, eyes on the table. "I'll eat in a little while."

"All right."

Reese exited the dining room as soon as she was able and took up her place by the window again. There was a chair nearby and she sat, thinking that nothing was worth this. If she couldn't calm down, she needed to give up this job. Her heart was pounding, and her face was flushed. She had been afraid just being in the same room with Conner Kingsley, and that wasn't fair to either of them.

Reese was in the midst of working this out, trying to be logical and remembering verses about God's love and care, when Conner walked into the kitchen, dishes in hand. He set them on the worktable. Reese made herself stand and thank him.

"It's I who should be thanking you. That was a very good meal."

It was quiet enough to hear him this time, and for a moment Reese wasn't so afraid. However, all she could manage was a nod.

Watching her, Conner felt compassion stealing in. He didn't know what it was about him that she feared, but he was sorry for her. Knowing firsthand how crippling fear could be, he simply said, "Have a good afternoon."

Reese managed another nod before Conner went on his way. His plate in hand, Troy came in as well, thanked her, and moved off.

Not until the men were outside, walking back to the bank, did they speak of her again.

"Was it any better?"

"No. She didn't even speak."

Troy wished he had an answer. This never occurred to him. She was a strong woman—he was sure of that. What was it about Conner that put her so far off track? They were almost back to the bank when Troy had a thought.

"Go see Dooner."

"What will he do?"

"He might know something and be of help to you."

Conner stood still for a moment, not sure if that was a good idea. Before the men entered the bank, a number of townsfolk passed by. Some greeted him and Troy, and some only stared, but no one looked afraid.

"I'll see you later," Conner said, a hand to Troy's shoulder before he stopped. "I don't know where he lives."

"Leffler will know," Troy said, smiling a little.

Conner shook his head and went inside for directions. Reese Thackery's reaction to him had him more rattled than he realized.

෨෧෨

Reese decided to work on the upstairs after lunch. She hadn't dusted there the day before and knew it probably needed some attention. What she hadn't counted on were unmade beds. First in one bedroom and then another. Reese had to smile as she bent over to tuck the covers into place. Both men were well dressed and seemed to have no item in their lives out of place. Their unmade beds told another story.

Conner had at least pulled the covers back into place a bit. Not so Troy. Clearly he'd tossed them off with little regard for where they landed in order to climb from the bed. And the chest of drawers in each room was in no better shape. The tops were littered with various items, none of which Reese stopped to study. She dusted around the interesting contents of a man's pocket and tried to make things as neat as possible.

Reese knew from the original cleaning of this house that the extra doors in both rooms were built-in closets. Both doors were shut, however, and the housekeeper didn't venture there. In fact, she tried not to linger long at all. Feeling a bit like she was invading their privacy, Reese finished the rooms as swiftly as she could and went on with the rest of her work.

෨෧෨

"Reese Thackery is afraid of me," Conner wasted no time saying once the study door was closed. "Why is that, Dooner?"

"I can't tell you that right now," Douglas said with regret.

Conner stared at him a moment, trying to gather his thoughts. This was not what he expected Douglas to say.

"Is it me specifically?" he tried next.

"Yes and no."

Conner's look was almost comical. "That was little help," he said slowly.

"I'm sorry, Conner. I wish I didn't have to be so cryptic, but I can't betray Reese's trust."

Conner thought about that for a moment. Clearly this was tied into something from the past, but what from the present: his size, his soft voice, his overall looks, or some combination of things? Or something he'd not even thought of.

Conner sighed a little before saying, "Maybe she was just tired."

"Reese is never tired," Douglas said in a dry voice.

"What do you mean?"

"Just that. I've never known anyone with such energy."

Conner did think about the fact that she'd cleaned the entire house by herself. And in about a week's time, if he was remembering correctly.

"I will give you this advice, Conner," Douglas added when Conner sat quietly. "Be yourself with her. Talk to her, be kind to her, whatever you think the moment demands. And when you think it's right, tease her the way you would me or Troy."

Conner thanked Douglas for his time and the wise words. He met Alison on his way out but didn't take any more of their time.

As he headed back to the bank, his mind was far from finance. It was still on Reese. Douglas couldn't tell him what was going on, and he thought Reese might die of fright if he tried to ask her. Nevertheless, he would find out. Conner had made several goals for himself before coming to Tucker Mills. Learning what went on inside that redheaded mind of Reese Thackery just made the list.

"How is Reese doing?" Hillary asked at tea that evening, not missing the way her parents looked at each other the moment she voiced the question.

"Well, she's still adjusting," Douglas replied tactfully. "It's all a bit new."

Hillary was not a little girl and heard more than her father said. That Reese would need to adjust when she was so good at this made no sense to her.

"But she's been cleaning and taking care of Mr. Zantow for years," Hillary pointed out.

"True," Douglas agreed slowly, "but every household is different, and there are new things to be learned."

"And that house is pretty large," Alison put in quietly.

"Have you ever been inside?" Joshua asked, unknowingly diverting the conversation. Hillary, however, was not put off. Once the evening moved on, her brothers in bed and only Jeffrey needing to be fed and put down, she landed herself on the foot of her parents' bed.

"What's going on with Reese?" she wasted no time in asking. Although Reese was a few years older, she still considered her a friend.

"Mr. Zantow wasn't always kind to Reese," her father said, coming directly to the point. "And she's had some fears that Mr. Kingsley would be the same way."

"Has he been unkind to her?"

"No, but sometimes old fears affect the present."

Hillary understood this. She hadn't seen Reese as much since the bank took her papers, and now she probably wouldn't see much of her because the Kingsley house was so large.

"Thank you for telling me," Hillary said, wishing her parents a good night.

"Are you sad, Hillary?"

"A little. For Reese."

"She'll appreciate your prayers."

The oldest of the Muldoon children nodded and took herself off to bed.

∞

"Could I bother you for some coffee?" Conner asked of Reese not 20 minutes after she arrived.

"It's not quite ready," she whispered back at him, her eyes never leaving his face.

"When should I come back?"

"In about five minutes."

"Thank you."

Reese stood watching the door out of which her employer had exited, not sure what to think. For the first time he'd been without a coat. At some point in the night she convinced herself that he wasn't all that large. She assumed his coat gave him a certain presence. She was wrong. Even in shirtsleeves, he was a large man. He had broad shoulders, a long torso, and long legs. Reese guessed him to be at least five inches taller than she was.

And all he wanted was coffee. You need to calm down.

Reese returned to breakfast preparations, her ear listening for Conner's return in hopes that she wouldn't look at him with such terror. Beyond the first day, he hadn't looked at her so intently, so maybe he wasn't noticing any longer. Reese hoped that her face was not giving anything away, but she knew the way her heart pounded could not be covered.

"Now?" Conner was suddenly beside her, asking quietly.

Reese started but went to get a mug, her hand shaking so badly that she put it on the table to pour.

"I don't expect you to wait on me," Conner said, taking the pot before she could get there. "Thank you anyway."

Reese nodded, feeling unnerved but remembering to offer cream.

"Thank you," Conner said, and Reese watched as he turned the color quite light and then added two heaping spoonfuls of sugar. She watched all of this in silence before looking up into his eyes. To her utter astonishment, he was smiling at her.

"I don't want to taste the coffee if I don't have to," he told her, taking a sip and moving on his way.

Reese actually moved so she could look into the dining room. He'd taken his place at the table, the coffee nearby and a Bible in front of him. She stared at the sight of him until she realized he was waiting to eat.

Wondering if any situation in her life had ever had her so baffled, she forced herself back to the task at hand.

Ten

"How have things been going?" Alison asked of Reese first thing Sunday morning, having prayed for her the entire week.

"Better, I think. I don't have to see too much of Mr. Kingsley, and that makes things a little easier." Reese looked down at the floor. "I feel guilty even having said that. I know he's not like Mr. Zantow."

Alison suddenly leaned toward her.

"I don't want you to be alarmed, but he just walked in with another man."

"He's here? In the meetinghouse?" Reese's breath quickened without warning. She told herself she was being foolish, but it didn't work.

"Yes. Don't you remember Douglas telling you he was a believer?"

"I must have missed that," Reese got out before Martin came looking for his mother.

"I'll talk to you afterward," Alison said, giving Reese's arm a squeeze and moving on her way.

Reese told herself to calm down. He was a fellow believer here to learn just as she was. It was time to be seated anyway. She took her normal place in one of the back pews and kept her eyes to the front. She was certain she could concentrate on everything that was said if she just didn't think about having to interact with Conner Kingsley.

132

∝∾

"Did I happen to notice you putting something in the offering plate?" Doc MacKay gently teased Reese after the service.

"Yes, you did," Reese answered, unable to stop the huge smile that stretched across her face.

"I don't mean to pry," he continued, his voice still light, "but I happened to be looking your way and thought I saw your hand move."

Reese bit her lip, trying not to laugh, but it wouldn't stay inside. She laughed in delight, and the doctor hugged her.

"It feels wonderful," she told him. "I had no idea."

"God doesn't have to look far to find a cheerful giver today," Doc complimented her.

"Thanks, Doc."

With a hand to her shoulder, he moved on his way. Reese was still smiling after him when Alison headed over to finish their conversation.

∝∾

"What would you say if I asked you to go with me to the meetinghouse some Sunday?" Reese asked of Mrs. Greenlowe over dinner.

The older woman looked at her but didn't immediately answer. Reese waited. She was tempted to apologize or start babbling but held her tongue.

"I might come," Mrs. Greenlowe said quietly, and then, "I think you need a new dress."

Reese didn't know if that was her way of changing the subject or not, but she allowed it.

"I probably need two," Reese agreed, "but I'm not sure when I'll shop for fabric."

"I'll get swatches from Doyle. You know he won't mind."

"All right. Look for something in blue or green."

"Not red?"

"No." Reese was firm.

"What about yellow?"

"It soils too easily."

"Well, you could just wear it on Sunday."

"I can't afford a dress I wear only one day."

"Not one day," Mrs. Greenlowe reasoned. "Fifty-two!"

Reese had not been expecting this comeback, and it made her laugh.

"I'll come with you sometime," Mrs. Greenlowe suddenly said, and just as suddenly stood, leaving the table and the kitchen. Reese stared after her, wishing she knew what had just happened. Was she supposed to ask her again or wait for her landlady to bring up the topic? Reese slowly finished her dinner, wondering how she would find out.

∞

"Reese," Conner began, coming into the kitchen first thing the next morning. "May I ask you a question?"

"Yes," she replied as she fell immediately to whispering.

"Who is the best carpenter in town?"

"Mr. Zantow," she answered without thinking. "I mean, it was Mr. Zantow . . . um, let me think."

Conner ignored the way her nerves seemed to take over. He waited patiently, not standing too close but still wanting to be heard, as Reese nearly wrung her hands and glanced at him in fear every few seconds.

"If you can't think of someone right now, maybe you could let me know."

"Oh, all right." Reese's voice was so comically relieved that Conner had to smile. Reese saw that smile and wished she knew what it meant.

"Something smells good," he commented before he could laugh.

"The potatoes, I think," she whispered.

"With onion?"

"Yes."

"Reese?"

"Yes."

"You don't have to whisper."

"Do I whisper?" she whispered to him, and Conner only smiled. He also took pity on her and moved from the kitchen.

∞

"Maddie?" Jace softly spoke his wife's name, bending over her on the settee. "Time for bed."

Jace smiled when she didn't answer. He didn't know why he tried. She did this every night and never had an answer for him. During the day she was hale and hearty, but after tea, she could not stay awake. Even on days when Clara was there to help, Maddie's day ended in the parlor, sleeping where she sat.

Jace lifted her, and she felt as boneless as a sleeping cat in his arms. Making sure her head and arms would not bump the walls on the stairs, he bore her off to bed. It occurred to him that by the time she delivered, he might have to get her awake in order to put her to bed.

"Jace?" Tonight she woke when the cool air from the bedroom hit her skin.

"Right here," he said, still helping her into a nightgown.

"I'm sleepy."

"Okay."

He knew she wouldn't remember a thing. In fact, she tended to frown at him in the morning, and he knew she was trying to remember getting from the parlor to their bed. She never remembered turning in.

Finally Jace crawled into bed beside her, trying to pray and not be frustrated with how tired she had been each night for the last few weeks. Before the baby, their evenings had been spent in a much different manner. They were not even to their first anniversary, but life had certainly changed.

He knew he was being selfish, but a little part of him wanted the old life back. He tried to remember if Clara was scheduled to come in the morning and then wondered if his chores could be done a little late.

※

Reese took several deep breaths, making herself concentrate. The men were already at the table having breakfast, and she'd been putting it off since she arrived. If she put it off any longer, she'd miss her chance. At last she made herself step to the doorway and speak.

"Mr. Betz."

Both men looked at her, but Reese's eyes were on Conner.

"What's that now?" he asked.

"Mr. Betz is a carpenter."

"Thank you, Reese," Conner said gravely, but his eyes just barely hid a twinkle.

Reese nodded and slipped out of sight. Conner looked to Troy to find him smiling.

"Progress?" the older man asked softly.

"Maybe," Conner replied, his heart hopeful, glancing toward the kitchen before going back to his meal.

※

"Gerald?" his mother tried for the second morning in a row. "What's the matter?"

"Nothing," he said, but Lillie knew it was a lie. Always a

good eater, Gerald had barely touched his food for several days, and Lillie feared that her husband's absence was starting to wear on him.

"What are you doing today?"

"I don't know." This was also his standard answer.

Lillie didn't worry that he would get in trouble—he wasn't that kind of boy—but she knew he was lonely, spending most days lying around the house or walking around town on his own. He didn't know what he wanted to do with his life, and Lillie had never been willing to push him. Victor had always bowed to her wishes on the subject.

Still worrying over a cup of tea after Gerald left the table, she determined to put on a wonderful dinner, hoping he would have an appetite by then.

∞

"How many documents have we read?" Troy asked mid-morning. He was at the desk this time.

"Maybe half."

"There's nothing here. Every account is in order."

"I noticed that." Conner's voice and face were thoughtful, but he wasn't coming up with any answers.

"So why did he rush off and say that he was ill? A man doesn't do that unless he has something to hide."

"Or so we assume?"

"What do you mean, Conner?"

"Just that, Troy. We assume it means guilt, but what if we're missing something? What if it's not about that?"

"What would it be?"

"I don't know, but clearly we're missing something."

Conner sat back a little, his long legs stretched out in front of him, the papers on the desk ignored. He was going to figure out

Victor Jenness; Conner had no plans to leave Tucker Mills until he did.

❦

"Do you have everything you need?" Reese asked when the men were a few minutes into their dinner.

"Yes, Reese, thank you."

"Everything is very good."

"Thank you. I'm going to work on the flower beds at the back of the house. I'll be out there if you need me."

The men thanked her again, and Reese nearly skipped through the wide hallway with her plan. Why it had never occurred to her, she didn't know. She was getting better concerning her fear, but if Mr. Kingsley was in the house, she was tense. She'd stepped out into the yard while they ate dinner the day before; she was going to try it again today.

Now Reese slipped quietly out the back door, trowel in hand, with plans to attack beds that had long needed weeding. Some flowers had survived well on their own, going to seed and even spreading, but it was plain to anyone who looked that they had been given no care in many years. Reese went the few steps down the back porch, her eyes already on the flowers.

When she missed the last step and stumbled, she braced herself for a twisted ankle. Her knee wrenched painfully in one direction, and a startled gasp escaped her. There was no railing to grab, so she landed on the ground, her twisted knee slamming painfully into the dirt.

Reese stared at the dirt just past her nose, still not sure how she got there. Her knee already throbbed, so she rolled painfully and tried to sit up. That required bending her knee, and even though she accomplished it, it left her panting with the pain.

"Oh, this is bad," she said softly, her breath coming in gasps. "I can't be hurt. I'll lose my job."

With this reminder, Reese knew she couldn't let this get the best of her. There was no railing to use, but Reese spotted the door handle and decided she could pull herself up the steps and to a standing position using that. Careful not to bend her knee, she twisted her body slowly that direction, not thinking about what she might be doing to her dress.

Using just her arms, she gained the bottom step. Had it not hurt so much, she would have laughed when she remembered that she still had one good leg. She made the next step by using her arms and one leg to push, concentrating with all her might not to bend that other leg.

She had just geared up to try for the landing when the door opened. Reese looked up from her awkward position, her heart thudding painfully, and saw Conner's face looming above her.

"Reese?"

That woman said nothing but turned her body so that it looked like she was simply sitting on the step.

Conner looked down at her hair, seeing it full of dried leaves and even some twigs. He didn't need to be a detective to know that something had gone wrong. He didn't try to speak but neatly stepped around her on the landing and went to stand on the ground, so that they faced each other. Reese glanced to make sure her legs were covered and then watched him with clear distrust.

"Do you want to tell me what happened?" Conner asked, taking in her flushed face.

"No."

Conner should have seen that coming.

"I want you to," he tried.

"I'm all right."

"I think that might be open for debate."

At the moment Reese was defensive enough to raise her chin, her eyes defiant not just with her employer but with the pain.

"Can you stand?" Conner tried.

"I'm sure I can."

"Have you tried?"

"You opened the door before I could reach the handle." She made it sound as though it was all his fault.

"Is your ankle hurt?"

"My knee."

"We need the small coach," Conner suddenly said, and Reese realized that Troy was in the house behind her.

"No," Reese began, but she was roundly ignored.

"Okay," the older man agreed. "It's been sitting a while and might take a little doing."

"No, really," Reese started again. "I think I can stand."

"Do you want me to help you to your feet?" Conner offered; Troy had gone to the stables.

"No!" Reese nearly shouted the word, panic filling her.

"All right," Conner agreed, thinking it was too bad that he scared her. "I'll go help with the coach, and maybe you'll be on your feet by the time I get back. Shall I shut this door?"

"Thank you," Reese said, humbled by his willingness to let her try. She sat very still until the door shut and then began to work her way to the landing again. Fear drove her, and she managed to reach the door handle swiftly. That was the last thing that went well. Try as she might, she could not pull herself up while only using one leg. Each time she tried, her other leg bent of its own volition, and she ended up gasping with the hurt. A few tries and she was more frustrated and crushed than she'd been in many long months, and so winded she didn't think she could go again. Conner found her like this.

"It didn't work," Reese volunteered, hands to her face in distress. "I'm going to lose my job."

"Why would you lose your job?"

Alarmed to see that Conner was coming her way, Reese could not force out an answer. Without apology or word, he lifted her into his arms. Reese's hands were still on her cheeks and she trembled with more than pain.

Conner didn't delay but walked swiftly toward the waiting

carriage around the house in the stable yard, and placed Reese inside. He climbed into the seat, took the reins from Troy, and put the horse into motion.

"Where to, Reese?" he asked, managing to be heard when he shifted to glance at her.

Reese gave instructions, trying to keep her knee straight, and in what felt like an eternity later, they were pulling up outside of Mrs. Greenlowe's white house.

That lady had come outside as soon as she spotted the carriage. "Why, Reese, what happened?"

"I wrenched my knee," Reese told her, feeling as though she could actually cry.

"Well, let me help you," Mrs. Greenlowe offered, but Conner was already there, lifting her and taking her up the steps into the open house door. He didn't wait for instructions but found the parlor and set Reese on the sofa. Still bent over her, he spoke.

"Come back to work when you're ready."

Conner then nodded to Mrs. Greenlowe, said goodbye, and exited, leaving those women to stare after him and then at each other.

"All set?" Troy asked Conner when he joined him at the bank.

"Yes. She was most upset about losing her job."

"I can see how she would be. What did you tell her?"

"To return when she's ready."

"And in the meantime, you'll have to eat my cooking," Troy offered.

"There's always the tavern," Conner teased before they got down to serious work.

"Have more tea," Mrs. Greenlowe ordered as she refilled Reese's cup with the drink she believed would cure all.

"Thank you."

Mrs. Greenlowe had done everything Reese would allow in order to make her comfortable. The knee was wrapped in cool cloths, but not wanting it to bend, Reese refused a pillow at first. Mrs. Greenlowe finally put it under Reese's foot. Reese also denied the poultice Mrs. Greenlowe wanted to try, not believing in such things when the skin wasn't broken.

"Did you have dinner?" Mrs. Greenlowe finally asked, always eager to feed someone.

"I don't think I did. I didn't get dinner cleaned up at the big house either."

"Well, if Mr. Kingsley can haul you around like you were a feather, he can lift a dish and take it to the kitchen."

For the first time in two hours Reese felt like laughing. She chuckled while Mrs. Greenlowe went to the kitchen to prepare a plate. All the time she worked, she shouted out to Reese.

"You didn't tell me he's the size of a small mountain. I don't know why you don't mention these things. And with that soft voice. I could barely hear him. And polite. I like a man who doesn't talk your ear off.

"That was a nice coach too. How many do they have? I thought they came by train. Has that been here all these years, or did it just come? I'll bet that was the horse he rides. It was a big one."

Reese only half listened. When she thought about being carried around so far off the ground, she lost her breath again. And Mr. Kingsley had been nice, even Reese had to admit that. He'd talked to her and not just given orders, and everything had gone very swiftly.

But most of all, he'd been right. She couldn't stand on her feet right now, and working had not been an option. She planned to be back on the job in the morning, but right now her knee was too swollen.

"I won't be able to climb stairs," Reese told Mrs. Greenlowe when she brought her a plate of food. "I'll need to camp out down here."

"You don't fit on that sofa, but we'll make you comfortable."

"Thank you."

"I picked these up just in time," Mrs. Greenlowe said, pulling a table close and setting out the fabric swatches. "Since you can't jump up and clean anything, you can look at the swatches I picked out."

"Is that red?" Reese asked with a frown, and Mrs. Greenlowe whipped that piece of fabric away.

"For an apron," the woman defended herself. "I look right snappy in red."

It was happening again. Even with the pain of her knee, Reese wanted to laugh.

Eleven

Troy was the one to hear the knock. He wasn't expecting anyone at this time of the morning, and curiosity more than anything else drove him swiftly to the front door. He found Reese.

"Reese!" Troy said with surprise. "What are you doing here?"

"I'm sorry to come to the front," she said, thinking that's what he meant.

"But what about your knee?"

"I can work today if I don't have to climb stairs, so I can still get your meals and work on the rooms on this level."

"Have you been using the side door all this time?"

"Yes."

"Why?"

"I thought it was best."

Troy stood aside, realizing he had left her on the stoop. He could certainly see why she felt that way after the way she'd been treated, but it was still very hard on his heart.

"Are you certain you're up to this?"

Before Reese could answer, Conner had spotted them by the front door and was coming their way.

"Reese?" he questioned, echoing Troy. "What are you doing here?"

"I'm here to make breakfast," she said, even managing to get her chin up a little; lately she felt safer if she allowed herself to become a bit defiant. While this was certainly not her normal personality, right now it felt like survival.

"I don't think you should do that," Conner said.

"You have to eat," Reese countered quietly, never dreaming they would object. Mr. Zantow hadn't cared how she felt.

The men only stared at her, and Reese, not knowing what to do with their expressions, backed toward the door, all defiance deserting her.

"I'll go," she said, trying to push away the thought of not being paid for a whole day, added to yesterday's half-day.

"We'll take you back," Troy offered.

"I can walk, thank you," Reese said and slipped out the door again.

Troy rarely saw Conner frustrated, but this was one of those times.

"What should we have done?" the younger man asked, his hands up in defeat.

"I don't know. I don't know why she felt so desperate to come."

Conner walked to a parlor window that let him see down the street. Reese was making her way methodically along, but not walking with her normal stride.

"How will she know when to come back?" Troy asked, but then he spotted something. "She's not going home."

"I see that." Conner followed her progress.

"She's headed into Shephard Store," Troy said, looking at Conner. The two men began to smile.

"I think she meant it. We should have let her stay."

"Will she come back tomorrow?"

"I hope so." Troy's look made Conner laugh. "Otherwise you're stuck with my cooking for more than one day."

"Well, Reese," Doyle greeted her with a smile. "What brings you out in the middle of the week?"

"I'm shopping for dress fabric, and then I want to look at shoes. Just look," she emphasized, not willing to touch her money in the bank unless she was desperate.

"Right over here," Doyle indicated with pleasure, not noticing that Reese was not having a very good time. Her knee did hurt, but more than that, she worried about the money she was losing. She had to have a new dress—there was no getting around it—but shoes would have to wait. Today she would just price them and plan.

If she'd only kept her head at the big house and not backed away, she might have been able to work. But she couldn't tell what Conner was thinking, and she had to be feeling very brave to cross that man. Trying not to dwell on it anymore, Reese brought out the swatches she'd stuffed into her pocket at the last minute and put Doyle to work.

⸎

"How are you feeling?" Alison asked of Maddie, who had stopped in soon after dinner with a recipe that Alison wanted to try. Maddie felt comfortable enough to stay while the pastor's wife started her baking.

"A little donsie now and then, but most days I'm good until evening. Then I fall asleep in the parlor each night."

"It's nice that you don't feel sick all the time."

"I'm not crazy about the taste of chicken right now, but nothing else has changed."

A baby's cry came from the stairway just then, and both women looked to see Peter coming from the back stairs, Jeffrey in his arms.

"He tipped over and bumped his head," Peter explained.

Tears of self-pity rolled down the baby's round cheeks,

intensifying when he spotted his mother. Alison took Jeffrey in her arms, cuddled him close, and told him all would be well. She smiled at a delighted-looking Maddie as the cries turned to sniffles and shudders.

"May I hold him?" Maddie offered, almost pleased that he was upset and she could comfort him.

"Certainly. He needs to eat, so you might not have a great time."

As soon as Alison said this, they all heard a knock on the front door.

"Pete, will you please get that?"

"Okay."

Peter skipped off in that direction and found Reese on the step.

"Hi, Reese."

"Hi, Pete. How are you?" she asked as he opened the door to allow her in.

"I'm fine. Are you limping?" he asked, having followed her through the parlor toward the kitchen.

"Yes. I fell on my knee at work yesterday."

"Hello," both Alison and Maddie greeted when Reese arrived in the kitchen. Reese kissed the top of Jeffrey's little head and took a seat nearby.

"Not working today?" Maddie asked.

Reese made a face. "I hurt my leg yesterday, and they didn't want me to work at the big house."

"Who are *they?*"

"Troy and Mr. Kingsley."

"I met them on Sunday," Maddie said. Jace had approached the new men, and Maddie had trailed after him. "They seem kind enough."

"They are," Reese said rather noncommittally.

"Why exactly didn't they want you to work?" Alison asked as Reese came to the worktable and started forming one of the piecrusts Alison had ready.

"I think they're concerned that I'm more hurt than I realize."

"Are you very hurt?" Alison made a point of asking.

"A little, but as long as I stay off stairs, I do all right."

"You limped, Reese," Peter mentioned.

"That's true," she agreed. "Bending it is a little tough."

"How did you fall?" This came from Maddie, who had gone to gently bouncing Jeffrey because he was showing the symptoms of hunger as Alison had predicted.

"Who fell?" Hillary asked, having just come in the side door, Joshua and Martin coming after her.

"I did," Reese explained. "I missed the back step at the big house and fell to the ground."

"You poor thing," Alison was in the midst of saying when someone else knocked on the front door.

"I'll go," Peter offered.

Peter had seen this man at church, or he might have shut the door in his face. The very large Conner Kingsley stood on the step, looming over Peter like a tree.

"Is your father home?" he asked in his quiet way.

"No," Peter whispered back.

"Your mother?"

"In the kitchen," Peter said, still whispering and backing up so Conner could enter. Not able to stop glancing at him, Peter led the way. The women were talking in complete comfort, Jeffrey still in Maddie's arms and Reese now filling one of the piecrusts, when Conner's frame filled the door.

For some reason, the first pair of eyes he met belonged to Reese Thackery. With no hesitation, her chin came up and her eyes grew slightly defiant.

"Please excuse me," Conner apologized when quiet descended on the group, and he finally found Alison's face in the mob. "My brother sent me a letter that I thought Dooner might enjoy reading. May I leave it for him?"

"Certainly," Alison said, wiping her hands and heading that way. "I'll tell him you stopped."

"Thank you." Conner managed to nod to all of them before his eyes found Reese again. He found her look still guarded.

Moments later, Conner was back out the door of the Muldoon house and headed to the bank. He went directly to Troy, who was doing something behind the counter.

"You'll never guess who's standing in the kitchen making pies at the Muldoon house this very moment."

"Do not tell me it's Reese," Troy warned. "Not after we ate cold leftovers."

Conner's only answer was an ironic raising of his dark brows.

"I'm heading over to make sure she knows she can come in the morning," Troy continued.

Conner laughed, certain he was joking, but Troy was shrugging into his coat and heading out the door.

∞

"He's so tall," Hillary mentioned. The boys had all wandered off, and Alison was nursing the baby.

"He is tall," Maddie agreed.

"How tall are you, Reese? I can't remember."

"I'm six feet."

"Even?"

"Maybe a quarter inch over, but I always just say six feet."

"How tall is Mr. Kingsley?"

"He must be five or six inches taller than I am," Reese guessed.

When the third knock sounded in a very short time, Alison laughed a little. She also shifted her chair in the corner of the kitchen, making her all but invisible to the door as Hillary went to answer. The young lady of the family returned with an apologetic Troy Thaden.

"Forgive me, Reese," he began, "for intruding on your time,

but I just wanted to make sure we didn't say anything that made you feel that you couldn't return to work in the morning."

Reese smiled. "I'll be there."

Troy's sigh made her laugh. It was on the tip of her tongue to offer to come that evening, but she remembered her dress fabric and decided against it.

"Thank you, and again, I'm sorry to invade your privacy."

The women held their laughter only until they'd heard the door close.

∞∞

Douglas and Jace were shirtless, backs glistening with sweat, as they worked alongside the wagon, forking hay into the bed. As they worked, they talked.

"I can't believe what I didn't know. Do you know how arrogant I was? I thought I had it all figured out, but I'd never even read the book of Genesis! I'd only heard the occasional story that I assumed to be part myth.

"When did you know, Douglas?" Jace suddenly straightened up and asked. "When did you understand that God is behind it all? That He's the creator?"

"I grew up in a Christian home, Jace. I was taught the book of Genesis, as well as the rest of the Bible, from the moment I could hear, but the defining point came for me when I was a teen. Two people in my life died, my grandfather and the sister of a friend. It was at that time that I had to face whether or not this belief was mine or my parents'."

"What did you do?"

"I read my Bible nonstop for about a week. All I did was sit and read, and everything I read, I knew that God had had a hand in it. I compared verses, the Old Testament with the New Testament. Books that had been written hundreds of years apart still proclaimed the same message. I realized that could only be

God directing the pens of each author until His message was clear.

"I also learned during that time that it was all right to grieve. Jesus mourned over Israel, and He forgave those who put Him to death. I knew that it was good and right that I hurt for a time but also that I put the past behind me and move on to the future."

"Is that when you knew you wanted to preach?"

"That came a few years later. I had learned so much as a result of those deaths that I wanted to share with all who would hear."

"And you shared with me," Jace smiled at him, the pitchfork going into motion again.

Douglas didn't comment, but he was pleased. He continued his bending and lifting, gaining new appreciation for the farmwork that was done in the area and asking God not to stop with saving Jace Randall but to continue His work in all of Tucker Mills and beyond.

∞

Reese returned home in the middle of the afternoon, ready to put her leg up, but Mrs. Greenlowe's form bending over the worktable in the kitchen stopped her. Reese could only stare at what had once been her dress fabric.

Mrs. Greenlowe had already begun to cut and sew, and as with everything else that woman did, this was done to perfection.

"You started," Reese stated the obvious and walked over for a closer look.

"Did you think I took your waist and arm measurements so I could make you a hat?"

Reese laughed and only shook her head. She picked up the length that would be the skirt and held it to the front of her. The warm-green floral fabric made her sigh. It had been a long time since she'd had a new dress, and never had she been allowed to choose the material.

"We won't be able to be around you after this," the landlady muttered. "You'll be so pretty that you'll preen yourself all over town."

"I doubt that," Reese said, the smile evident in her voice.

"You just wait," Mrs. Greenlowe warned mischievously. "You'll be catching some man's eye in this dress, and before you know it, you'll be cleaning your own house and not someone else's."

For a moment, Reese allowed herself to dream about falling in love with a man who loved her in return. They would live in a small house with an equally small kitchen, but it would be theirs.

"I still say you should have gone with red," Mrs. Greenlowe had to get in.

"I'm going to put my leg up." Reese exited on that note, not forgetting that she'd told Troy she'd be at the big house in the morning.

∞

It took until Saturday for Reese's leg to feel normal again and for all the swelling to go down. And when it did, she went at the big house with a vengeance. She'd dealt with meals all week, but some of the cleaning had been forced to wait. No longer.

Reese was finished with the upstairs before dinner, and as soon as the dinner dishes were dried and put away, she attacked the main-level parlors. There were two of them, one quite large and one smaller. Dust was always an issue, and Reese determined not to leave a speck in sight. She gathered up small rugs to be taken out and beaten, keeping them carefully contained until she reached the back porch, taking more care with the steps than usual.

Her mind on the dirty task ahead, along with the hymn she

was humming, Reese had just touched the ground with both feet when Gerald Jenness stepped around the corner of the building.

"Gerald, what are you doing here?"

"I came to see you."

"Why?" Reese put it bluntly.

"Why not?" Gerald asked, and Reese had it in her heart to feel sorry for him.

"I'm working, Gerald." She kept her voice kind. "I can't visit right now."

Gerald heard the words but was nowhere near ready to leave. Indeed, he'd been so lonely for weeks now that it only just occurred to him that he could seek out Reese and not wait until he ran into her in town.

"What's it like inside?"

"That's none of your business."

"Do you go in all the rooms?" Gerald asked, looking as though he was going to head toward the door.

"Gerald, I have work to do."

"I won't get in the way."

"You're going to get me fired," Reece stated, her hands coming to her waist. "You can't be here."

"What's he's like? Kingsley?"

"That is also none of your business. Now go."

Gerald's look became stubborn.

"You have to leave," Reese repeated.

"You're afraid of him, aren't you?"

Reese's gaze narrowed and her voice grew firm. "You're going to be the one filled with fear if you don't leave. I'll chase you off with the broom."

Gerald looked into her face and knew she meant it. And in truth, he didn't want to get her into trouble. He opened his mouth to say he'd be back, but Reese had held her arm out, pointing him away from the house.

Gerald's own face registered anger then. She was treating

him like a child. Without another word, he stomped his way around the corner and left.

"You handled that well."

Reese heard the softly spoken words behind her and started violently. She turned to the man whose voice didn't match his size.

"Excuse me, sir?" Reese questioned, wondering what she had missed and if indeed she was about to be fired.

"You avoided his question about your fear of me very nicely," Conner explained, his face open. "That was crafty. I'll have to remember that about you."

Eyeing him a moment, Reese asked, "Remember what exactly?"

"That you're crafty."

Reese thought she would be sacked at any moment, but Conner's smile was kind, warm even, as he turned and went back inside.

Reese didn't move for at least a minute. She'd thought she was alone; she hadn't heard a thing. And what exactly had Conner Kingsley heard?

Turning her back on the house, she set to beating the rugs, her mind too unsettled to hum. It wouldn't do any good to wonder. If he was going to fire her, he'd certainly let her know.

☙

"Thanks for letting me read this," Douglas remarked to Conner on Sunday morning when he returned the letter before services. "It's good to hear that your niece is out of the woods."

"Isn't it? She's been on my mind a lot. Dalton and Susie too," Conner said, mentioning his sister-in-law.

"Maybe he'll come and visit," Douglas suggested. "I thought he hinted at that."

Conner smiled. "A surprise visit. He's not very subtle, is he?"

Douglas laughed and asked, "How is it going with Reese?"

Conner's eyes got large. "She's moved from fear to defiance. If I even look at her, that chin comes up. If I was a man spoiling for a fight, I'd know just where to go."

"Good," Douglas surprised him by saying.

"Why is it good?"

"Because that's a little more normal. Reese is not afraid of much."

"So you often find her contentious?"

"No, not really, but Reese doesn't suffer fools lightly, and she can't stand to be treated like one. If ever you underestimate her, you might find yourself being told where you've gone wrong."

"I sure ended up in trouble over not wanting her to work this week, and she didn't have to say a word."

Douglas had to smile, having heard the entire account. "I understand she was at my house."

Conner shook his head, thinking he'd been completely blind that day.

"She even made us a pie when she came back. Now is that forgiveness or not?"

It was time for Douglas to check on his family and get up front. Smiling all the while, he reached up to put a warm hand on Conner's shoulder, giving it a squeeze before moving on his way.

∞

Troy and Conner had left laundry for Reese. Laundry was not her favorite chore—the table was always too low and her back would ache miserably. But Reese was planning to work on it as soon as she got done with the kitchen floor.

On her hands and knees, working in one corner, she was unaware of the way Troy came upon her. Just taking a short cut through that room, he stopped short.

Troy stood and looked at the hole in the bottom of Reese's right shoe and couldn't help but notice the lack of stockings. He could not have helped but notice her new dress on Sunday, but at work it was the same two dresses day after day. In fact, since the fall she'd been only in the brown dress, and Troy realized she must have ruined the other.

His shortcut forgotten, he began to back out of the room, but Reese heard him.

"Did you need something?" she asked, turning on her knees a little.

"No, just taking a shortcut."

"Don't slip on the wet floor," she warned cheerfully, returning her focus to the corner.

Troy thanked her, made sure he still had the papers he'd come home for, and exited the house to walk back to the bank.

He didn't know how, but he had to find a way to get shoes for Reese. He thought about giving her extra money for another dress as well but knew he shouldn't push the issue.

He was going to be gone over the weekend to Linden Heights, but as soon as he next saw Alison Muldoon, he would ask her whether she had any ideas concerning shoes for Reese Thackery.

Twelve

"I made you some sandwiches for your trip," Reese told Troy on Friday morning. The two were standing in the downstairs hall. "They're wrapped in this cloth, along with some fruit and cookies."

"Thank you," Troy said, taking them from her before looking into her eyes.

"You can't go hungry on the train," Reese spoke softly, feeling self-conscious.

When Troy continued to stare, Reese couldn't hold her tongue.

"What's the matter?"

"I was going to ask you something stupid."

"What was it?"

"I was going to ask why you haven't married, but then I remembered your papers."

"Mrs. Greenlowe just mentioned marriage to me," Reese said, her voice sounding young with wonder. "I don't know why."

"Don't you want to be married?"

"I don't know if I'm the marrying kind," Reese admitted, making herself not think about her dreams.

"Why would you say that?"

"I'm too tall, too thin, and too redheaded. It's a not a good combination."

"Says who?"

"I don't know," Reese shrugged.

"Conner mentioned that a young man came to see you."

"That was Gerald," Reese said softly, still feeling bad for him. "He's Mr. Jenness' son. He's in his teens and very lonely."

"And you don't want him pining after you?"

"He's a good deal younger than I am and not a believer, so no, I don't."

"You're wise to wait."

Reese smiled a little. "I don't think I have a choice about that."

Troy smiled back at her and told her to enjoy the weekend.

"Don't be afraid of Conner," he warned her. "He won't bite."

Reese was able to laugh a little, finding it to be true. He wasn't as frightening lately, and Reese didn't really think he was out to harm her, especially since he didn't drink. On the other hand, she didn't know how a man that large could get around without making any noise.

"Have a good time," Reese said.

"Thank you for the food."

Reese didn't move when Troy took his leave. She stood in the hall, feeling almost sad to see him go. Conner had come from the study to walk him to the door, and Reese couldn't hear their conversation. However, she was still standing in the hall when Conner came back.

"Where is Troy's wife?" she asked, her voice quiet and thoughtful.

"She died more than three years ago."

Reese figured as much.

"But he'll see his daughters this weekend?"

"Yes, and his granddaughters."

Reese nodded, feeling happy for him.

"I've been meaning to ask you something," Conner suddenly said.

Reese looked at him, a bit of her guard returning.

"What did your father do for Mr. Zantow?"

Reese looked surprised.

"I mean," Conner clarified, "Mr. Zantow didn't run a large business or farm. It's hard to imagine him needing a male servant when he himself was a carpenter."

Reese nodded. "My father spent the first six months working on the house. He was fairly handy with a hammer, and the house needed lots of repairs. After that he would go for wood and do a lot of cutting and splitting, the back-breaking type that Mr. Zantow hated."

Reese fell quiet for a moment. "He didn't live much longer than that, so I don't know what he would have done all these years."

"And did you work the whole time or only until the contract became yours?"

"I did the cooking, but I didn't start cleaning before my papers."

"No wonder you're such a good cook," Conner complimented, and Reese looked surprised again. "You see," Conner added, "sometimes I'm not scary at all."

Always feeling a need to leave before things grew awkward, Conner told her he'd be at the bank until dinner, gathered his satchel, and went out the front door.

∞

"You're showing!" Cathy Shephard exclaimed with excitement when she went to the farm to visit Maddie.

"I can't be showing," Maddie disagreed, looking down at herself. "It's barely three months."

Cathy looked again. "Maybe you're not."

"Wishful thinking?" Maddie suggested.

"Probably." Cathy smiled at the thought and then looked serious. "I want to be Granny."

Maddie frowned. "What else would you be?"

"I mean, I want to be called Granny, even though you've never called me Mama."

Maddie smiled, not expecting this side of her aunt.

"And what does Doyle want to be called?"

"You'll have to ask him. He's excited about this but in a quiet sort of way, so he might not know what he wants."

"Why is he quiet about it?"

"Worried about you, I expect."

"Worried how?"

"That you won't be all right or that the baby won't."

Cathy's own penchant toward worry was surfacing at this point, and Maddie knew that Doyle was not the only one.

"I'm going to be fine," Maddie assured her with quiet conviction. "So will the baby."

"Well, of course you are!" Cathy retorted bracingly.

"That's not what I mean," Maddie pushed the point. "No matter what, whether I live or not, or even if the baby dies, we'll be all right."

Cathy didn't see how that could be true, but keeping Maddie's condition in mind, she didn't say anything. She had carried a basket of baked goods in with her and turned to where it sat on the table.

Maddie didn't know what to do. She hated to let the topic drop, but if Cathy didn't want to hear, there was no point in speaking. Or was there?

The decision was taken from her. Jace had seen the wagon and had come from the yard to have dinner and say hello.

∞

It was dinnertime at the big house in town too. Reese nearly had the food ready for the table when she heard the front door. She hurried so it would be ready and waiting, but Conner beat her to the door. Filling the door frame that led from the hallway, he stood, a paper in his hand. Reese froze, fingers still holding the serving dishes, and stared at him.

"Charisse V. Thackery," he read, his voice curious. "What does the V stand for?"

Instantly Reese's look became stubborn, and she remained mute. Conner, however, was not put off. Readying for the challenge, his brows rose, and he leaned against the frame as if he had all day.

"Victoria?" Conner detected a small shake of Reese's head, but she didn't make a sound.

"Virginia?" he tried.

Another shake of the head told him he was wrong.

"Valerie?"

"No. I have work to do," Reese reported, effectively closing the conversation and moving to put food on the table. Conner watched her go back and forth between the dining room and the kitchen but didn't get in her way or interrupt. But as usual he was thinking. *I'll find out.*

∞

Victor Jenness stood outside the bank window in the dark shadows of the building, furious with himself that he'd forgotten his keys. It was equally dark inside, but still his eyes were just beginning to catch something new. Squinting toward the alcove, he realized the furniture had been moved around.

His heart beating painfully, he felt his entire frame flush with heat as fresh anger filled him. This was his bank! They had no right to come in and interfere in this way.

Victor had planned to sneak back to his own home, check on Gerald and his wife, and then swear them to secrecy, but he didn't know right now if he could control himself. Slipping even deeper into the shadows, this time behind the bank, Victor stood to catch his breath and try to figure out his next move.

⌘

Conner was weary, and the house was still. He'd given almost no thought to Troy being away for the weekend but now realized the house was very quiet without him. After those first few days of adjusting to the memories and being back after so many years, Conner had weathered the transition very well.

But not tonight. Tonight it seemed he saw his favorite sister everywhere he looked. She had died when he was 12, and Conner's last memories of her had been here, enjoying their grandmother together, and feeling as though they could stay forever.

Reese had already left for the day, or Conner might have sought her out just to get his mind from the thoughts crowding in. If only he could keep his mind on the time in the house and not the coach ride that followed.

Conner's temple began to throb. He wondered if reading his Bible for a while might be the answer. Conner hoped that studying God's Word and getting to sleep early would remedy the situation.

⌘

Reese let herself in the side door, already thinking about what she would prepare for breakfast and dinner. With Troy missing, she would adjust the amount some, but not by much. Conner could eat at least twice what she could consume and never look as though he'd fallen into gluttony.

She started the coffee as usual and then began mixing eggs and ham. The coffee was brewed and sending its aroma around the house and the eggs were nearly done when Reese realized that Conner usually made an appearance by now.

Not wishing to intrude but wanting his breakfast to be hot, Reese slipped across the wide hallway and peeked into the study. She was surprised to find it empty. Being as quiet as she could manage, Reese checked all the downstairs rooms. Conner Kingsley was nowhere to be found.

Reese stood at the bottom of the stairs, knowing she could never do it. She bit her lip, hoping he would suddenly appear at the top of the stairs and put Reese's mind at ease. It didn't happen.

Reese slipped back to the kitchen and made sure the fire was safe, going to the window to see if he was out by the barn. She then used the front door to save time. This was a job for Doc MacKay.

∞

Leaving a very sober Reese at the bottom of the stairs, Doc went quietly up the staircase, not thrilled with this invasion of privacy but willing to check on Conner, not just out of concern, but for Reese's sake as well.

"Conner?" Doc called quietly after coming to a closed door. He knocked softly before opening it. A large figure lay in the bed, but there was no sound or movement.

"Conner?" the doctor tried again, this time approaching the bed. Not until he touched the banker's shoulder did Conner stir.

"I'm sorry," Doc MacKay wasted no time in saying. "Reese was concerned when you didn't come downstairs."

"What time is it?"

"Nearly 8:00."

"Oh," Conner groaned a little, shifted on the mattress, and attempted to clear his throat. "I didn't get to sleep until early this morning, and Troy wasn't here to wake me."

"Why don't you rest a bit more?"

"I should get to the bank."

"Not if you're unwell."

"I'm not; I'm just tired." Conner scrubbed at his face, feeling as though he'd had no sleep at all. "Maybe Reese could run over and tell Leffler I'll be there later."

"I'll take care of it," Doc assured him. "Can I get you something? Reese has breakfast and coffee ready."

"Tell her I'll be down later, after I've slept some more."

"All right."

Slipping back out the door and closing it, the older man made his way to the stairs where Reese still waited on the bottom step. That man kept his voice low when he stopped beside her.

"He didn't sleep well. He wants you to go to the bank and tell Mr. Leffler that he'll be in later today." Reese opened her mouth to say she would be happy to, but the doctor continued. "I'll take care of that. I think you should just go about your chores on this level, and when he comes down, fix him something to eat."

"He didn't want anything right now?"

"Just sleep."

Reese nodded, but she felt helpless. It was her nature to do more. What if he called for help? No one would hear him.

"What's the matter?" Doc asked.

Reese told him where her imagination had run.

"He assured me that he's not ill, Reese. We've got to take him at his word."

"But he doesn't know you that well. For all he knows, telling you that might give you ideas of bleeding him."

The doctor had to admit that Reese had a point, but he would still not go back upstairs.

"What if he doesn't come down at all?" Reese finally asked.

"If he's not downstairs by the time you're ready to leave for the day, come and get me."

This was not what she wanted to hear, but Reese still nodded and let the matter drop. She could have used some time in the buttery, but that room seemed too far away. Keeping to the kitchen where she washed tablecloths and napkins and did some baking, Reese worked, half-listening for steps on the stairs.

∞

"We're glad you could join us," Douglas told Doc MacKay during dinner. "It's been a few weeks since we could talk."

"It has, and I've made a decision about that matter we talked about a few months ago. My nephew is going to join me here as soon as he can. If he likes it and settles in with the townsfolk, I'll go to live with my brother in South Carolina."

"How soon will it be?" Alison asked.

"No one's in a big hurry, so we'll wait and see how it all comes together."

"Well, whenever it does," Douglas said with a smile, "it will be our loss and your family's gain."

Doc smiled at the compliment, almost hoping it wouldn't transpire too swiftly. He wasn't in a hurry to leave Tucker Mills and its wonderful inhabitants, but the cold winters that visited the area made staying very hard.

He wasn't a young man anymore, and an old back injury was growing more and more difficult to deal with, especially in freezing temperatures. For the moment, however, he would enjoy the time he had. Be it six months or two more years, he knew this was where God wanted him.

∞

Reese's arms were buried in the washtub when Conner finally came downstairs. He was dressed but without his coat, and although he looked a bit pale, his eyes were bright and he seemed alert.

"How are you?" she asked, very real concern in her face and voice.

Conner was surprised by this but didn't allow her to see.

"I'm fine, thank you. Just a bit hungry."

"I'll make you something right now."

"I'd be happy to fix something for myself," Conner offered. "I don't need to interrupt you."

Reese found herself suddenly interested. "What would you fix?"

Conner hadn't expected that and was at a sudden loss for words. He spotted some bread and cheese on the table and was going to mention that but instead looked up to find Reese just holding laughter.

Conner smiled a little before saying, "I guess I will interrupt you, Reese. If you would be so kind."

"I'll just be a few minutes," Reese told him and went to work as soon as he exited to the dining room.

∞

Reese was longer than a few minutes, but it was worth the wait. She delivered a bowl of fluffy eggs with ham, a berry pastry, and a potato and cheese dish. She went back for the coffeepot as soon as she'd set the food down, refilling Conner's mug and making sure the cream was in reach.

"You're not very afraid of me these days," Conner observed, knowing he would not have mentioned it if Troy had been at the table with him.

"No, I guess I'm not," Reese agreed, even going so far as to look at him.

"Why is that? What changed?"

Reese had been thinking about that very thing and was able to give a logical answer.

"I wish I could say that I had prayed through it or claimed

Scripture and understood that fear is a serious sin, but it didn't happen like that."

"How did it happen?"

"You're just not like that," Reese said, knowing it was a strange comment.

"Like what?"

She shrugged a little, looking for words that would explain.

"Not like Mr. Zantow?" Conner helped.

"No." Reese was back to whispering again. "You're nothing like him."

"Was he difficult all the time?"

Conner saw the brief shake of her head before she added, "Just when he'd been drinking."

"And is that what you waited to see? If I would get drunk?"

"I must have. I'm ashamed to say that I didn't believe Douglas. He assured me it was all right. He said he'd send Alison or Hillary here, but I was still frightened."

"Maybe Alison and Hillary haven't been through the things you have."

"I hope not," she said. "I wouldn't want that for them."

Conner had many things he could have said to that, but he didn't know if they'd be welcome. He wanted to tell her how sorry he was for the way she'd been treated, and that he was glad she felt safe here.

"Oh!" Reese suddenly saw what she had done. She jumped up from her place at the table, her eyes large as she looked at Conner. "I didn't mean to sit down. I'm sorry."

"It doesn't matter," Conner tried, but Reese still looked upset.

"I need to let you eat," she declared just before exiting with more haste than needed. Once in the kitchen and away from Conner Kingsley's eyes, Reese put a hand to her forehead. She didn't know what had come over her. She hadn't even felt herself sitting down. They were talking, and for the first time he wasn't her employer but just another person who seemed to care what she felt and thought.

Reese shook her head, still thinking about what she'd done. *You have work to do,* she finally told herself. *He didn't seem upset, so you need to drop it. Get back to work.*

Reese took a deep breath and then took her own advice.

❧

"I'm headed to the bank," Conner said a short time later.

Humming quietly, Reese's hands were back in the washtub. "All right. I'll leave food for your tea and your meals tomorrow."

"Thank you."

Conner began to turn away but came right back.

"Charisse Violet?" he asked.

"No." Reese's reply was nothing if not thankful.

Conner laughed a little and went on his way.

❧

"I'm headed to the meetinghouse in a few minutes," Reese informed Mrs. Greenlowe on Sunday morning.

"All right," the lady agreed from her place at the stove.

"Did you want to come?"

Not turning from the stove for a moment, Reese waited, looking at her landlady's back. When she did turn, it was only her head, speaking to Reese in profile.

"Not today, Reese. Thank you."

"Should I check with you again or wait for you to ask me?" Reese had to get this settled.

"You can ask," Mrs. Greenlowe simply said, turning back to the stove and giving Reese the impression that she was done talking about it.

Reese walked slowly to the meetinghouse, not even concerned whether she was late. She prayed all the while for Mrs. Greenlowe, her heart aching for that woman to know Christ.

When I moved in, Lord, I was just glad to have a place. It took some time for me to realize that I might have a chance to speak with Mrs. Greenlowe about You. I thank You for her interest. I ask You to give her more. I think her heart is searching. You rescued me. You saved me when I was drowning in pain. I know that Mrs. Greenlowe's life is easier than mine was, Lord, but if You could just soften her . . . touch her and let her know how much she's loved.

Reese knew if she kept on, she would be in tears. She made herself think about changes she might make in her own life and ways she could be a better example. Not until she got to the meetinghouse, found it rather full, and took a seat very near Conner Kingsley, did she realize how arrogant she had been.

I told Mr. Kingsley that I needed only to see his behavior and the fear went away, Reese prayed. *I'm so self-sufficient at times that I forget the great work You do in my heart. It's only been a few weeks— not even a month. I know I wouldn't be sitting here if You hadn't worked in my heart.*

Thank You, Lord, for saving me. Thank You for saving me each day. Help me to be such a light to Mrs. Greenlowe that she can't help but see it. Change me until everything about me says I'm Your child.

Douglas was speaking this whole time, and Reese had missed it. She turned her attention to the front, but not before she noticed Conner watching her. He waited only until she looked his way and then nodded in greeting. Reese softly greeted him the same way, seeing again that only God could have done this.

Thirteen

"How was Linden Heights?" Conner asked of Troy when the afternoon train arrived and that man came straight to the bank.

"Everyone and everything is fine. Your family sends their love."

"That's good to hear. How is my niece?"

"She was at the meetinghouse yesterday, looking a bit pale but holding her own."

"Good."

"They want to know when you're going to visit."

Conner looked surprised.

"What is that look about?" Troy asked.

"I just didn't think I'd be here long enough to need a visit home."

"I just went," Troy reasoned.

"You're a father and a grandfather," Conner reasoned back.

"In other words, you don't have anyone special enough to visit in Linden Heights."

"Precisely."

"And what about here? Any reason to stay longer?"

Mr. Leffler interrupted them just then, but the look Conner gave Troy told him they would be getting back to this subject.

170

Lillie heard a noise in the kitchen as she was turning in for the night. It was not a new house so such noises were not that unusual, but when it sounded again, she realized Gerald was up and felt she needed to check on him.

Carrying the candle in front of her, Lillie made her way back downstairs and saw a glow coming from the kitchen. When she stepped into that room and found her husband at the table, she nearly set her nightdress on fire.

"Victor!" she all but shouted.

"Shh," he hushed her, agitation in his every move.

"You're here!" Lillie's voice had lowered some, but her husband was still tense.

"Sit down," he ordered, coming to take the candle from her.

Lillie did as she was told, unable to stop staring at her spouse. He was thinner and ill kept. Victor Jenness prided himself on his appearance, and Lillie was more afraid of this than anything else.

"Where have you been?" Lillie suddenly found her voice. "And why did you leave?"

"Have you seen the bank?" he shot back with a question of his own. "They've changed my office around. They had no right!"

The light in her husband's eyes now snagged Lillie's full attention. He had always been an intense man, a passionate man, but right now he looked beyond reason. And it was a look Lillie recognized.

"I've been around town the past few days," he spoke, his voice low with rage. "Do you know where Reese Thackery is working? At the big house! They questioned me and made me feel like a fool, but what do they have the bank's indentured servant do? Work for the bank owner. Hypocrisy."

"She's free, Victor," Lillie put in gently. "They gave Reese her papers. She works there, and they pay her."

"What? That can't be right. We could have kept her for almost two more years! It was an excellent idea."

Lillie had never understood the plan to begin with so she

didn't comment, but she had never seen it as such a great idea, especially when it meant having Reese coming to her house. Lillie shuddered at the very thought.

"What's the matter?" Victor asked, and for the first time Lillie realized he hadn't even asked about their son.

"Nothing," she murmured quietly. "Where have you been?" she tried again.

"Around" was all he would offer.

"Would you like something to eat?"

"No, I've got to go."

"But you just got here," Lillie argued. "And what was this business you had to see to?"

"Don't you understand?" Victor suddenly stood. "I was the finest bank manager this town has ever known. They're trying to take my bank, and I won't allow it."

"They just want to talk to you, Victor. Just come to bed now and go see them in the morning."

The change in Victor's face was frightening. He came toward Lillie as though he would harm her.

"Did they speak to you about me? What did they say?"

"Victor!" Lillie snapped at him, coming to her feet as well. She had never let anyone bully her, and she wasn't going to start now. Her husband saw the set of her chin and backed down a bit.

"Every time they talk to me," Lillie began, only slightly calmer, "they ask how you're doing. They came to the house out of concern because you said you were ill. They've only wanted to see how you're doing and to discuss bank business with you.

"If you've done nothing wrong, then go and see them. And if you have committed a crime, turn yourself in."

"Of course I've done nothing wrong," Victor told his wife, his voice quiet and controlled, "but I don't owe them any kind of explanation."

"They own the bank, Victor."

The look Victor gave his wife could only be labeled as superior.

"They changed my office around. I was the best bank manager this town has ever known."

"Victor," Lillie began again, but he cut her off.

"Tell no one I was here, not even Gerald. I don't want him burdened with all of this."

"All of what?"

"I'll get my job back, Lillie. Just see if I don't."

He was to the door before she could anticipate him.

"Victor," Lillie rushed that way, but he'd slipped outside and into the night. Lillie went as far as the backyard, but he seemed to have disappeared. She whispered his name a few more times, but there was no answer.

Going back inside, she saw that he'd forgotten his hat. He never went out without his hat. Lillie didn't want to cry until she saw it abandoned on the table.

When at last she climbed the stairs again, it was not for sleep. She lay awake all night on her bed, reminding herself that she had no choice but to go to the bank.

∞

"Maddie," Jace called on Monday morning, having been to town and brought the mail back. "Are you around?"

"Upstairs," she called down to him, and Jace went that way.

"I've got mail," he announced when he found her in his old bedroom.

"Anything interesting?" Maddie asked. Having added things to an old trunk, she was pushing it back against the wall.

"It looks like one from Boston and one from my sister."

"You didn't read them?"

"They're not to me." Jace's voice was dry, and Maddie began to smile. "Yes, you go right ahead and laugh about it. A woman gets ready to have a baby, and suddenly her husband is invisible."

Maddie didn't laugh, but she did have to cover her mouth with one hand.

"I've heard of husbands getting jealous about babies," she teased him.

"What husband?" he asked with great exaggeration. "I don't exist, remember? At Doyle and Cathy's yesterday, all you and your aunt could talk about was baby stuff."

"Well, Doyle was there."

"He fell asleep in the chair," Jace reminded her.

"So did you," Maddie pointed out.

"There's only so many hours I can hear debates on first foods and scalp treatment."

Maddie had to laugh then. She put her arms around her husband and laughed against his chest.

"I'm not sensing any real sympathy here, Mrs. Randall."

"Does this help?" she asked, composing herself long enough to kiss him.

"Maybe a little," Jace's arms had come up to hold her.

Maddie kissed him again, and Jace pulled her even closer. His fingers were making a mess of her hair when they heard a door downstairs.

"I forgot Clara was coming today," Jace whispered.

"I forgot too."

Arms wrapped around each other, Jace planned to revisit this scene right after tea that evening. Maddie was working to be thankful that she had Clara's help, even when it meant the occasional interruption.

❧❧❧

Lillie found her feet slowing as she approached the bank building. She had lost a lot of sleep over this decision and was suddenly finding it harder to accomplish than think about.

Not knowing what she expected Mr. Thaden to do, she

remembered that so far he had been compassionate. Lillie felt she was betraying Victor but also felt she had no choice. Gathering her courage, she made herself go inside. Asking Mr. Leffler if she could speak to the men in the alcove, Lillie worked to keep calm.

∞∞

"I didn't think you would ever come outside," Gerald spoke to Reese from out of nowhere and startled her into dropping her basket.

"Where did you come from, Gerald?" Reese exclaimed, fighting the irritation she felt, even though none of the clothing had spilled into the dirt.

"You didn't see me?" He looked pleased with the thought.

"Gerald," Reese kept her voice patient. "Nothing has changed. I'm working."

"I know a secret," Gerald boasted, having ignored Reese's words.

"That's nice," Reese acknowledged, not wanting to patronize him but heading out to hang up the shirts she'd scrubbed, not caring if he followed or not.

"Aren't you even a little bit curious?" Gerald asked, trailing her.

"A little, I guess," Reese said absently, pegging out wash as she went.

"My father was here last night."

Reese turned to look at her visitor, knowing he would be pleased to have gained her attention.

"Is he all right?" Reese asked, not really knowing what happened.

"Of course." Gerald's voice held more bluster than he felt. In fact his father's voice had scared him last night, but he would never tell Reese that.

"Is he at the bank today?" Reese asked.

"No, but he will be soon. You know he's the best bank manager this town has ever had."

Reese didn't know that, but neither did she argue.

"Well, I'm sure Mr. Kingsley will be happy about that. They only came to check on the bank and see how it was doing."

"He didn't do anything wrong!" Gerald stated emphatically, some agitation coming to the surface.

"Gerald, I never said he did."

The young man felt foolish then. Last time he left, he had left in anger, and he didn't want to do that again, but he didn't know any other way out of the conversation.

As it was, Reese didn't know what to think. She watched Gerald move off, not sure what had just happened. The only thing she was certain of at the moment was that she needed to stay here at the house until the bank closed and tell the men about Gerald's announcement.

✣

The men were in deep conversation as they walked home. Neither of them noticed Reese standing at the parlor window watching them come up the walk, but when they opened the door, she was standing in the hall waiting for them.

"I'm sorry to be here so late," Reese began, feeling she needed to apologize. "But something happened today with Gerald Jenness, and I thought I should tell you."

"That's fine." Conner was the one to speak up. "Go ahead."

"He said his father was in town, but he wasn't at the bank. I asked if he was all right, and Gerald said yes. I then said something that made Gerald think I was accusing his father, and he became very upset. He left in a huff."

"Did he say where his father is now?" Troy asked.

"No, but he insisted that his father was the best bank manger

Tucker Mills has ever had, and he would be back in the bank soon."

"Thank you, Reese," Troy said, thinking about the fact that Mrs. Jenness was under the impression that her son knew nothing of his father's visit. "We appreciate your staying to tell us."

Reese nodded and started toward the kitchen, which led to the stairway she used to come and go.

"Did you have more work you have to do, Reese?" Conner stepped close enough to ask.

"No, I was just leaving."

"Do you have something to collect at the side door?"

"No."

Conner used a thumb to point behind him. "Use the front door."

Reese hesitated.

"Use it all the time," he pressed further. "Use it every time you come and go."

"Why?" she finally managed to ask.

"Because I want you to."

Reese looked stubborn. She just didn't know if this was the right thing.

"I'll make a deal with you," Conner watched her carefully as he spoke. "You tell me what the V stands for, and you can use any door you like."

Reese's chin went instantly into the air. She marched to the front door, glanced back long enough to find both men smiling, and sailed outside.

Conner laughed, looking at the door for several moments. When he glanced over at Troy, that man had an odd look on his face.

"I don't want to know what you're thinking, do I?" the younger man asked.

"Probably not," Troy smiled before admitting. Conner let the matter drop so both men could enjoy their tea.

"Hey, Troy," Conner said, opening that man's door after they both turned in. "Are you awake?"

"Yeah."

Troy listened as Conner entered the room.

"Something just occurred to me."

"About what?"

"Jenness. What if we're not dealing with a sane man? What if the things his wife described are pointing to the fact that he's no longer in his right mind, if he ever was?"

"What made you think along that line? I mean, you've never even met the man."

"Believe it or not, the layout of the alcove. We're not finding anything amiss in the files. His business dealings were completely legal, but the way he had those bookshelves arranged makes me think of someone very insecure. Someone who wants privacy but not because he's up to something.

"That and the fact that he left the bank in a panic and has not even tried to reclaim his job, not to mention return to his family. It just makes sense to me that something might have set him off that day, something his mind cannot handle."

"You have a very interesting point. I hadn't thought about it from that view because he seemed so normal."

"But not when he left," Conner reminded him. "What you described to me was a man on the edge, who'd just been pushed."

"But there was no evidence of that beforehand," Troy thought out loud, "which makes your theory completely believable."

Conner didn't say anything. For a moment, both men silently worked the details through their minds.

"I'll let you sleep," Conner said around a yawn.

"I'm going to need it," Troy agreed, thinking that Conner's prognosis was entirely plausible but unsettling nonetheless.

Reese had shopping to do. Kitchen supplies in the big house were running a bit low, so she headed out first thing Thursday morning. She started at Shephard Store, a list in hand, along with a large basket.

Her mind was completely on the list, so much so in fact that when Mr. Somer suddenly appeared in front of her ready to talk about his latest ailment, Reese had to force her mind to the moment.

"It's my back today," he revealed, and Reese did her best to listen. "Acted up first thing this morning, right out of bed. I would have blamed it on the eggs my wife made, but it happened before then."

"Eggs bother your back?" Reese had to ask; she'd not heard this.

"It can happen," he said before opening his mouth to add more. Reese bent a little, trying to hear him, when she realized that his eyes looked a little surprised.

"Mr. Somer?" Reese called, but he only stared at her.

"What is it, Reese?" Doyle had heard her tone and was coming their way.

"Mr. Somer?" Reese tried again, but by now he was beginning to fall.

Doyle caught the smaller man as he began to crumple and laid him gently on the floor. Reese bent over him, feeling his neck for a pulse, the way she'd seen Doc do it, her own pulse pounding with fear.

"Go for Doc!" Doyle shouted to a customer, and Reese tried talking to the little man, whom no one ever believed to be truly ill.

"Mr. Somer, can you wake up? Can you hear me? It's Reese. You were telling me about your back. Mr. Somer, wake up now."

Reese thought she felt a pulse, so she whipped her apron off and balled it up to go under his head. He looked a little more normal then, but his color was very bad, and Reese begged God to send Doc in a hurry.

It felt like forever. Doc did not push Reese aside but knelt opposite her and began to check on the patient.

"What happened?" he asked while he worked, and Reese told him what she'd seen.

"What's wrong with him, Doc?" Doyle bent over the three of them and asked.

"His heart, I think. I can't make him comfortable on this floor, Doyle. We need to get him home."

"I'll get the wagon."

It never once occurred to Reese to do anything but accompany Mr. Somer and the doctor to the Somers' home. She sat in the back of the wagon, her apron still in use, and went to the door to warn Mrs. Somer when they arrived.

The news shook that lady, but she kept her head and swiftly prepared the bed that was in the small room off their kitchen. Doc MacKay and Opal Berglund's oldest son, Harry, who had been in the store, carried him from the wagon directly to the bed.

Reese made her way to the kitchen, where she could see that Mrs. Somer had been readying wax for candles. Reese put water on for tea and kept out of the way. Beyond that she prayed, hoping that if she was called on to do more, she would know what to do and when.

∞

It was unusual for the men to arrive home for dinner and not have aromas wafting through the house the moment they stepped in the front door. Nevertheless, they didn't jump to conclusions but waited until they were in the dining room and then the kitchen before facing facts: Reese had not made dinner. A pie sat on the table, one they were sure was for dinner, but nothing else was ready.

"Will we get in trouble if we eat the pie?" Conner asked, always starved by noon.

"I don't think so," Troy reasoned, already looking for plates and forks. "I'm sure she meant it for dinner."

Conner's piece was gone with amazing speed, but he didn't go for another one. He grabbed a slice of bread from the loaf they'd had for breakfast, not even bothering with the butter.

"I'm going to search the house and then head through town," Conner mumbled around a mouthful of bread.

"For Reese?"

"Yes. Stay here in case she comes back."

Troy helped him search the house but then did as Conner asked. He planted himself back in the kitchen and tried to make a meal from what he could find.

ᖚ

"Here, Mrs. Somer," Reese offered. "I made some tea."

"Thank you, Reese," she said, still shaking a little. Reese held the chair for her to sit down.

"How does Doc think he's doing?"

"He's not sure right now. His breathing is strong, but he's not waking up." The tired and worried woman suddenly reached for Reese's hand. "You were there, Reese! What happened?"

"He was talking to me about his back hurting, and then he slowly collapsed. Doyle caught him and put him on the floor."

Mrs. Somer bit her lip. "He always says he's sick, but he never is. He's never been sick a day that I've known him. His mother was like this, and I think he thought it was his place to carry on the tradition."

Reese smiled at the description just as someone knocked at the door.

"I'll go," Reese offered and was surprised to find Conner Kingsley on the front porch.

"Mr. Kingsley." Reese looked as surprised as she was. "What brings you to the Somer home?"

"You," he stated calmly, and Reese slipped outside to speak with him. She then realized the time.

"I'm sorry I didn't get your dinner."

"It doesn't matter. I'm making sure you're all right."

Reese blinked. She didn't know why this was a surprise, but it was.

"So . . . are you all right?" Conner checked with her.

"Yes, I'm fine, but Mr. Somer collapsed at Doyle's, and I came to help."

"Of course you did," Conner said.

"What did that mean?"

"Just that helping is what you do best. It wouldn't occur to you to do otherwise."

Reese didn't know if she was being mocked or not. She studied the tall man in front of her, trying to weigh the issue.

"What did I say that's causing that look?"

"What look?"

Conner smiled. "Have you ever noticed that we tend to talk in circles?"

Reese nodded, looking slightly embarrassed.

"How did you know where I was?" she asked.

"One of the few advantages of being this size is that your questions are all answered very quickly."

"And you asked in town?"

"Certainly. We've never gone without dinner, so I knew something had to have come up. I just hoped you weren't injured or ill. How is the man doing?"

"We're not sure yet, but thank you for asking" was all Reese could think to say, still surprised that he'd come across town to check on her.

"I'll let you go," Conner said, putting his hat back on his head.

"All right. I'll be back to the house as soon as I can."

Conner nodded, and Reese began to turn away.

"Reese?" he said her name.

That woman turned back.

"Vanessa?" Conner asked.

"No," Reese said yet again, but this time her eyes were brimming with suppressed laughter. She was still smiling when she slipped back inside the Somer home.

Fourteen

"It was like seeing myself," Doyle said to Cathy that night as they readied for bed. "I remembered how sick I was."

"But you're not sick anymore," Cathy reasoned.

"But I could be. Any of us could all go at any time."

"That's true, Doyle, but you've nothing to worry about," Cathy argued.

"How do you know?" Doyle asked his wife, thinking back on a conversation he'd had with Jace just two weeks past. How could anyone know? Jace seemed to think that he could. Doyle had to ask himself, as the older man, why he didn't seem to know.

"What has put these thoughts in your head?" Cathy asked, sounding and feeling a bit impatient.

"Just seeing Mr. Somer lying there. We all only half listen to him when he tells us how he's doing, and then he's on the floor. It could have been me."

Cathy had no answer. She wanted to argue with her husband and tell him he was just tired, but in her mind, without even being there, she could see Mr. Somer on the floor too. It was a scary thought.

And the image of an unconscious Mr. Somer was not one she wanted to sleep on! Cathy Shephard finished brushing her hair and climbed into bed. Doyle would have to trouble this one through on his own. Cathy didn't want to think about it. She planned to fall asleep as fast as she could.

෨෨

"How was Mr. Somer when you left the house yesterday?" Troy asked of Reese while she worked on breakfast.

"Actually I stopped in this morning, and he was awake and resting comfortably."

"That's good to hear."

"I'm sorry you didn't get dinner," Reese added.

"I filled up on pie."

"Pie?" Reese confirmed, having wondered about its disappearance. "Was that all you had?"

"Pretty much," Troy admitted almost proudly, causing Reese to smile.

While these two spoke downstairs and Reese worked, Conner finished dressing in his bedroom. Yesterday's schedule had been an odd one; so odd, in fact, that Conner had just found a letter from his brother. He'd put it in his coat pocket, and never gotten around to reading it.

Taking a seat on the edge of the bed, he opened it to see what Dalton had to say.

It's tough not having you around was how the letter opened. *I'm used to having you to pick on and tease and confide in, but I know your work there is important.*

I was reminded as I sat down to write this that just a few months ago Mother was alive. Do you think of her often? Is it a burden to you, or are you too busy with the bank business there?

Conner stopped reading. He did think of his mother—he thought of her at some point every day—but a sense of unreality had come over him since coming to Tucker Mills. At times it felt as though she was still waiting for him in Linden Heights. His heart would think of her welcoming him home and know instantly that it wasn't true, but each time the image caught him short.

For just a moment he went back. Back to a time when her mind was still lucid. Her body had become weak and frail, but the fear had not set in yet, and she still looked at him with tenderness, remembering that she was the mother and he the child.

I never saw you marry, she said on one occasion. *I always thought I would.*

You sound like you're going somewhere, Conner had teased her gently.

Thankfully, I am, she teased back. *So tell me, why have you never married, Conner? Please don't say it's because of me.*

It's not. I just never found someone who would have me.

I still say you should have married Ruth or Eliza Thaden.

They're like sisters and you know it.

She had taken his hand then. *It would be wonderful for me to see you give your heart away.*

Conner folded Dalton's letter, knowing that finishing it right now was not a good idea. The memory of his mother's death was too fresh. Mabelle Kingsley had dealt with fear off and on for most of Conner's life. At times it had been very hard, but until the very end of her life she'd been more than a mother; she'd been his friend, the person who had been with him during the hardest days of his life.

Conner put the letter on the dresser, grabbed his coat, and headed for the stairs. He wanted to hear all that Dalton had to say and planned to write back, but for now it would have to wait.

∞

Reese was headed back to Doyle's to finish yesterday's list when Alison called to her.

"Can you stop in?" the pastor's wife asked when Reese met her in the yard.

"Not this morning. I've got to fill this list that didn't get taken care of yesterday."

"Douglas and I stopped by the house last night. Mr. Somer was sleeping, but we had a nice visit with Mrs. Somer."

"I'm sure she appreciated it. It's been pretty upsetting."

"Before I forget, can you join us for dinner after services on Sunday? Would Mrs. Greenlowe mind?"

"I don't think so. Can I bring something?"

"One of your pies if you have time to bake."

"All right. I'll plan on it."

Reese didn't linger but moved on to Doyle's, her mind on the list.

"Back to finish your list, Reese?" Doyle asked when he saw her come in.

"Yes. It seemed more important yesterday than today, but I still need things."

Doyle nodded, and Reese watched his face.

"Are you all right, Doyle?"

"Just thinking," he responded as though he were in a world of his own. Shaking his head a little, he asked, "What's first?"

Reese began reading her list, assuming he didn't want to speak of his thoughts, but she was wrong. When her basket was full and all seemed to be in order, Doyle said a bit more.

"You just never know, do you?"

"That's true," Reese agreed, understanding what he meant; you couldn't be in the store and not think of it. "It certainly compels us to know our eternity is in order."

"If we can know," Doyle said, his voice low.

"I guess that's determined by whether we believe the Bible or not."

"I believe the Bible."

"The Bible says we can know, Doyle," Reese told him, shifting items in her basket to make it easier to carry.

"Where does it say that?"

"Lots of places, but I don't have those verses memorized. Do you want me to ask Douglas about it?"

Doyle hesitated. "Would Jace know?"

"Probably, or he could find out."

"I'll check with Jace," Doyle confirmed, not growing embarrassed with Reese's matter-of-fact way.

"Thanks for everything, Doyle."

"Thank you, Reese."

Reese went on her way. The basket was heavy, but that was a good reminder of how heavy sin was. She asked God to keep Doyle's hunger alive and to give Jace the answers.

❧❧❧

"Vera?"

Reese turned to the large man who had come into her kitchen after dinner and tried not to smile.

"No," she told him softly.

"All right." He wasn't put off in the least; indeed, he looked like a man with a mission. "Next question: Why is he Troy, and I'm Mr. Kingsley?"

Reese didn't even remember using the men's names when they came home to eat, but her employer clearly wanted to know.

"Why do you ask?"

"Just curious how you decide. You call Dooner Douglas, but use Mr. Leffler and Mr. Jenness for those men. How do you decide which name to use?"

"Troy asked me to call him Troy, and I didn't meet Douglas as a pastor. They were just Douglas and Alison, so I've never used their formal names."

"So if I told you to call me Conner, would you do it?"

Reese had to think about this. "I don't know," she admitted.

"You don't seem to have an issue with Troy."

"He's a grandpa," Reese said, mentioning the first thing that came to mind.

The lift of Conner's brows was hysterical. Reese put her hand to her mouth, but the laugh still escaped.

"On second thought," Conner spoke when she was quiet, "your logic might scare me, so don't tell me."

"I won't," Reese agreed, but she was still smiling.

Conner shook his head as he exited, not sure what had compelled him to ask but glad that he had. Her answer had given him another glimpse of her personality, a personality that was beginning to captivate him.

∽∾

Reese did not expect to see Conner and Troy at the Muldoon house, but she still had a smile for both men before going to the kitchen to see what she could do. As usual, Alison was very organized, but Reese's hands still joined Alison's and Hillary's, and soon they were sitting down to eat.

Reese was between Martin and Peter. Douglas prayed to thank God for the food, and the dishes were passed. Reese waited only until she'd served herself to stand and go to Alison. She took Jeffrey from his mother's arms and went back to her seat. Happy to eat with one hand and hold the baby with the other, Reese managed both tasks, gaining an adoring smile from Jeffrey every time she looked his way. At the same time, both Peter and Martin talked to her.

Troy was sitting across from Reese, quietly taking all of this in. Not certain when he'd last met someone of Reese's skills, he shot subtle glances her way unless a question was put to him. In the course of the meal, Reese worked on her food, put her nose in the baby's cheek whenever she could, and rubbed until he smiled. And when Martin needed something, Reese managed that as well.

Amazed just watching her, Troy knew in his heart that she was the woman for Conner Kingsley. He knew that saying something would never work, but in the time he'd known Reese, he was very impressed.

A question came his way from Douglas, and Troy was glad for the diversion. The thoughts running through his mind were very emotionally draining. It was far easier to answer a question concerning banking.

When everyone had eaten their fill, Reese and Hillary offered to do the dishes. The parlor door was closed, and the women went to work. There was quite a bit to wash, but the youngest women in the house were making quick work of it when Hillary had a question for Reese.

"Do you ever think about getting married?"

"Sometimes," Reese answered. "How about you, Hillary?"

"Sometimes," Hillary echoed, a smile in her voice.

"What made you think of that?"

"Oh, I don't know," Hillary hedged. "I just got to daydreaming about seeing you married."

"Why me?"

"I just think I could find a great husband for you."

"Is that right?" Reese teased, not taking her seriously.

"Um hm."

Hearing her very satisfied tone, Reese turned completely away from the dishpan in order to face the younger woman.

"You have someone in mind," she accused.

"Did I say that?" Hillary asked with all the innocence she could muster, but her act didn't work.

"Hillary Muldoon, you do have someone in mind!"

Hillary didn't answer, but neither could she stop smiling.

Douglas chose that moment to come into the kitchen, and Reese turned to him.

"Douglas, since I'm the older woman, does Hillary have to do what I say?"

Douglas laughed and said, "I'm not going to get into this."

"She has a husband picked out for me and won't tell me who it is," Reese complained, and Douglas was all at once interested.

"As a matter of fact, Hillary, I think it only right that you respect Reese's age and tell her what she wants to know."

His mock serious tone and face sent his daughter into gales of laughter, and she couldn't say a word. Her laughter only caused Reese and Douglas to start, and this was the way Conner found them.

"This sounds fun," he said, eyes taking in all of them.

"Ignore us, Conner," Douglas contained himself long enough to say. "What can I get you?"

"A glass of water, please."

Conner's needs were taken care of, and he and Douglas returned to the parlor.

"Are you ever going to tell me?" Reese asked when they were finally alone.

"I don't know," Hillary smiled, never intending to tease or make fun. "Maybe in time."

Reese asked a few more times, even trying to gain a hint while they finished in the kitchen, but not at any point would Hillary reveal who she had in mind.

∞

"What did you do this afternoon?" Reese asked her landlady after she had taken a seat in the parlor. She had once again invited her to the meetinghouse, but the older woman had again declined.

"Just some sewing," Mrs. Greenlowe answered, looking a little tired. "Who was at Muldoons'?"

"Just Mr. Thaden and Mr. Kingsley."

"Was that a little strange for you?"

"No," Reese said sincerely. "I see them off and on all day, and they're at the meetinghouse on Sundays, so it's not that unusual."

As soon as the words were out of Reese's mouth, she realized how true they were. Life around the two men had become very routine. And in a very short time. It wasn't too many days ago that she feared displeasing Troy Thaden. At the same time, terror was the only way she could have described her feelings for Conner Kingsley, but she'd been all wrong about that.

"I'm going to head over and see Mr. Somer," Reese announced when the room stayed quiet. "I'll come home in time to put tea on."

"You're a good girl, Reese," Mrs. Greenlowe said, once again giving her the long-standing compliment. Reese thought about it as she walked to the Somer home. One day she'd be thinking fast enough to ask Mrs. Greenlowe what she meant by that.

❧

"Come and see me this week," Doyle said softly to Jace as he and Maddie were leaving the Shephard home.

"Okay," Jace agreed, but his eyes were full of questions. He was about to voice his thoughts when Cathy came back from seeing Maddie into the wagon. The very small shake of Doyle's head arrested all ideas of that. Jace simply thanked Doyle and gave Cathy a hug.

Once in the wagon, Maddie didn't seem to notice that Jace was quiet and thoughtful. It was just as well. He didn't know what was going on and really had nothing to report.

❧

"Are you asleep?" Douglas asked his daughter when he checked on her that night.

"No, I just put the light out."

Douglas sat on the side of Hillary's bed and found her hand.

"Do you really have someone in mind for Reese?"

Hillary's laughter sounded in the darkness, and Douglas, having to soften his own laughter, hushed her.

"You're going to wake the boys."

"I can't help it. You were the one to come in and start that subject again."

"That's true, but I'm also the one who wants an answer."

"In the morning," Hillary said.

"Why then?"

"I can't see your face right now."

Hillary's whole bed shook with silent laughter as she heard her father finding the flint to light her bedside candle. When he had it lit, he held it close to his face and grinned at her. Hillary, who was not normally a silly girl, found herself giggling.

"Come on now," Douglas coaxed. "Let's have it."

"Mr. Kingsley."

Hillary would not have missed her father's expression for a fortune. He looked surprised, doubtful, and then thoughtful, all in the space of a few moments.

"You know," he said slowly. "You might be right."

"I think they already care for each other and don't know it."

"Why do you say that?"

"Just the way he watches her, and the looks she sometimes gives him."

Douglas had put the candle back on the table, but Hillary could see that he was still thinking.

"She's certainly not afraid of him anymore," Douglas said thoughtfully.

"Why was she afraid?" Hillary asked.

"Oh, just remembering Mr. Zantow. She worried that Conner would be the same way."

"I think about Mr. Zantow sometimes," Hillary admitted. "I wonder if at any time he humbled himself before God."

"I've wondered that too. I've also been thankful that God is in charge, and I can trust Him for Mr. Zantow's eternity."

The two fell silent then—a comfortable silence, one of love and security.

"I'd better let you sleep." Douglas bent to kiss her cheek.

"Goodnight," Hillary said.

Douglas gave her hand a squeeze before blowing out the candle and making his way from the room.

∽⌒

September was half over, and signs of the harvest began to emerge. Jace was beginning to be very busy on the farm, but Doyle's words to him on Sunday would not escape his mind. As soon as he could spare a few hours, he went to town. It was Wednesday.

Jace walked into the store, not sure what he would find but surprised to see that Doyle didn't seem all that pleased with his appearance. Jace didn't push in—Doyle was waiting on someone—but took a seat by the stove. Having come all the way to town, he was willing to wait.

It took some time, but Doyle eventually joined him.

"You came," Doyle said.

"Yes, I did. You don't seem too pleased."

"It has nothing to do with you," Doyle replied, his face clearly registering his unhappiness.

"What's going on?" Jace asked, not willing to beat about the bush any longer.

Doyle's look grew even fiercer, and Jace starting asking himself what he'd done. He kept silent this time, however, and before they could be interrupted, Doyle spoke.

"I don't want to die."

"Are you feeling poorly again?" Jace asked.

"No, but I could be. I keep telling Cathy that, but she won't listen."

"Is this about Mr. Somer?" Jace asked, having heard the whole story and knowing it must have been unsettling.

"It could have been me!" Doyle snapped in frustration, but before he could continue a woman came in, a little girl at her side.

Jace came to his feet and walked around a bit, asking God to give him words, but it never came to that. Cathy arrived after the woman was done, and Jace remembered Doyle's reticence to talk in her presence on Sunday. The two men exchanged a look, but only one had a plan. Jace would get Doyle alone this coming Sunday, so the older man felt free to talk. He wasn't sure how, but he wouldn't go home until he'd accomplished at least that.

ᴥ

"I want Reese to get some new shoes," Troy told Conner as they walked to work on Thursday morning. "I was going to work something out when I went to Linden Heights, but it completely slipped my mind."

"Have you told her you want her to have new shoes?"

"No. I'm trying to think of a subtle way to go about it."

"Maybe you could give her a little more money when you pay her."

"I haven't paid her," Troy said. "I was going to suggest you give her a little more."

Conner came to a stop, Troy with him.

"We've not paid Reese," Conner confirmed, his eyes telling of his surprise. "I haven't even been keeping track of what we owe her, thinking you were taking care of it."

"I assumed you were."

Without another word, Conner turned for home, doing sums in his head. His long legs eating the distance, he was stepping back through the front door of the big house in just a matter of minutes. He couldn't call for Reese but stood still trying to hear her. When the downstairs seemed quiet, he walked halfway up the stairs and heard humming. Going up, he found her dusting in Troy's bedroom. She had heard steps and was facing the door when he came in, so he didn't startle her.

"We haven't paid you." Conner wasted no time in stating the reason for his surprise return.

Reese had no idea what she was supposed to say to this, so she stood still, the dust rag in hand.

"Were you going to say anything?" Conner asked and immediately wished he could take the words back.

"I just assumed," Reese began, but Conner's hand in the air stopped her.

"I apologize. I should not have asked you that. This is not your fault, and Troy and I are sorry to have overlooked this. There is no excuse."

"It's all right. Mrs. Greenlowe is very understanding."

"You can't even pay your rent," Conner said, still amazed that this had been missed. Was he a banker or not?

"She won't throw me out," Reese assured him, not serious at all, but Conner looked upset. Reese tried to make amends. "It is all right, Mr. Kingsley. Truly. I would have checked with you eventually, I'm sure."

Conner wanted to argue that there should have been no need to check, but he kept this thought to himself. Instead he decided to go for broke about the shoes.

"There will be extra money because of this error," Conner began, sounding like the businessman he was.

Reese opened her mouth to protest, but Conner did not let her speak.

"You will use that money for shoes. Troy wants you to have new shoes."

Reese did not know what she was expecting, but this wasn't it. Her mouth opened, but no sound came out. Conner found it amusing.

"Speechless," he teased her. "I don't see that too often."

"Troy wants me to have new shoes?"

"Yes. He didn't want to offend you but found there is no subtle way to go about it. You do need shoes, don't you, Reese?"

"Yes, but how did he know?"

"He didn't say."

Reese looked thoughtful, not able to remember Troy ever seeing her feet.

"Are we agreed?" Conner checked.

"What exactly am I agreeing to?" Reese asked, mischief rising in her. "To be paid for my work, or to spend the money where I'm told?"

Conner would not back down, but a sparkle lit his own eye when he answered.

"Just this once, you're agreeing to both."

"And if I refuse?"

"I'll tell Troy."

Reese had to smile. He had figured her out. For some reason, she would stand up to Conner, but not Troy. She couldn't bear the thought of disappointing him.

"Does Doyle Shephard have what you need?" Conner asked.

"Yes. I've already seen them," she admitted quietly. "The black ones are prettier, but the brown ones are sturdy. I'll get those."

Conner suddenly wanted her to have both but knew he couldn't suggest such a thing. It didn't seem that anyone ever spoiled this woman, and suddenly he wanted to.

"Stop by the bank when you have a chance," Conner suggested instead, "and pick up your pay. In fact, take some time away from the house today and get your shoes."

"If I had known you were going to be this bossy," Reese teased him, "I might not have taken the job."

Conner laughed a little, taking it in stride but also not wanting to think about what life would be like right now if she hadn't taken the job.

Fifteen

On Friday the men had eaten dinner and returned to the bank at the normal time. Reese cleaned the kitchen and even readied things for tea, but her mind was on the shopping she needed to do to remedy the low food supply and the cleaning she wanted to get done in the dining room and kitchen. When someone knocked at the front door, it took a moment for her to realize she needed to answer.

The man standing on the porch was a stranger to her, and yet he wasn't. Reese stared at a smile she knew well, but when he spoke, it was not with the voice she expected.

"You must be Reese Thackery." He did not whisper. "I'm Dalton Kingsley."

His hand came out, and Reese shook it before speaking.

"Hello, Mr. Kingsley."

Reese was opening the door wide when he said, "Please call me Dalton."

Reese shut the door and watched him look around, his hat and bag still in hand. His head went back so he could view the ceiling and stairway, his mouth smiling as he took in the orthogonal lines of the hall.

"Everything looks great." He turned back to Reese, still smiling with pleasure. "Troy said you were doing an excellent job."

"Thank you," Reese acknowledged quietly, still taking in his presence—not just his appearance at the door, but his size. Were all the men in the family huge? He wasn't quite as large as Conner, but he was still a big man.

As Reese watched, he moved to the sideboard in the entry hall and studied the oil painting of the man there. The fond smile on his face told Reese that Dalton had known this man.

"Conner and Troy must be at the bank," Dalton suddenly turned and guessed.

"Yes. They've had dinner, but I'd be happy to make you something."

"I am quite hungry if it's no bother."

"Not at all," Reese said, leaving him in the hallway to make her way back to the kitchen. She didn't think he would follow, but then she didn't know about the private conversation he'd had with Troy during his visit back to Linden Heights. Dalton had put his hat and bag down, arriving in the kitchen just a few seconds behind her.

"I feel I need to personally apologize for the bank's having held your papers."

Reese was slicing ham but stopped when he made this announcement.

"It's all right," Reese said, not sure how to reply. "I was glad when it was all done."

"I'm sure you were. I hope Conner is paying you well."

Reese said yes, but the small, breathless laugh that escaped on that word did not get explained. Dalton made a mental note to ask his brother.

"Has Conner told you that you're taller than our sisters?"

"I didn't know you had sisters," Reese told him.

"Four of them, and they're all quite tall, but no one has you beat."

Reese smiled and continued adding food to the plate she was fixing. She kept the biscuits and butter separate but soon presented a full plate to Dalton Kingsley.

"Would you like a piece of cake? It's chocolate."

"Just one?" he asked in a way that so reminded her of Conner that Reese had to bite her lip to keep from laughing.

"I'll bring it to you," Reese offered, her way of telling Dalton he could go to the dining room and eat. He took the hint but was calling for her before she could even get a knife out. Reese went to the door.

"I'd like to ask you a huge favor," Dalton began. "Would you sit down?"

Reese wanted to decline but instead took a seat by the wall.

"Here." Dalton stood and pulled out the chair across from him. "Sit here, Reese."

In silence, Reese did as she was told, slightly overwhelmed by how relaxed and friendly he was.

"Douglas Muldoon and I go way back. He's the one who wrote about your situation."

Dalton could have gone on, but the look on Reese's face stopped him.

"Reese?" he said with slight impatience. "Doesn't anyone tell you anything?"

Thinking he was upset with her, Reese only shrugged.

"Honestly, Conner," he went on, cutting meat into smaller pieces and talking to the men who were not there. "Troy, what were you thinking? And Dooner!"

Reese only watched him, trying to take in his eccentric behavior as well as this new but significant bit of information.

"Anyway," he continued, getting back to business, "I would like to have the Muldoon family come for dinner on Sunday, but that means more work for you tomorrow. I want you to join us as well, but will you have enough time and energy to take care of it?"

"Certainly," Reese replied, giving her standard reply, her mind on other things.

"Are you sure? Is there someone who could help you?"

"It'll be fine." She forced her mind back to the moment. "What would you like to have?"

"Anything. They have how many children, five?"

"Yes, but one is still a baby."

"All right. Well, actually, I'd best check with them before I ask you to do all that work. I'll do that before I stop by the bank."

Reese nodded, thinking she might have met someone with her energy level. She thought he was finished with her then and began to rise, but he kept on talking between bites.

"I've just realized that you might not be able to buy meat on such short notice. Does someone in Tucker Mills have something readily available?"

"Yes. I was thinking beef or pork, and both can be purchased right now," Reese was pleased to say, but her mind was more on the stop she needed to make as soon as she was done for the day.

Dalton finished his meal without Reese even noticing and sat looking at her. Reese looked back, not catching on.

"Did you say there was chocolate cake?" he finally asked.

Grinning like a schoolboy when Reese laughed a little, he stayed in his place and waited for the cake to arrive. It was a very large piece, and Reese had all she could do not to laugh again when he looked so pleased.

"Did you need anything else?" she asked.

"No, Reese, but thank you. I've taken enough of your time."

Reese only smiled and went back to work, a little bit glad that Conner and Dalton were so different. She didn't know if having a tornado in the house was something she could manage on a daily basis.

❧

Dalton was busy in the next hour. He finished his cake, found the Muldoon home and settled those plans, went back to the big house to inform Reese, and then headed to the bank. He'd not told anyone he was coming and couldn't hide the satisfaction he felt when he stepped in the door, knowing that both Conner and Troy would be surprised.

Dalton walked into the bank building and, much as he had done at the house, stood and took it in. That was when Troy spotted him.

"Well, now," the older man said good-naturedly. "Look who's come to Tucker Mills."

Dalton had to laugh. Troy came out to shake his hand, and as soon as Conner was close enough, Dalton gave him a great hug. In the next few moments he was introduced to Mr. Leffler before the three bankers sat in the alcove to talk.

"How is Jamie?" was the first thing Conner wanted to know.

"Very well. She's not back to full strength, but she's on her way."

"That's great news," the younger brother said sincerely.

"How long will you stay?" Troy asked.

"For a week," Dalton committed. "I thought about just coming for the weekend but realized it wasn't enough. We're having Dooner and the family over for dinner on Sunday, by the way."

"How are we managing that?" Conner asked, knowing none of them knew how to cook for a crowd.

"Reese is handling it."

"You've met Reese?"

"She fed me dinner. It was delicious."

"And you know she's willing to handle a Sunday dinner?"

"Certainly," Dalton spoke with confidence. "She'll join us, of course."

"Of course," Conner echoed, shaking his head a little.

Dalton didn't appear to notice, and when Mr. Leffler sought Conner's assistance a few minutes later, Dalton was able to tell Troy what was really on his mind.

"He's got to marry her."

"Absolutely," Troy agreed, "but it can't be rushed. It's just been a short time, but I think they're more aware of each other than they realize."

"His concern about her doing Sunday dinner is a good sign."

"Yes, it is."

"How does she do around him? Not still afraid?"

"No," Troy smiled. "You'll have to watch them in action, but be subtle. I'm not always able to pull it off, and Conner will ask me what my looks mean."

Conner was returning, so they changed the topic to affairs of the bank for the rest of the afternoon. The men talked about what Troy and Conner were finding in the accounts, the situation with Mr. Jenness, and the future of the Tucker Mills Bank.

∽∾

When Reese left the big house on Friday afternoon, she did not go directly home. Dalton's words still in her head, she made a beeline for the Muldoon house and asked to see Douglas. He came from the study to speak with her in the kitchen, baby Jeffrey already in her arms.

"I just learned that you wrote to Dalton Kingsley about my situation."

"That's true, I did," Douglas admitted. "Did it never come up between the two of us?"

"No, I had no idea."

Douglas sat down in the kitchen. Alison was working at the table, wondering how her husband would explain.

"I felt terrible pain the day that Mr. Jenness announced the bank would keep your papers," Douglas started. "I went for a walk to pray and ask God to help me accept this for your life. While I was on the walk, I remembered who owned the bank.

"I go way back with the Kingsley family. Dalton and I were in school together. We hadn't had much contact in recent years, and I mostly wrote asking for his advice. Without warning,

Conner and Troy came to town. Not until I'd heard they were here did I realize my letter had been received and acted upon."

"And evidently they found the bank's owning papers as odd as the rest of us did," Reese figured thoughtfully. "Thank you, Douglas. I had no idea, and as you can imagine, I'm very grateful."

Douglas only inclined his head modestly as his wife spoke up. "So what did you think of Dalton?"

Reese smiled. "He's a kind man, but he and Conner are different. I think I'm glad about that."

"The only thing larger than Dalton is his personality," Douglas said fondly, remembering some times from the past.

"We'll have to get these two talking during dinner on Sunday," Alison said to Reese, who agreed with a mischievous lift of her brows.

Much as she wanted to sit and hear stories now, Reese made herself leave. After giving the baby a last cuddle, she handed him off and headed for home.

∞

Friday evening at the Greenlowe house was quiet. Both women were in the parlor, Mrs. Greenlowe with handwork in her lap and Reese with her Bible and the book she was reading. When someone knocked on the kitchen door, the landlady was the closest and went to answer it. She was back just a moment later, telling Reese she had a visitor. Reese found Conner on the porch.

"You're welcome to come in," Reese invited.

"I don't wish to intrude on your evening," Conner replied, but then in his quiet way he got right down to business. "You met Dalton."

Reese smiled before saying, "Yes, I did."

"Did the word 'hurricane' come to mind?"

"No, it was 'tornado.'"

Conner smiled. "I'm actually here for a reason. I heard about Dalton's plans for Sunday and wanted to make sure that was all right with you."

"Yes, I told him it was."

"But Dalton can be hard to say no to. Are you sure about Sunday, Reese?"

"It's fine."

"And you understand that you're there to join us, not work?"

This gave Reese pause. "Who will put things on the table and take care of the dishes?"

"Dalton, Troy, and I."

Reese's look was so skeptical that Conner's own brows rose.

"You think we can't take care of it?" He sounded as outraged as he could manage but still only drew a disbelieving look from Reese.

"Let's just say," Reese tried tactfully, her voice having dropped to whispering, "that I'll be available should you need me."

Conner had to smile as he studied her. His head tipped to one side when he asked, "Douglas said you're never tired. It's true, isn't it?"

"Of course it's not true," Reese said, trying to dismiss the matter.

"Are you tired right now?" Conner pressed her.

"No."

"Were you tired when you got up this morning?"

"No." She sounded surprised at the very idea.

Conner was shaking his head in amazement when he thought of something.

"Velma? Is it Velma?"

"No," Reese said emphatically.

"Verna?"

"No," Reese repeated.

"Why don't you just tell me?"

"Because it's an awful name, and you're too curious for your own good."

"I'll find out," he teased her, leaning against the porch railing as if he had all night.

"I don't think so," she teased back.

"We'll just see about that."

"Do you know what I just found out?" Reese was the one to change the subject this time.

"What?"

"Douglas wrote to your brother about my situation with the bank."

"You didn't know that?"

"Not until today when your brother mentioned it." Reese suddenly smiled. "You and Troy and Douglas were all in trouble when he realized you hadn't told me."

"Let me guess." Conner was smiling hugely. "He did a lot of talking to us when we weren't in the room."

"You know him very well."

"Yes, I do."

"I also found out today that you have four sisters, all of whom are quite tall."

"My, my, Dalton did do a lot of talking. Did he also tell you that you're taller than all of them?"

"Yes, he did. He seemed to think I would be pleased."

"Were you?"

Reese shrugged. "It doesn't make any difference to me. I don't know a woman as tall as I am, but I wouldn't mind."

"Would you have been afraid of me at first if I hadn't been so big?"

"No." Reese knew it to be true.

"Why did it matter?"

Reese weighed her words and came up with what she felt was a reasonable answer.

"I'm used to being able to protect myself. Had you been a different kind of man, I wouldn't have been able to do that."

"How did you come to Christ?" Conner asked.

"One day I talked with Douglas and Alison. After listening to what they said, I believed," Reese said, careful not to add more.

Conner watched the way her face sobered and her eyes went to the wood at their feet.

"Maybe someday I can hear the whole story," Conner ventured.

"Maybe," Reese echoed, her eyes on a faraway spot. "How about you? Did you grow up in a believing home?"

"I did, yes. I remember praying with my father one night, and he asked me how I knew my prayers were being heard by God. I didn't have a good answer, so he got his Bible out and showed me how I could have God's Spirit living inside of me, as His child, and if I was His child, then my righteous prayers would always be heard by Him.

"That night I told God I believed in Him and needed Him to save me. I was only about six at the time, but I know it was real. When hard things came into my life after that point, I would be tempted to doubt God's love for me, but that night was always the memory that came to mind."

"At the risk of sounding insulting, you don't seem like someone who's ever known hard things," Reese theorized, even as she wondered what he was like as a child.

"I can see why it might seem that way. Someday I'll have to tell you about it. Maybe when you tell me your whole story."

Reese nodded, thinking the future a good idea. She certainly didn't want to discuss it tonight, not here and now.

"I'd better let you go," Conner said when the breeze picked up and he realized Reese was not wearing a sweater or coat.

"I'll see you in the morning."

"Goodnight, Reese."

"Goodnight."

Conner waited until she was inside before replacing his hat and walking home very slowly.

ॐ

Reese had her hands full on Saturday, but she was up to the challenge. She had done laundry earlier in the week, so plenty of linens were fresh. She took extra care with the dining room table once the men had had dinner and gone on their way. She knew they would want their tea but was also fairly certain they would leave things in good order for the guests.

Reese counted people in her mind before counting places at the table. Including herself, she needed ten chairs. The table was comfortable for twelve, so Reese knew that if the Kingsley men each wanted to take an end, they would have elbow room to spare.

Not until Reese went outside to shake a rug did she become distracted from her mission. She had just finished, knowing her hair had taken the lion's share of dust, when she looked up to see Gerald walking her way.

"Hello," Reese greeted him kindly, not nearly so cross to see him this time.

"Hey," he said when he neared, and Reese thought he seemed down.

"What are you doing today?"

"Nothing," he said, his look going south. "All you ever do is work."

"I like to work," Reese felt a need to tell him, biting her tongue from saying he could use a job himself.

"I don't like the man you work for," Gerald suddenly said.

"Do you know the man I work for?" Reese asked, when what she really wanted to do was defend Conner Kingsley.

"He sent my father away," Gerald retorted, sounding as sulky as he felt.

Again Reese wanted to jump to Conner's defense but controlled herself.

"Maybe you should talk to Mr. Kingsley or Mr. Thaden and

ask one of them about it," Reese suggested, realizing she didn't know all the details.

"They would just treat me like they treated my father!" Gerald sounded belligerent now, and Reese knew there would be no reasoning with him.

When silence settled around them for a moment, Reese was on the verge of excusing herself, but Gerald spoke, his tone softened.

"Why don't we do something together sometime?"

"That's not a good idea, Gerald. I'm complimented that you would want to do something with me, but you and I have very little in common."

"My mother says you're too old for me and not good enough, but she's wrong."

"Your mother just wants to protect you," Reese replied, not allowing herself to be offended. "And she doesn't know me well enough to know if I'd be good for you. It's natural that she'd feel that way."

Gerald looked at her, his heart aching inside of him. He knew he didn't stand a chance. Even though she was only a servant in town, there was something special about her, something he was drawn to.

"Just say you'll go with me, even on a walk," Gerald tried again, not surprised to see Reese shaking her head no.

"I've got to get back to work, Gerald. Thanks for stopping to see me."

"But you don't want me to stop in anymore, do you?"

"If it's only going to give you ideas about us, then you'd better not."

Gerald left without another word, and Reese prayed but also asked herself what she could have said differently. She hated this attachment he'd developed to her, but never did she want to see him hurt.

Without warning, Reese felt the hair pick up on the back of her neck. She glanced around, feeling as though she was being watched. She even went around the edge of the house to look for Gerald and spotted him down the green. Going back to the door she'd used to come outside, Reese took a moment to look around.

The feeling was lessening, but something wasn't right. Had she not just seen Gerald on the green, she would swear he'd hidden in order to watch her. Reese finally went back inside, her heart a little worried.

∞

Conner's mind registered concern the moment he walked in to find Reese waiting for them in the hall. The last time she'd done this, Gerald Jenness had visited.

"Has something happened?" he asked as soon as he was close enough. Reese explained Gerald's visit, not being overly specific but telling Conner, Troy, and Dalton about her sense of being watched.

"I don't want you outside in the back by yourself," Conner immediately began. "If you can't do something out front, don't worry about it unless we're here."

"I'm not the issue," Reese took no time in saying. "If Mr. Jenness is lurking about, he doesn't care about me. You're the reason he left his job—at least that's what his son thinks. I only stayed to warn you. I'm not in danger."

Troy and Dalton had stayed quiet, fascinated with the way Reese spoke up to Conner. Conner, on the other hand, had more to say.

"You will do as I ask. I don't want you outside where no one can see you."

"And you're not listening," Reese emphasized. "I'm not the issue, and even if I was, it's only Mr. Jenness."

"What does that mean?" Conner asked, his face registering confusion.

"I'm much bigger than he is."

Dalton's hand came to his upper lip, and Troy turned a laugh into a cough. Conner and Reese, however, were not laughing.

"I have to get home," Reese said. "I'll see you tomorrow."

"And we'll talk again on Monday" were Conner's parting words.

Reese only eyed him before heading to the door. When she was gone, both Dalton and Troy took one look at Conner's face and decided to leave their comments for another time.

Sixteen

Reese had never tried to figure out why, but she always sat in the rear pew. She didn't hurry away when the service ended, nor did she want to avoid people, but the back pew somehow fit her needs.

She had noticed on past Sundays that Troy and Conner also seemed the most comfortable in that row. And on this Sunday, with Dalton accompanying them, it became something of a tight squeeze. In fact, Conner ended up sitting on the side of Reese's skirt. She didn't notice at first. It took her wanting to shift a bit to realize she couldn't move. She was just about to say something to him when he leaned toward her.

"Vesta?"

"No," Reese said, wanting to laugh.

"Why don't you just tell me?"

"What's your middle name?" Reese suddenly asked.

"James."

"You see?" she whispered. "It's normal. Mine is not."

Conner looked down at her. Reese looked up at him.

"By the way," she said, having almost forgotten, "you're on my skirt."

To her utter astonishment he didn't shift over but smiled at her.

"I'm comfortable."

Reese bit her lip and turned away to keep from laughing. Conner, almost in laughter himself, shifted enough to let her pull the fabric closer to her side.

The action made Conner more aware of her than ever before. He'd flirted with her just now, something he'd not even attempted in more years than he could remember, and even as the sermon got underway, he knew why.

Reese Thackery was the most intriguing woman he'd ever met. Conner didn't live in a small town, so knowing folks well was more difficult. He was close to the people in his church family, but there were no women his age who were also unmarried.

Reese Thackery had brought out something inside of him that he didn't know existed. She was hard-working and smart, easily the most capable woman of his acquaintance. There was also something altogether vulnerable about her, something that caused Conner to wish he could protect her forever.

"Now let's look at a few verses in Psalm 25," Conner finally heard Douglas say, and he realized he needed to listen.

"I'm going to read just four verses to you, but I don't want you to miss a few elements. In these four verses, 'thy,' 'thou,' or 'thee' is used ten times. David, the author of these words, is speaking in complete humility, understanding that his salvation is all about God: God's desire to save and God's desire to keep us. David understands this. I'm going to start in verse four and just point out a few things as we go along.

"'Show me thy ways, O Lord; teach me thy paths.' Now this is not a complicated verse. It seems pretty straightforward, but we tend to be blind to the seriousness of our sin. When we ask God to show and teach us, we're not always ready for that prayer to be answered.

"Verse five says, 'Lead me in thy truth, and teach me; for thou art the God of my salvation; on thee do I wait all the day.' Just in case you've forgotten, we've already covered five of the thy-thou-thee references to God. There's no missing them in these verses. God's presence, His will, and His power will not be ignored.

"Okay, verses six and seven. 'Remember, O Lord, thy tender mercies and thy lovingkindness; for they have been ever of old. Remember not the sins of my youth, nor my transgressions; according to thy mercy remember thou me for thy goodness' sake, O Lord.'

"Did you catch the 'remembers'? First David asks that God remember, then he asks Him not to remember, and then he wants Him to remember again. How many of us have sins from the past that we never want to have to think about again? David is asking God to let those stay in the past.

"And all for God's glory. David will certainly know the benefits of God's goodness, but the ultimate glory will be God's. Did you notice the phrase 'they have been ever of old'? We don't talk like that anymore, but I love those words. They remind me that God is the Creator. They tell us that even before creation, God was merciful and that his kindness was the most loving type."

Sitting in the front row, his heart soaking in every word, Jace Randall found himself asking God to be His most loving that day. Jace had something to take care of, and he knew that nothing good could come of it without God's kindness and mercy.

∞

The Muldoons' visit to the big house started with a tour. Reese felt a certain measure of pride that things looked nice, and as she had expected, Alison and Hillary fell in love with the house and furnishings as fast as she had.

Reminding herself to act like a guest—Troy had made a point of telling her that this morning—Reese followed along, happy to do that until it was time for the food to go on the table. She started out sitting with the others in the dining room, but male voices, all sounding confused and coming from the kitchen, caused her to excuse herself and head that way.

"What's the matter?"

"You're not supposed to be in here," Troy started.

"Okay," she agreed, and began to put rolls in a low bowl.

"Reese," Troy tried again, only to have her agree and begin giving orders.

"Let's put that fork with the meat. Good. Now those salads need spoons. Right there. Good."

A few minutes later Reese looked things over, not speaking or looking at the men, and then went back to her seat. The Muldoon family was more than a little amused by all of this, and their smiles almost started Reese to laughing. Instead, she smiled at Joshua, who sat next to her, and looked up to see the men trooping in with all the platters and bowls.

The compliments were many, but the men were all careful to give credit to Reese. She was glad when Dalton prayed and everyone began to eat, taking the focus off of her.

Not for another five minutes did she see that the men had made no plans for drinks. Reese discreetly stood and went to Dalton.

"Shall I make some tea?"

His face was comical.

"I forgot we needed something to drink."

"I'll take care of it," Reese assured him and slipped from the room.

If Dalton had looked at his brother just then, he would have found himself scowled at. Certainly it was Dalton's idea to have Reese be a guest, but without someone to handle the details, it just didn't work. Conner ate a little more of his meal, seeing that Reese had enjoyed little of hers, excused himself, and joined her in the kitchen.

"I knew this would happen," he said, wasting no time displaying his feelings.

"What's that?" Reese had gone right to whispering.

"You would have to work."

"If I recall, you were the one who assured me that the three of you could handle it."

"That lasted until I walked off Mrs. Greenlowe's porch and realized what I'd said."

Reese only smiled, checking the milk for freshness before putting it into a small pitcher.

"I don't mind," she countered.

"You're doing it again," Conner said.

"What am I doing?"

"Whispering."

Reese looked at him. "Do I do that when I talk to you?"

"Often."

"Why do you whisper?" Reese decided to ask.

"My throat was damaged when I was young."

"So you can't speak any louder?"

"No. In fact, some days my vocal cords wear out, and only rest brings my voice back."

Reese nodded thoughtfully as she realized that he always wore his cravat quite high. She wondered if he was scarred but was careful not to drop her eyes away from his. Nevertheless, her curiosity about this man only increased.

A few seconds later Reese realized she was looking into his eyes. They were kind eyes, light blue, amid a handsome, almost boyish face, and right now those eyes were looking right back at her.

"What can I do to help?" Conner brought them back to the moment.

"I'll load the tray," Reese suggested, surprised at where her thoughts had gone. "And you can carry it."

The job was accomplished a short time later, and water and tea were served at the table. Reese returned to her meal, ready to eat and glad to have tea with it. She was also thankful she had something to do with her hands and eyes; otherwise she would have gone right back to staring at Conner Kingsley, who occupied one end of the table.

∞

"Hey, Doyle," Jace said as soon as there was an opening. "Would you mind showing me a pair of boots in the store? I might not have time to come in this week."

"Not at all," Doyle agreed, leaving the women to their talk and slipping out the side door.

Jace felt terrible for the deceit; he didn't need boots and planned to tell Doyle that. But the afternoon was wearing on, and he knew they wouldn't be in town that much longer.

"I'm sorry I lied," Jace confessed as soon as the door shut behind them.

"I'm not," Doyle said bluntly, and Jace looked closely into his face, as he had been doing all day. Doyle appeared tired and older, and in only a few days' time.

"You've got yourself all worked up. I can see it."

"I'm not sleeping, and I'm having to hide that from Cathy."

"Tell me what's on your mind, Doyle. Explain it to me."

"I'm not sick now, but as you know I was sick, and not that long ago. I didn't fear death then, but I do now. I don't know what to do about that."

"Well, you're asking at the right time," Jace said. "If you think you can wait and argue your way into heaven at a later time, you're in for a horrible surprise."

Doyle looked at the man married to his niece and knew he would not play games with him.

"I've always seen myself as a good man," Doyle confessed. "I don't cheat my customers, and I'm generous when I can be. I love my wife, and I feel like I've done all right."

"Then why all this fear now?"

Doyle's heart sank. It was a powerful question, and one that he could not answer.

"If I drop dead right now, Jace, I don't know what God will say to me. I don't know if I'll be in heaven."

"But you can know. I learned that early this year. It took a long time, but the blinders are off my eyes. I can see exactly what the Bible was saying all along."

"What has it said?"

"That I'm condemned unless God saves me, no matter how well I think I'm doing on this earth. My sin separates me from God, and without the shed blood of His Son, I'll be lost for all of eternity."

Doyle paled, but Jace's expression was kind.

"I can tell you about what happened to me, Doyle. There's a lot I don't understand, but I can tell you my story."

"Tell me," the older man urged, and Jace began. He told Doyle how thankful he was that Maddie had had questions all those years and that she wasn't able to let the subject rest. He explained to him how he'd not seen how serious his sin was, and then how frightened he'd been when he realized how great and powerful God was; that He could have taken his life at any time.

"That's me, Jace." Doyle was breathing hard. "It was Mr. Somer this time. It could have been me, and not just collapsing but dying. I'm not ready for that."

"Would you like to be ready?" Jace asked, hoping he had the right words.

"More than anything, but I'm afraid. I'm so afraid that I can't work or think straight."

"This is what I said to God, Doyle. I told Him that I'm a sinner, and I believe that Jesus Christ is His Son. I told Him I believe that His blood alone can save me."

"That's all?" Doyle asked.

"No, Doyle, that's not all. I didn't come with my mind made up—I came in humility and desperation. The words weren't complicated, but that doesn't diminish the huge work Christ performed on my behalf when He died to save all men. I had to see my need, Doyle, and until I did, I couldn't go to God with a repentant heart."

"So I have to believe that my sin will condemn me?"

"Yes, and that God has the only answer through His Son."

The word *answer* got Doyle's attention as nothing else had. He was full of questions, and Jace had been answering those questions, but he didn't like what he was hearing. Nothing Jace could tell him would work if he wasn't willing to listen.

"Tell me one more time," Doyle asked.

"Do you know you're a sinner, Doyle, or do you think you're all right?"

"I know I sin," Doyle admitted, his heart paining him.

"There is no hope outside of the saving blood of Christ. He provided a path to God through belief in Him. When we confess our sin and need to God, and believe that His Son will save us, He does."

"How will I know it's true, Jace? How will I *know?*"

"You'll be changed. On days when your heart doubts, you must go to Scripture and not rely on feelings or experience, but if your belief is true, you'll be a changed man."

"I have to do this," Doyle whispered. "I have to take care of this now."

"You can, Doyle," Jace told him with a smile. "I found out that God doesn't turn anyone away."

And in the quiet store, with a sense of aloneness in the world, Doyle Shephard confessed his need to God and asked God to save him. Jace said little but listened as this man he cared for, his first friend in Tucker Mills, accepted the gift that only God could provide, and nearly cried himself when Doyle finished praying and wept like a child.

"Tell them about the time you helped old Mrs. Hyde," Douglas urged Dalton once the adults had finished dinner and settled in the large parlor.

"With her dog?" he clarified.

"Yes, that one."

Dalton rolled his eyes, and Conner's shoulders began to shake.

"Mrs. Hyde was the meanest woman in Linden Heights. It's true!" Dalton declared when the group began to smile, sure he was exaggerating. "She watched out her window to make sure we stayed out of her yard, and when we didn't she'd send the dog out after us."

"And he was mean," Conner put in.

"He certainly was. Well, anyway, my father had been talking to me about doing good works and thinking of others, so I went to Mrs. Hyde and offered to cut down an old tree she had in her front yard. At first she seemed pleased, so I went to work. The tree wasn't that large, and I could reach all the branches from the ground, but my work only lasted about ten minutes before she sent the dog after me.

"I heard this terrible growling and barking, so I climbed the tree I was cutting, but it was old and rotting, and I wasn't small. On top of that, this dog could jump. Every branch sounded like it was going to break with me on it, so I kept moving and yelling for help, and all this time the dog was going crazy, jumping up and trying to bite me."

Dalton shuddered with the memory. "I thought I was a goner."

"So what happened?" Alison asked.

"It gets worse," Dalton said. "The branch I was on gave way, and both the branch and I fell on the dog."

"Was he hurt?" Reese asked this time.

"He was more than hurt—he died," Dalton revealed, still horrified at the memory. "Mrs. Hyde must have been watching from the window, because suddenly she came out with the broom and chased me off the property."

Every mouth in the group was open with shock and laughter. Dalton was in his element, recounting the old story.

"I ran all the way to the bank and told my father what had happened. He went to see Mrs. Hyde, and we buried the dog for her, but she never forgave me. Thankfully she didn't replace the dog, but I still gave her yard a wide berth until she died about five years later."

"Is that all true?" Reese asked, still laughing at Dalton's voice and antics.

"Every word. You can ask Dooner."

"Where were you in all of this, Conner?" Douglas asked. "I can't remember."

"Probably at home. I remember hearing about it at tea that night and being relieved that the dog couldn't bite me anymore."

Voices could be heard just then coming down the hallway from the small parlor where the three boys played. Douglas got up to check on them, and Reese, not thinking about whether or not it was her place, offered coffee and dessert.

Dalton was all for that, so she went off to do the honors, cutting the pie she'd made as well as the berry crisp that Alison had brought. Hillary went to help her, and the Muldoons stayed for another two hours.

Reese walked as far as their house with them and then continued on home, looking forward to spending the evening with her landlady and even telling her some of Dalton Kingsley's stories.

❧

That night when Reese climbed into bed, she realized that life had taken on a pattern that varied little. Reese liked change, and even enjoyed the unexpected, but she was not discontented right now with her schedule.

The days were predictable, seeing the same people all the time, but she wasn't the same person she was a year ago. How many years did she stand in Doyle's store and never once think about praying for him? Such a thing had never occurred to her. But now God's Spirit lived inside, and she was aware of people, how much God loved them, and how important His death was because of them.

Fatigue finally set in. Remembering the words from the sermon just that morning, Reese drifted off to sleep with the Psalm 25 verses on her mind and her nightly prayer that God would save Mrs. Greenlowe.

❧

"I need to tell you something," Jace said to Maddie as soon as they were back at the house. "I'll put these two up," he referred to the horses, "and be right in."

"All right," Maddie agreed, wondering at the odd expression on her husband's face. He looked excited and tense at the same time.

Maddie didn't want to go inside but forced herself into the kitchen and waited right next to the door for Jace to come. The wait felt longer than it was, and even more confusion set in when Jace stepped in the door and hugged her, holding her tightly.

"Come here," he said at last, taking her hand and leading her to the parlor sofa.

"What is it, Jace?"

"It's Doyle. He believes in Jesus Christ."

Maddie's hands came to her mouth, and tears filled her eyes. She had so many questions but couldn't speak one of them.

"I regret lying and saying I needed to look at boots, but your

Aunt Cathy is having a hard time with Doyle's questions, and I knew he wanted to see me alone."

"And he prayed with you?"

"Yes. He was terrified of dying in his sin."

Maddie wanted to throw her arms around Jace, but something in his face held her back.

"What is it, Jace? What's bothering you?"

"I don't know enough, Maddie. What if I told him the wrong thing? What if I didn't present it right?"

Maddie did hug her husband then.

"It's all right. You don't have to save him. God does that. I'm sure you just told him what you did, and he understood, didn't he?"

"Yes," Jace agreed, relaxing a little.

"Now tell me," Maddie moved away a little. "What's this about Cathy not wanting to hear Doyle's questions?"

"He didn't go into detail, but he didn't want her to know we had talked."

Maddie nodded. This made sense. Cathy would not want to think about death or someone not being good enough to go to heaven.

"I'm busy right now, Maddie," Jace suddenly said. "The fields own me at this time of the year. I need you to go to town this week, maybe Wednesday, and see how he's doing."

"I'll do it. Maybe he'll have told Cathy by then."

"Maybe," Jace said, needing to hold his wife again.

They sat, just holding each other, neither one speaking for a long time. Eventually, Jace began to pray, but it was brief, his heart overwhelmed with what had happened that afternoon. He asked God to let Doyle's heart be real and to keep his and Maddie's hearts forever His.

∞

"Good morning," Conner said as soon as he tracked Reese down. She was working on breakfast but also bringing some things up from the buttery.

"Good morning," she greeted him on the stairway, stepping aside so he could go down.

"I'm not going down. I'm looking for you."

"Oh?" Reese questioned, her eyes watching him. Conner backed against one wall so she could pass and then followed her back to the kitchen.

"Did you want something specific for breakfast?" Reese asked, knowing this was not the case.

"I'm sure I'll enjoy whatever you're making."

"Something special cleaned?" Reese now suggested, not quite able to hide a glimmer of a smile in her eyes.

"No." Conner was fighting his own smile. "Something more serious than that."

"I have to go outside to do my work," Reese said, coming right to the point. "You can see that, can't you?"

"I can see that you need to stay visible. You can still do your work, just not at the back."

"That's the best place for some jobs," Reese began, but Conner shook his head.

"I can move all of my work home until we know what's going on."

"I don't want you to do that," Reese returned, becoming very sober. "And I'll do as you ask, but you're still not listening to me."

"Tell me again what I'm not hearing."

"I'm not the one in danger. It's you and Troy."

"You don't know that."

"Yes, I do. I didn't do anything to Mr. Jenness. You, on the other hand, seem to have taken his bank from him."

"You might be right, but I'm not willing to take that chance. If you're not inside, stay where you can be seen from the green. Please, Reese."

Reese nodded and turned back to the oven. Conner watched

her, guessing she wasn't very happy with him. Leaving her to do her work, Conner wondered if she was upset with him or just getting back to business. He hoped he would know before he left for the bank.

෨෨෪

"Hello, Maddie," Reese said when she answered her knock. "Come in."

"Thank you, Reese," she said, stepping inside. "Oh, my, this is beautiful."

"You haven't been here?"

"Not for many years. I'd forgotten how large it was." She turned and smiled at Reese. "I'm glad you have to clean it, Reese. I'm not sure I'd ever get done."

"There's always something to do," Reese explained, completely at ease with the whole idea. "Come in the kitchen."

"Thank you. I came for that recipe. Did you remember it?"

"No, but I can write it down for you now."

Maddie looked as they walked. As with everyone else, she wanted to ask for a tour but remembered that this was not Reese's home.

"How are you feeling?" Reese asked, writing down the ingredients for a basting sauce to put on pork.

"Mostly just tired. Sometimes my stomach is upset, but not often."

"What do you do for that?"

"Eating sometimes helps."

"I've never had a stomachache a day in my life. I wonder what it will be like when I'm pregnant."

"Well, Reese," Maddie said softly. "Is there something you want to tell me?"

Reese's laughter sounded in the room, and Maddie looked pleased. She also said she couldn't linger.

"Let me know how it turns out," Reese said, seeing her off through the front door.

"I will. Thanks, Reese."

Maddie started down the walk toward her wagon but stopped. She turned and looked back at the house, still seeing Reese in her mind and the comfortable way she'd let her out the elegant front door.

Almost like she lives here was the thought in Maddie's head. *Or should live here.*

Maddie eventually turned for the wagon to begin her errands, but her mind had stumbled onto an idea, one she thought was most intriguing.

ↆↄ

Lillie Jenness had taken Monday morning to run errands. She had quite a long list, not having shopped for a time, and it was nearly dinnertime when she got back. She'd worked ahead of time, however, and knew it would just take a few minutes to put the meal on the table.

She was shocked to find that Gerald had already been in the stew, his dirty bowl and spoon discarded on the worktable. It wasn't like him to do such a thing, and Lillie wondered why he'd been so hungry. Shaking her head a little, she went ahead and put the meal on, quite certain he would not be around to join her but also planning to confront him over the act as soon as he arrived home.

Not until she'd eaten and gone upstairs to put some things away did she began to doubt her own conclusion. Someone had been in her bedroom. A meticulous housekeeper, leaving everything in order each day, Lillie noticed that the closet door was slightly ajar. And the quilt on the bed looked as if someone had sat down on it.

Lillie's next thoughts caused her heart to race. She would

not ask Gerald if he knew something, since that might make him ask questions in return, but she was pretty sure that Victor had come home. Lillie looked in the closet to see if clothing was missing but couldn't remember exactly what had been there.

Going back downstairs to sit in the parlor and watch for Gerald, Lillie debated her next move. Did she tell someone at the bank? After all, she wasn't positive that Victor had been home. Her head began to pound. What was the man doing? Why not just come home and be done with the matter?

Lillie lay back on the sofa. When her thoughts turned to unanswered questions about her spouse, they always caused anxiety. She knew the thinking was fruitless, but her mind still tried to picture Victor in some unknown location. Wishing Gerald was home to distract her, Lillie closed her eyes and actually hoped sleep would come.

Seventeen

"Is this safe to eat?" Troy teased Reese when she put dinner on the table.

"Why wouldn't it be?"

"Well, you were upset with Conner earlier today, and you might have given me his plate."

Reese found this highly amusing. She laughed as she met Troy's eyes and then looked over to Conner.

"Is that what you think—that I'm upset with you?"

"It did cross my mind," he stated calmly, his eyes watchful as always.

Reese laughed as she went back to the kitchen and then remembered something important. She returned to the dining room and went directly to Troy.

"I forgot to thank you for the shoes," she said. "I'm sorry it's taken so long, but each time I remembered, you weren't around."

"You're welcome," Troy responded, pleased that she accepted the extra money. "They fit well?"

"Yes," Reese said, biting her lip in pleasure before slipping back into the kitchen.

Conner hadn't missed a moment of that exchange, and Dalton had not taken his eyes from his brother.

"Something on your mind, Dalton?" Conner asked rather mysteriously, his eyes on his food.

"What would be on my mind?" the older Kingsley asked when Conner finally looked at him.

"I'm afraid to find out" was all Conner would say before going back to his meal.

Troy and Dalton exchanged a brief but knowing look. There was no point in confirming to Conner what he already knew was on their minds.

ᘒᘓ

Reese was in Mrs. Greenlowe's garden after tea on Monday, checking on the pumpkins and fall squash, when Conner came walking up. She had not been expecting him, but at the same time was not surprised that he'd come.

"Good evening," she greeted when he came to the fence.

"Good evening to you," Conner answered in kind, watching her bend one last time. "It's at this time of the year that I feel lazy as a banker."

"Why is that?" Reese had come to the fence.

"Jace Randall will be working every moment of daylight, and I have my evenings free."

"He loves it," Reese said. "And I suspect you have a certain affinity for numbers."

"Ever since I was young. Math was always my favorite subject."

"Was it because your family was in banking, do you think?"

"It might have been. My sister Nell isn't great with numbers. So math didn't come easily for all of us."

"Is Nell older than you?"

"Yes. They're all older than I am."

"The baby," Reese said, smiling at him. "You wouldn't know it to look at you."

"I ended up larger than my father," he shared. "You can't believe how proud I was to grow taller than he was. I would go shoulder to shoulder with him every time I could manage it, just to measure. He teased me and said it would never happen. I loved proving him wrong."

"And he was proud," Reese guessed.

"Yes, he certainly was." Conner smiled fondly. "I'd already passed Dalton, who took it very well, so my father was the last milestone."

"And what will you do when your own son passes you?"

"Just like my father, I can't imagine it ever happening."

"It would take a lot of food," Reese said practically, making Conner laugh. He then noticed the vegetables in Reese's hands.

"Here, give me those," he said, taking them to the back door, which suddenly opened.

"Thank you," Mrs. Greenlowe said, taking the produce and shutting the door before Conner could say a word. Reese had watched from down by the fence and laughed, knowing her landlady had kept the door open a crack, hoping to catch a few words.

"It's almost too much for her that we whisper," Reese said when Conner got back to her side.

"You don't have to," Conner informed her.

Reese shrugged. "It just sort of happens, I guess."

For a moment they didn't speak, but Reese had something on her mind, and she was ready to ask it.

"Can you tell me now? Can you tell me what happened to your voice?"

"It's not a very fun story," Conner began, but Reese didn't interrupt. Instead she went to sit on the porch steps, and Conner joined her.

"My sister Maggie and I had just finished a visit here at my grandmother's. We were a little late leaving for home in the coach, so darkness came fast. We hadn't been on the road all that long when some men stopped us. They demanded money, but we didn't have any.

"I remember the rain starting and my sister screaming. The

next thing I knew I was in a farmer's cottage. My throat had been cut and I couldn't say a word, but at least I was alive. The drivers and my sister were killed."

"I'm sorry, Conner," Reese whispered even more softly than usual.

"It was a rough time. I had to learn to talk all over again. And since Maggie and I were closest in age, I felt like I'd lost my best friend."

"How old were you?"

"Twelve. Maggie was four years older. We'd never had a bit of trouble traveling in the past. It seemed completely safe in our large coach. My mother grew fearful after that, and none of us came to Tucker Mills again. This is the first time I've visited in 14 years."

"The memories must be overwhelming."

"They're awful and wonderful all at the same time. When I first arrived I kept seeing Maggie. This was the last place she was alive. I didn't expect to feel the way I did after so much time."

"But you had your faith, even as a child, didn't you?" Reese asked. "I mean, it wasn't completely hopeless, was it, Conner?"

"No, Reese, it wasn't," Conner answered, thankful for the reminder. "My sister had the sweetest spirit. Her love for Scripture was genuine, and her desire to serve was evident to all. I hadn't read my Bible much until that time, but when I was well enough, reading it made me feel closer to her. In time, I grew closer to the Lord, and I'm still thankful for the way God used Maggie's death to teach me so much."

"How old were you when your voice worked again?"

"Almost 14," Conner smiled. "I was bursting with words by then, and they were all about what I'd been reading in my Bible. When my mother died earlier this year, she had a rough go of things, but if she was having a good day, she often talked about my wanting to read my Bible all evening long."

"I didn't grow up knowing the Bible," Reese confessed. "I feel like I've missed so much."

"In some ways you have, but you're in the place God wants you right now."

"That's what Douglas has told me."

"We're running out of light," Conner said.

"For what?"

"I was going to ask you about your belief in Christ."

Reese looked away from him.

"It might be better in the dark," she said, her voice barely audible.

"I don't think so," Conner disagreed, and then let the silence fall. It was growing dark fast, and Reese knew she should get inside.

"I'll be back," Conner said as he stood. "Maybe tomorrow night or Wednesday. Will that work out for you?"

"Yes. I'm free both nights."

"Maybe I'll be back both nights," Conner suggested with a smile, put his hat on his head, and walked into the dusk.

Reese stood and watched him until he was out of sight. It had been wonderful to sit and talk, and Reese wondered if that might be another area of her life where she'd missed out.

As she walked inside, she remembered that Tucker Mills was not Conner's home. He was not here to stay. Reese didn't let herself think about what life would be like when he and Troy left town.

∞

"How is Reese Thackery this evening?" Troy asked when Conner returned to the big house.

"Did I say I was going to see Reese?"

"Well, you didn't go to the tavern," Troy began, "and if you'd been at the Muldoons', you would have said so. So that leaves one other place in town."

Conner smiled but didn't answer. Troy didn't press him. Had

Dalton been in the room, he might have, but the older man knew when to let things be.

∞

"Mrs. Greenlowe wants you to come to tea this evening," Reese told Conner on Tuesday morning. "But don't feel like you have to."

"Why would I feel that way?"

"For the obvious reasons," Reese stated.

"Which are?" Conner was still not getting it.

"When a person is asked over, he feels a certain obligation to the person asking. You don't know Mrs. Greenlowe, so you might be even more afraid of offending her by saying no."

Conner was taken with her logic and nodded thoughtfully. He forgot there was a question to be answered.

"I'll just tell her it didn't work out for you," Reese put in next.

"Don't do that," Conner was swift to say, realizing what he'd missed. "I'd be pleased to come. What time?"

"Five-thirty."

"I'll be there."

"All right, but only if you want to."

Conner nodded, seeing she was not convinced.

"Five-thirty it is."

Reese watched him for just a moment and then went back to work. It wasn't like her to worry about such things, but her conversation with Mrs. Greenlowe was still fresh in her mind.

Is he sweet on you?

No, it's not like that.

How do you know?

I just do.

He needs to come to tea, and I'll see for myself.

We don't need to do that.

You ask him in the morning. I'll expect him tomorrow night.

Reese had tried to argue, but it had done no good. Her landlady had made up her mind and was going to have her way on this. And Reese didn't mind his coming—she enjoyed his company. She just didn't want him arriving out of obligation.

Reese pushed the whole event out of her mind. Conner Kingsley was not the type of person who let people manipulate him. He was coming because he wanted to. Arranging the tin kitchen that held today's roast closer to the fireplace, Reese asked herself how often she would have to say it before she believed.

"How many more files do you have to research?" Dalton asked Conner and Troy.

"We're nearly done," Conner explained. "If it weren't for this issue with Mr. Jenness, we would be back in Linden Heights in just a few weeks."

"And what of Mr. Leffler? Can he take over for Mr. Jenness, who by all accounts has deserted his post and in effect terminated himself?"

"He's perfectly happy as a teller," Troy informed Dalton. "He doesn't want the job of bank manager. If we don't stay, someone will need to be hired."

"Are you interested in staying?" Dalton asked of Troy.

"I like Tucker Mills," Troy said. "It's a bit far from my girls, but from a business standpoint, it works very well."

"And you, Conner?" Dalton asked next.

"I could live out my days in Tucker Mills, but that begs the question about who will be in charge at our bank in Linden Heights," Conner responded, referring to the bank that he and Troy managed. "We've got an excellent staff there, but the distance could be a factor."

"But someone from the main bank could always step in,"

Troy inserted, not ready to leave town. "You checked before you came, Dalton, and said it was going very well."

"It is. You've got a treasure in Morris Rane. He's dedicated and completely honest."

"And he would manage things indefinitely," Conner added. "When Mother was dying, he was invaluable to Troy."

"That he was." Troy remembered it well. Conner had been forced to leave the bank for more than two months.

"I leave Friday," Dalton said next. "I don't have to know what we're going to do—you can always put it in a letter—but if we could have some idea in the next 24 hours, I would be glad of that."

"I'm not sure exactly how to go about it," Conner admitted. "Deserting his post or not, Mr. Jenness needs to make another appearance. If I could make that happen, I would be ready with several suggestions for this bank."

"All right," Dalton agreed, his mind busy. "If Mr. Jenness should appear before I leave, fine. If not, I'd still like to hear those suggestions no later than Thursday at tea."

Conner and Troy agreed. It wasn't fair to all involved to leave the situation in limbo. Whether there was an appearance from Mr. Jenness or not, bank business had to go on.

༄༈

Doyle closed up the shop on Tuesday evening, his movements slow. He wasn't feeling poorly; indeed, he'd never felt better, but he had prayed with Jace two days before and still didn't know how to tell Cathy about the change in him.

And there was a change. Cathy had already noticed and commented on his good humor and color. Doyle knew that his demeanor before praying with Jace was that of a man getting old or ill, so her comments were no surprise. However, he still had not had the courage to tell her the real reason. She had become so agitated whenever he'd mentioned his fear of dying.

I need help, Lord God, Doyle prayed, closing the door behind him and heading toward the house. *I want my relationship with Cathy to be as good as it's always been, but I'm doing what Jace warned me about: I'm coming to You with my own terms. Help me, Lord God. Please help me.*

Doyle was at the door of his house before he knew what he was going to say, but he determined to find a way to tell her of the decision he'd made before bedtime.

❧

For Conner, Tuesday evening took much longer than a day to arrive. From the moment Reese had asked him, even knowing the invitation was from Mrs. Greenlowe, Conner thought about it.

He couldn't tell what Reese thought of him, but each time they spoke, she was a little more open, a little more relaxed around him. Conner knew he might be headed for heartache but took Reese's demeanor around him as a good sign.

All of this and more was on his mind as the day ended and he walked home with Troy and Dalton. He planned to clean up a bit and head right back out. What he hadn't banked on was his housemates' reaction.

"I'll see you later," Conner stuck his head in the dining room long enough to say.

"Where are you going?" Dalton asked.

"I've been invited to tea at Mrs. Greenlowe's."

"The Mrs. Greenlowe who is Reese Thackery's landlady?" Dalton clarified.

"The very one."

"Why were Troy and I not informed of this?" Dalton asked.

"Did you need to be informed?" Conner came back, his face calm and a little amused.

"Come now, Conner," Troy spoke up. "You know that Dalton is even more curious than you are."

"True," Conner agreed and began to turn away. "Have a good evening."

"Wait a minute." Dalton was on his feet, Troy not far behind. They caught up with Conner in the hallway. "Who invited you? Reese?"

"As a matter of fact, the invitation came from Mrs. Green-lowe."

"But Reese will be there, right?" Dalton had to know the details.

"I imagine so."

"Is this the best coat you have?" Dalton asked suddenly circling his brother, his eyes critical. "Maybe you should change."

"That would make me late. And besides, she didn't mind last night."

"Last night?" Dalton frowned at Conner, then Troy, then Conner again. "You were there last night?"

"Yes."

"Where was I?"

"Writing letters in the study," Troy informed him, having lived through these episodes with the brothers for years. It was always amusing.

"I've got to go," Conner said, his voice indicating he meant it.

"Wait a minute." Dalton stopped him, putting his hands on his shoulders. Conner waited, knowing he had something to say, but Dalton was silent.

"I have to go," Conner repeated.

"I wanted to give you advice, but it's been too long since I courted my Susie."

"I'm not sure this is courtship, Dalton, but thank you for caring."

Sorry that he had no words, Dalton nodded, not about to let Conner leave before giving him a hug. Conner accepted the embrace gratefully, as he always did, and this time he made it out the door.

⬦

"I need to tell you something," Hillary whispered to her father in the corner of the parlor; the rest of the family was scattered around the house.

"What is it?"

"When I was outside just now, I watched Conner Kingsley walking down the green. He looked very nice."

"Was he going home?"

Hillary shook her head. "Away from the big house."

"Was he walking in such a way that he would eventually pass Mrs. Greenlowe's?"

Hillary nodded this time, looking more than a little pleased. Douglas had to smile at her. She was so certain that this could work, and Douglas hoped it would, but unlike his starry-eyed daughter, he was slightly more practical.

"How can we find out?" Hillary suddenly asked, causing her father to laugh.

"We can't. It's none of our business."

"If Reese is involved, it's our business."

Douglas thought she had a point but still had no suggestions.

"What are you two up to in the corner?" Alison asked, spotting them.

The innocent looks they gave her only made her more suspicious and ready to ask more questions, but neither one would offer an iota of information.

⬦

"Thank you," Conner said to Mrs. Greenlowe when she made

sure that all food was within his reach. "You've prepared a feast, Mrs. Greenlowe."

"Well, we can't have you going away hungry. That won't do!"

Conner was learning in a hurry that the changes in her voice had nothing to do with the conversation or anything happening during tea. It was simply how she was feeling at the moment and the way she expressed herself.

"Here, Reese, try some of this custard. It's the one you like."

"My favorite? Thank you."

"How is bank business?" Mrs. Greenlowe suddenly asked, her opinion about banks having changed some.

"It's going well," Conner answered.

"What was that?"

"It's going well," Conner repeated, careful to keep his face to her so she could hear him.

"Is Jenness around these days?"

"No. He's still away," Conner said tactfully, and at the same time, began to wonder why Reese wasn't saying anything. Conner passed a plate of bread to Reese and got a thank you from her but noticed that she went back to being quiet. Mrs. Greenlowe noticed about the same time.

"You're not saying anything, Reese," that lady proclaimed a bit loudly.

"I've nothing to say right now."

"Well, tell us about your day," Mrs. Greenlowe pressed.

"I told you when I got home, and Mr. Kingsley sees what I've done every time he walks into his house."

This got Reese frowned at, but she only smiled, having decided not to pretend during this meal. Conner knew who she was, as did Mrs. Greenlowe. Reese was confident enough not to have to be entertaining.

"Well, you certainly had a lot to say to each other last night." Mrs. Greenlowe's voice was grumpy as she got to the crux of the matter.

"We were talking about things we've each learned about

God," Reese told her, not holding back. "I wasn't sure if you would be interested in that."

"Some days I am," she admitted, "but not today."

Reese nodded, careful to be respectful.

"My brother is here for a visit," Conner offered, trying to think of something the landlady might not know.

"Older brother is he?"

"Yes. The oldest in the family."

"How many are there?"

"Six are living."

"And your parents?"

"Both dead."

"And what town do you live in?"

"Linden Heights. It's not too far from Boston."

"I've been to Boston, and I've heard of Linden Heights but haven't been there."

"It's quite a bit larger than Tucker Mills."

"Which do you like best?"

"I like both," Conner said honestly, even knowing he was leaning toward his present location.

"And do you bank in Linden Heights?"

"Yes. We own four banks, three of which are in Linden Heights, and I manage one of those with my business partner."

"Why don't you just stay here?"

"Well," Conner worked to be tactful, "until we talk to Mr. Jenness, it's hard to say exactly what the plans will be."

"How tall are you?" The subject changed quickly.

"Six feet, six inches."

"Reese is tall."

"Yes," Conner couldn't hold his smile. He glanced at Reese, who was looking fondly at Mrs. Greenlowe, and appreciated her all the more. The temptation would have been to hush the older woman or make excuses for her, but Reese sat still, respectfully attentive to the conversation going on around her, not opting to interrupt in any way.

And the meal progressed in just that manner. Conner conversed until his throat threatened to give out and stayed until he felt it was the proper time to leave. If Mrs. Greenlowe had hoped to hear the two of them talk, she was to be disappointed. When Reese walked Conner to the road, she confirmed his thoughts on that matter.

"Thank you for coming and putting up with that."

"I don't feel that I put up with anything."

"She's protective of me and has a hard time not knowing what we say to each other," Reese said, now willing to offer an explanation. "If I spend too much time out here, I'll be in trouble for not having said all of this to you indoors."

Conner smiled. "I'll let you go then. We don't want you in trouble."

Reese smiled, still surprised at how wrong she was about him. Conner smiled back, wanting to touch her arm or make some gesture to show that he cared, but he quelled the desire.

Putting his hat on his head, he said, "I'll plan on tomorrow night."

"I'll be in the garden," Reese said in reply, watching again as he walked into the evening dusk.

Eighteen

Reese had done as Conner asked. She had not used the back door for work of any kind, not even going out to sweep that porch or tend the flowers that had grown at the rear of the house. The back entrance was the door she preferred for several tasks, but she didn't feel inconvenienced.

The side doors, the one that led from the kitchen and the one that exited to the yard from the buttery work area, had become the doors she used when needing to be outside. She emptied water out these doors, shook out brooms, rags, and rugs, and today she even ate her dinner on the bench that sat against that side of the house.

It was getting cold in Tucker Mills, October nearly on them, but today Reese was hot, and after making a sandwich for herself, took it outside with a large mug of tea. Reese loved the smell of fall. The leaves were changing and the crispness of the air was intoxicating. She prayed for a long time, thanking God for the wonder of the seasons and for the good job He'd given her.

Conner came to mind as she began to eat, but she didn't pray about him, asking God only to help her be wise and not take her feelings to a place where they would sit alone. She thought about what she knew about Conner Kingsley and even Dalton, and realized she'd learned much by cleaning their house.

There was no pretense in them. The men she saw at the

meetinghouse and at the bank were the same men she saw in the privacy of their home. Reese felt this said a lot for their character and was pleased to know them.

In the midst of these thoughts, the prickly feeling came on her again, and not just a feeling this time but sound to go with it. Reese studied the barn. Someone was out there. She heard another noise, like a door opening, and stood to go that way. She was only about halfway across the yard when all grew quiet. Staying very still, she studied the buildings but saw nothing.

Much as she wanted to tell herself her imagination was overactive, she knew it wasn't true. Someone had been in the barn. Debating whether to go for Conner and Troy right then, Reese realized that whoever it was was probably long gone.

Not wanting to sit outside any longer, Reese went back indoors, locking the door behind her. She knew what she had to do: She had to tell Conner. Just as soon as she did that, however, the doors to that side of the house would be barred to her as well.

∞

"All alone?" Maddie asked when she stepped into the store.

Doyle smiled hugely at the sight of his niece and came around the counter to hug her.

"Sit down," he invited, and they took chairs by the wood stove. He hadn't needed to fire it up yet, but summer or winter, it was everyone's favorite place to sit.

"How are you?" Maddie asked.

"I'm all right. Did Jace tell you?"

"Yes, and I know just what you're feeling. You're full of questions and a little bit afraid that it's not real."

"That just about sums it up. I didn't know, Maddie. I didn't realize God could be so personal. I read in my Bible yesterday about Zacchaeus and how short he was. I had heard that story from the time I was young, and always the emphasis was put on

Zacchaeus. I never saw the compassion of Jesus before yesterday. He could have condemned Zacchaeus for his sin but saved him instead."

Maddie couldn't stop the tears that came to her eyes.

"Now, don't do that," Doyle begged. "You'll get me going, and then Cathy will come, and we'll both have some explaining to do."

Maddie laughed a little and brushed at her face.

"How is it going with Cathy?"

"I can't tell. I told her last night. I asked God to help me, and then I told her how I believed in His Son to save me." Doyle shook his head with regret. "She didn't get it, Maddie. She stared at me and wanted to know what I was hiding. I couldn't get her to understand that what I was saying was real. She was pretty quiet at breakfast and again when she brought my dinner."

"It might take some time," Maddie said.

"Will you be seeing her?"

"I plan to stop there before I head home."

"Maybe she'll talk to you."

When Doyle uttered these words, he didn't know how close he was to the mark. Maddie visited with her uncle for a while longer and then headed next door to the house. Cathy was very sober, and Maddie wondered whether she would even want company, but that didn't take long to change.

"Have you been to see your uncle?" Cathy asked, anger punctuating every word.

"I just came from there."

"Did he tell you about his experience with *God?*" The words were spat out. "I think he's sick again and won't tell me!" Her voice broke a little. "What am I going to do, Maddie?"

"Sit down, Cathy," Maddie urged her with compassion. "I want to tell you something."

It took some coaxing and Maddie making tea to get Cathy to settle at the worktable in the kitchen.

"I want you to listen to me," Maddie began, seeing that her aunt was beyond agitated. "I have something to explain to you."

"About Doyle?" Cathy looked afraid.

"In a way," Maddie tried but then shook her head because Cathy was trying to talk again. "Just listen."

"All right," Cathy agreed. Remembering Maddie's condition made her sit still.

"At first this won't make sense to you, Cathy, but I want you to keep listening."

Cathy nodded, wondering where this could be going.

"Not all beliefs are the same, Cathy. And as much as we might want that to be okay, God says it's not. Some pastors are not teaching what the Bible says."

Cathy wanted to ask her what she was talking about but made herself stay quiet.

"We can know where we stand with God. And we can know if we're good enough for heaven. The answer to that is that none of us is good enough for heaven."

"Well, I know we sin, Maddie, but not like some people."

"It doesn't work like that, Cathy. When God asks you about your sin, you won't be able to bring up someone else who you think was worse. You will have to answer for your own sins, and that's what Doyle realized."

"So he is going to die?"

"Of course he's going to die." Maddie kept her voice gentle. "We're all going to die. And by that time, it's too late. Eternity has to be settled here and now, on earth, and Doyle took care of that."

Cathy looked thoughtful but not angry. Maddie gave her a moment of silence and then kept talking.

"It scared Doyle to see Mr. Somer fall like that. He's still not out of bed, by the way. Doyle was reminded of how swiftly our lives can end here. And he knew he wasn't ready to meet God."

"But he's been a good man."

"I challenge you to find any Scripture that says being a good person is enough to let you stand before a holy God," Maddie said.

Cathy licked her lips. Maddie sounded so sure. And lately she had been different. A lot of women changed when they were in the family way, but that didn't explain the changes she'd also seen in Jace.

"So what's a person to do?" Cathy asked.

"What you just did. Ask questions until you have all the information you need. Ask questions with a searching heart until you know that your goodness isn't worth anything and that salvation is because of Christ's shed blood."

"Maddie," Cathy said, her voice amazed. "I've never heard you talk this way."

Maddie reached over and took her aunt's hand. "I can't take anything to heaven with me but the people I love, and only then if they agree with God. I don't want you to be left out, Cathy. That would break my heart."

"Maddie, I just don't know. It's all so new."

"Yes, it is, and I'm not asking that you decide in one day, but please listen to Doyle. He can help you understand, even though it's new to him."

"He's wanted to talk since Mr. Somer was in the store," Cathy admitted, "and I haven't let him."

"It's not too late to listen."

"I've got to go and see him," Cathy said as she stood. "You understand, don't you?"

"Of course. I'll see you later. Maybe Jace and I can come in on Friday or Saturday night."

Cathy barely said goodbye, but Maddie didn't notice. She was out in the wagon as fast as her legs could carry her, wanting to run the horses all the way home.

I'll plan on tomorrow night had been Conner's words to Reese
when he'd left after tea Tuesday night.

I'll be in the garden Reese had said in return. And now the
moment had arrived. The evening was cool, and there was little
to do outside, but Reese's wait paid off when Conner's long legs
brought him back to the fence.

"More vegetables?" he asked.

"Not tonight," Reese said, already moving for the porch
stairs. Conner sat beside her.

"How is Mrs. Greenlowe tonight?"

"Doing fine. I told her you'd be coming. She seemed all right
with it as soon as I explained that we'd be talking about spiritual
things."

"I hoped you hadn't forgotten about that."

Reese shook her head, not able to look at him just then.

"Will it be too hard for you?" Conner studied her profile.

"Not if you don't look at me," Reese said, glancing up and
finding him with a huge grin on his face. While she still watched,
he shifted so his face was in profile to her, and Reese began,
even though she wished it were dark.

"I think you know that I was at Mr. Zantow's from the time I
was 17."

"Troy told me about the papers."

"Well, Mr. Zantow had certain patterns, and I learned them
well, even before my father died."

"Like what, for example?" Conner asked, still turned to the
side.

"I could count on him leaving for the tavern soon after tea.
He never came home until he was very drunk. Before my father
died he all but ignored me, but once I was alone, Mr. Zantow's
attention turned to me. He never seemed to remember a thing
during the day, but at night, when he was deep in his cups, he
would seek me out.

"I never had trouble holding the door against him or getting
away if I wasn't in my room. He wasn't a large man, and when he

was drunk, I was much stronger. All of that worked until one night when I thought I had plenty of time. I was bathing by the kitchen fireplace when he suddenly came barging in the door."

Reese paused, and Conner had a hard time not looking at her. He also thought that if Mr. Zantow had been on the premises just then, Conner would have become violent.

"Seeing me like that must have given him some kind of strength." Reese's voice was very soft. "We wrestled until I found enough balance to push him. I pushed hard. He went back against the stones on the fireplace and then slumped to the floor. There was a lot of blood, and I thought I'd killed him. I threw my clothing on and went for Doc MacKay. He checked Mr. Zantow, who wasn't dead but just bleeding from a head wound.

"Doc made sure he was going to be all right, and I took myself off to bed. I didn't sleep. The next morning I went to see Alison Muldoon. I knew her husband was a pastor, and I was so shook up about what had happened that for the first time in my life I wanted someone to pray for me. Douglas said he would be happy to but that I also could pray for myself. He explained God's plan of salvation that morning, and I believed."

Reese took a huge breath. Conner thought she might be crying, but when she went on, her voice was normal.

"It was an awful night in one sense, but completely freeing in another. I don't know how I found a way to tell an almost-stranger about what happened to me, but I did it. And Douglas was so compassionate. Alison cried, and I couldn't remember anyone ever crying over me before."

Conner had not banked on what this would do to his heart. His chest hurt just listening to her voice and having to think about what a lonely, desperate life she had lived, prey to a man who didn't know what a treasure she was.

"Well, anyway," Reese continued, her voice growing even softer, "I don't know what else to tell you, except that I'm glad Mr. Zantow didn't die that night. It would have been awful, and hard as it was, the whole ordeal led me to Douglas and Alison and then to Jesus Christ."

Conner had to look at her. She was sitting very still, her eyes on her lap.

"Thank you for telling me."

Reese knew from the sound of his voice that he was now facing her. It wasn't a story she shared very often because the memory was hard, and a woman didn't tell a man about being undressed or bathing. But with Conner it was different. When he'd cared enough to ask, Reese had wanted to answer.

"We've run out of daylight again," Conner observed.

"It's happening early these days."

"I'd better let you get inside."

"Oh, Conner," Reese suddenly remembered. "I have to tell you something. I can't believe it slipped my mind so completely, but someone was in the barn today. I'm sure of it."

"You saw someone?"

"No, but I heard something, and when I started that way, all fell quiet."

"Were the horses restless? Was that the noise?"

"It wasn't anywhere near where you keep the horses. It was over in the deserted area."

Conner thanked her, already on his feet and making plans in his head.

"I want to discuss this with Troy, and then we'll talk in the morning. All right?"

"All right. Goodnight."

Conner bid Reese goodnight as well and thanked her again for telling him. For the third night in a row, she watched him walk into the dusk.

As soon as he was out of sight, Reese went indoors. She spoke for a few minutes to Mrs. Greenlowe but then bid that lady goodnight. Not normally wearied by anything, Reese felt as though the wind had been knocked completely out of her. For the first time since she'd come to Christ, she didn't take time to pray but crawled into bed and slept immediately.

The crack of dawn found all three men searching the barn and outbuildings that stood near the big house.

"Look here," Troy called to Conner in the middle building. He showed him footprints and the core of an apple.

"Someone's recently been camped out in here," Conner concluded. He walked outside and looked at the doors. "Let's air these buildings out," Conner suggested, swinging each door open wide, so that most of the interiors were visible to the green.

"What did you find?" Dalton asked as he came upon them, not having spotted anything in the haymow of the barn.

"Reese was right," Troy said, heading that way to show Dalton.

The older brother nodded and asked, "Will Reese be all right with one of us around all the time?"

Conner heard and answered, "My greater fear is that she won't be all right if we're not around."

This was not a hard point for the men to agree upon. Conner planned to tell Reese about it as soon as she arrived.

"So tell me," Dalton quizzed Reese from the doorway of one of the bedrooms upstairs; it was midmorning. "Do you like children?"

"I do like children," Reese said patiently, even though this was the fourth time he had found her to ask a question. "Do you like children?" she asked in turn, just as she'd done the three other times.

"Very much. I have five."

"That's a fun number."

"Okay," Dalton said enthusiastically. "I'll let you get back to work."

"Okay," Reese agreed, holding her laughter until he was out of the room.

The men had told Reese their plan was to be around for however long it took to discover the identity of their intruder, and not seeing any help for it, she had agreed graciously. What she hadn't expected was for Dalton to volunteer for the first shift. Not that it mattered. Reese simply avoided the study where he worked on his business papers. Little did she know that he would seek her out.

And he was being so obvious. Reese thought if Conner knew about it, he wouldn't be happy at all. She would never tell, but that didn't mean that he wouldn't learn of it.

"What about housework? I mean, I know you do it, but do you enjoy it?"

Reese turned, amazed that he was back.

"Yes," she answered, still managing not to laugh. "I like almost all housework."

"What don't you like?"

"The laundry."

"Why is that?"

"Because it's hard on the hands, but mostly because the table is high enough that I can't sit and low enough that it makes my back ache."

"Okay," Dalton said before he slipped away.

Reese did some slipping of her own down the back stairs as it was time to check on dinner. She thought if she moved quietly enough, she might get some work done in the kitchen without being disturbed.

⊗⊗

"What about celebrating Christmas? Some people think it's wrong." Cathy had come to the store to check with Doyle.

"I'm not sure about that. We can ask Jace."

Cathy's intent look was becoming familiar to Doyle. Ever since she'd come to see him the day before, she had been asking questions. Most he couldn't answer, but for once she kept thinking instead of trying to prove her point.

Doyle now waited for the next question, but it didn't come. He wondered what his expression had been when Cathy defended herself.

"Maddie said I should ask questions."

"You should. I just wish I knew more."

"Doyle," Cathy came close now, her eyes worried. "Are you really all right?"

He put his hands on her shoulders and answered calmly, "Yes. It was a spiritual and emotional issue, not a physical one."

Her heart still worried, Cathy nodded, but she also still pondered her niece's words. Doyle watched the expressions chase across her face and put his arms around her.

"We'll get it, Cathy," he spoke reassuringly. "Don't you worry. God won't give up on us yet."

∞

"How do you like big cities?" Dalton asked when he found Reese an hour after the last question.

"I don't know. I've never been to one."

Reese was familiar with the sounds of the house and heard the front door just then. Dalton didn't seem to notice. Nor did he notice when Conner appeared in the kitchen doorway a short time later.

"You'll have to visit," Dalton was saying. "I think you'd like it."

"I might," Reese agreed.

"And what about families visiting? Is that something that sounds fun to you?"

"Well," Reese said honestly, "I don't have any family."

"But what if your husband had family?"

Reese caught the astonished look on Conner's face and had to smile.

"I think it would fine," Reese said.

"Okay," Dalton said with pleasure and turned to the door. The way he jerked to a halt was one of the funniest things Reese had ever seen. She bit her lip hard to keep from laughing, not wanting to miss this interchange.

"Conner!" Dalton's voice was evidence enough that he'd been caught in the act. "I didn't see you."

"Clearly," Conner said, somewhere between amusement and frustration.

"I was just heading back to the study," Dalton muttered, attempting to restore some of his dignity. "Reese will call me when dinner is ready."

Conner moved out of the way so his brother could pass and then walked very deliberately into the kitchen.

"Do not tell me that he's been like that all morning."

Remaining silent, Reese only looked at him.

"Reese?"

"You said not to tell you."

Conner shook his head.

"What did he want to know?"

"What *didn't* he want to know?" Reese said with a smile, not willing to tell all.

"Is tomorrow Friday?" Conner asked suddenly.

"Yes."

Conner smiled a smile that was a bit wicked and headed toward the dining room.

Reese knew that Alison would be working on tea preparations and that Mrs. Greenlowe was also expecting her home soon, but she had to talk to the pastor's wife. Going around to the kitchen door, she knocked and slipped inside, happy to find only Alison and Martin.

"Hi, Reese. Done at the big house for today?"

"All done."

"What will you and Mrs. Greenlowe do tonight?"

"Alison, should I cut off some of my hair?"

Alison, who had been half attending while putting the kettle on, stopped and looked at her guest.

"Your hair is beautiful. Why would you cut some off?"

"Oh, just in case."

"In case of what?"

"It might look better."

"Marty, run along upstairs for a moment, will you?" his mother asked.

"Okay," the little boy agreed, and Alison came to sit next to Reese. She wanted Reese to tell her what was going on but didn't know quite how to find out.

"Is there anything you want to tell me?" Alison tried.

"About what?" Reese asked, not able to meet the older woman's eyes.

"About why you're suddenly worried over your appearance."

"Did you never worry about your looks when you first met Douglas?"

Alison nodded and admitted, "When he became interested, I did worry, yes."

Reese didn't comment.

"Is there someone whose opinion you're worried about?"

"Maybe," Reese answered, not willing to tell all just yet. But in truth Alison didn't need much more. Reese's eyes were filled with longing and questions, and Alison's heart melted a little at the sight. She also made a swift decision not to pry.

"If you decide you want me to have more details, you know you can share with me."

"Thank you, Alison." Reese stood. "I'd best get home."

"Tell Mrs. Greenlowe I said hello. And as for the hair, if I were you I'd think about it a bit longer."

"I'll do that," Reese replied and was gone a moment later.

Alison meant what she said: She would be there if Reese wanted to talk, but waiting might be harder than she first imagined.

Nineteen

"Will you see if Doyle has any more of this fabric?" Reese asked Mrs. Greenlowe. She had run upstairs as soon as she got home and grabbed the other swatch she'd been eyeing. This one had a navy background with a coral design and tiny white flowers for accent.

"Sure, I will," the older woman agreed. "You want another dress?"

Reese nodded.

"It's him, isn't it?" Mrs. Greenlowe asked, her voice thoughtful. "He's getting to your heart, isn't he?"

"Maybe a little," Reese admitted, her face more vulnerable than she would have believed.

"You're a good girl, Reese," Mrs. Greenlowe said, and Reese saw her opportunity. "And don't deny it," the landlady put in before she could speak.

"I want to," Reese said quietly.

"There's no reason," Mrs. Greenlowe replied, looking a little agitated, and Reese knew it was not the time. Indeed she needed to face the fact that it might never be time.

"What can I help with?" Reese offered instead, seeing that tea was almost ready.

"Grab those plates and that teapot, and we'll eat."

Reese did as she was told, taking heart in the fact that

whenever they ate together, Mrs. Greenlowe never objected to her praying.

∞∾

"I'm leaving tomorrow," Dalton told Douglas, sitting in that man's study at the end of the workday.

"It's been great to see you," Douglas said sincerely. "You must miss your family."

"I do miss them. I don't travel much without them, and they've been on my mind almost constantly."

"And it seems that your daughter is going to be fine?"

"Yes. The doctors never did figure out what gave her such a high fever and made her so tired, but she's getting life back into her now, and I'm thankful."

"Well, you know I pray for you."

"And I you," Dalton told him.

The men said goodbye then, both having enjoyed the times of reliving memories and making new ones. After saying a swift goodbye to Alison and the Muldoon children, Dalton headed home for tea and a meeting with Troy and Conner about the future of the bank.

∞∾

"I made some sandwiches and cookies for your trip," Reese told Dalton on Friday morning, rendering that man speechless.

When he didn't say anything, Reese looked to Troy.

"He's pleased, Reese. Just give him a moment."

"Thank you," Dalton spoke quietly, sounding much like Conner. "May I say that if I had a son old enough, I would bring him to Tucker Mills to meet you."

Reese felt her face heat, something that didn't happen often, but she still managed to smile and murmur a thank-you.

"Why is Reese blushing?" Conner asked as soon as he walked into the room.

"I embarrassed her," his brother confessed.

Conner's eyes were on Reese. With a lift of his brows, he asked if she was all right.

Managing a small smile, Reese said her goodbyes and headed to the kitchen.

The men left for the train station a short time later, both Troy and Conner going to see Dalton off.

"Tell Susie I said hello, and kiss my nieces and hug my nephews," Conner made a point of saying.

"And tell my family I'll visit when I can," Troy added.

"I'll do it. And Conner, you do something about Reese."

"What exactly do you suggest I do?" Conner asked, brows raised in amusement.

Always so full of words and advice, Dalton just looked at Conner for a moment.

"This one isn't easy, is it?" he said.

"You noticed, did you?"

"Yes. She's hard to read, and since she's in your employ, you don't want her to feel that she can't say no about seeing you. If you do start to see each other, what will that do to her reputation?"

"Just up and marry her," Troy suggested, bringing laughter from both brothers.

The train was ready to leave. Dalton hugged Troy and then turned to his brother, once again searching for words.

"I love you, Conner," he finally managed. "And if God sees fit to bless you with a life spent with Reese Thackery, you'll be the only man on earth happier about it than me."

The brothers hugged unashamedly on the train station platform before Dalton had to board. Conner and Troy waved to him once he appeared in the window and then started back toward the green, Conner with plans to go to the bank, and Troy back to the house.

"Are you going to be all right?" Troy asked.

"Why would you ask that?"

"Oh, I'm just a little concerned that without Dalton here, you might not know how to proceed."

Conner stopped walking and looked at him.

"He did give me more excuses to talk to Reese, didn't he?"

Troy only smiled.

"I'll see you at dinner." Conner ended up saying less than he was thinking, but he did ponder the matter all the way to the bank.

On his way back to the big house and knowing the morning would rush by, Troy also knew that if he wanted to say more, it would hold until dinnertime.

᷇᷇

"Vashti," Conner tried at dinnertime, only to have Reese look at him in horror.

"As in the first queen in the book of Esther?"

"Yes," Conner said, his look sheepish. "I'm running out of names."

"Well, it's not Vashti," Reese told him in no uncertain terms. "My mother wasn't that eccentric."

"So this isn't a normal name?"

"No, it's not. In fact, I've never heard anyone with this name."

"Is it something she made up?"

"It might be," Reese said with a shrug, not certain what her mother had been thinking.

"You never asked her?" Conner questioned next.

"She died when I was six," Reese explained.

"How did she die?"

"Having my sister."

"You have a sister?"

"No, she died with her."

Conner could only nod. He had come into a family with both parents hale and hearty, not to mention six older siblings. He couldn't imagine being so alone in the world.

"And when your father was alive, did the two of you get on well?"

"Most of the time. He would fall into bouts of serious discouragement, and then I would feel left out because he wouldn't want to talk or do anything."

"Was that before or after he indentured himself?"

"In my memory it started right after my mother and sister died. But then he would remember he had me and snap out of it for a while. Sometimes he would even go months in a normal way, but then he might get down and sit around the house for as much as two weeks, not doing anything or talking."

"What would you do?"

"I just kept going to school and cooking what I knew how to make. It was usually when we ran completely out of food that he would snap out of it because I would start crying and carrying on until he responded."

"Are there any good memories, Reese, or are they all overshadowed by the pain of the past?"

"There are some good memories. I can actually see my mother reading her Bible by the fire. I have no memory of her talking to me about it, but it gives me hope that she might have believed.

"And the same goes with my father. He didn't do well with teaching me, but when he remembered, we prayed before meals. I'm not sure if it was some sort of tradition for him or he had a genuine belief in Christ.

"And too, Mr. Zantow was never a threat to me before my father died, and I feel comforted knowing that if he'd been there to protect me, my father would never have let me be harmed."

I want to be here to protect her now, heavenly Father, Conner found his heart praying. *I want to take care of her. Please help me know how to proceed. Please help me be wise, and put Your hand on my heart—Reese's as well.*

"I'd better put dinner on," Reese remembered when she heard Troy come out of his office. There was a particular board that always creaked.

When the men sat down to eat a short time later, Reese sat in the kitchen and ate her own meal. Conner was under the impression that she liked to eat later, or he would have invited her to join them.

Enjoying the food she made in the warmth of the kitchen, Reese realized she was beginning to care for Conner Kingsley in a very significant way. She had no idea that the feelings were being reciprocated no small amount.

⚬⚬⚬

"I'm getting fat," Maddie told her husband over dinner.

"Is that right?" Jace smiled, rather enjoying her rounder curves.

"Don't you dare look so pleased, Jace Randall. I've got months to go."

"You work too hard to get fat" were Jace's words of comfort, and Maddie took them. She did manage to get into town fairly often, but chores at the farm were nonstop, even with Clara's help.

"Well, you'll have to tell me if I start to repulse you."

Jace's brows rose. "Did I seem repulsed last night?" he asked.

"Shh," Maddie hushed him, just covering a laugh. "Clara's in the kitchen."

Jace only smiled at her, his look warm. Had he shared them, his thoughts were not about physical intimacy, but about the way God had blessed him. He loved his wife, and she was going to have their baby. Jace now knew how sweet life could be. And not because he'd done anything, but because Christ had done it all.

With the crops waiting, cool temperatures or not Jace could not dawdle at the dinner table. He gave Maddie a lingering kiss before going back to work, still thinking about the work God could do in a repentant heart.

∞

"I'm going to be in the side yard," Reese popped her head into the office long enough to tell Conner, just as they agreed that she would. Conner had not insisted that she never venture outdoors but only that she tell whomever was at the house during the time when she did go.

"All right," he agreed, and tried to take his mind back to the papers in front of him. It didn't work. Giving up just ten minutes later, Conner went all the way down to the buttery workroom and out the door to find her.

To his surprise, she was eating her dinner on the bench. Conner didn't wait to be invited but sat down, once again trapping her skirt.

"It's a little cold out here," he said, taking in her coat. It was rather threadbare in places.

"It is, but the fresh air is worth it."

Conner smiled as his head went back, and he looked across at the trees that changed a bit more every week. The colors were amazing, colors only God could have imagined.

"Do you have a scar?" Reese asked, and Conner looked down to find her staring up at him.

"I do, yes."

"Does it ever pain you?"

"Not anymore. It itched and hurt for many years, but not now."

"Do you get tried of wearing your cravat all the time? Or are you used to it?"

"I'm used to it. It was more of a problem when I was a boy and none of the other boys wore them."

Reese smiled. "It's nice that your family is in banking. It would make you awfully hot on a farm."

Conner smiled in return, more pleased than he revealed that she was relaxed with the subject.

"Well, I'd better get back to work," Reese commented, having finished the last of her food and coffee. She started to stand but found her skirt trapped. She looked to Conner, who was taking a long look at the sky, seeming not to notice her predicament. After some moments he looked down and pretended to be startled.

"You're still here."

"As you see," Reese said, fighting a smile.

"Problems?"

"Just one large one."

Conner's head went back as he laughed, and Reese found that she liked the quiet sound. He also shifted over and freed her skirt. Then with one fluid move he stood, reached for her plate and cup, and held the door to allow her back inside.

Watching from the cover of a few nearby trees, Gerald felt cold, much colder than the weather would merit. Deep in his heart he'd known that Reese Thackery was not going to fall for him, but somehow he'd hoped. And even today—arriving just before Conner made an appearance and hiding in the trees—he hadn't heard the conversation, but he could see what was happening.

Just to be on the safe side, Gerald waited for them to go indoors before he slipped away. With every step that took him away from the big house, he asked himself what he was going to do.

"How are you doing?" Maddie asked her aunt when they stopped in for dinner on Sunday afternoon.

"We didn't go to the meetinghouse today," Cathy wasted no time in sharing quietly while the women finished putting the final touches on dinner. "Doyle's not sure he wants to go to the meetinghouse on the green anymore, and I'm not sure I can go to the new one."

"I go to the new one. Does that help?"

"That's what Doyle asked me, and I just don't know yet."

"It's a huge decision, and you must still have questions."

"Yes, I do. Doyle can't answer them all, but he keeps reading his Bible and telling me things."

"Like what?"

"Did you know that in the first chapter of Genesis, God talks as though He's more than one person? Doyle says that's Jesus and the Holy Ghost too."

Maddie nodded. "Jace and I read that not too long ago."

"I never knew that."

"Why did it strike you as important?"

"I think of Jesus having a beginning, but He doesn't. I mean, I know He was born at Christmas, but it seems He was also present at creation."

Maddie's heart was smiling in amazement to hear these words coming from her aunt. She had been so angry just a few days before and was now willing to discuss Scripture. Maddie stayed quiet when her aunt brought up some more facts that Doyle had uncovered, completely unaware that the same conversation was going on in the parlor.

※

"How are things going?" Jace asked of Doyle.

"Pretty well, I think. I have questions, and so does Cathy, most of which I can't answer."

"That sounds familiar. Maddie and I still have questions every Sunday for Douglas Muldoon."

"And has it helped? Have you gotten answers?"

"Every time. If he has to think about something, he gets back to us, but he usually has what we want to know."

"How does he do it?"

"He's just spent so much time studying, Doyle."

"But how do you know you can trust what he says?"

"Because he shows me in the Bible. There's no denying it when the written words are in front of me."

"Like me seeing Jesus' forgiveness of Zacchaeus and not just seeing that Zacchaeus was a short little man?"

"Exactly. God's Spirit is opening your eyes to truths that have been there all along. And He's given all of us good minds to understand."

Doyle smiled, knowing that more questions would come, but right now he was at peace. He'd read the Bible off and on for years, but now, for the first time, it was making sense to him. And even at this moment, Maddie was talking to Cathy in the kitchen. Doyle prayed that God would see fit to open her eyes as well.

∞

With a rather spur-of-the-moment decision and just a week after Dalton left, Troy decided to visit Linden Heights for the weekend. He was missing his family so much, especially his granddaughters who were changing from week to week, that he didn't want to delay.

Reese didn't have as much notice as before but still managed to make sandwiches and pack a nice meal for Troy to enjoy on the train. The ride was not overly long, but the weather had become very cold, and she was confident that having something to eat would keep his body warmer.

Conner did not see Troy off at the train station, but after asking Reese whether she could work indoors for a while, he ran errands on the green concerning some printing and the wood railing for the bank alcove. Reese took that opportunity to do some extra cleaning in Troy's room. She moved all the furniture she could manage and left the room in sparkling order. Dust was always an issue, but she got what she could.

She finished just in time to put dinner on the table for Conner, who left again as soon as he was done, leaving Reese to her next big task for the day: the fireplace in the large parlor. The ashes had built up since the men were in there most nights, and Reese wanted it off her list. Swathing herself in an oversized apron and covering her hair, Reese went to work on a job that took the remainder of the day.

∞

It was not a warm walk down the green for Reese when she left the big house that evening, but then her long legs always made fast work of the distance wherever she was going. She hadn't visited Mr. and Mrs. Somer for a time and decided to stop in on her way home. It was a bit out of the way, but that didn't deter her. And indeed, as soon as Mrs. Somer saw Reese, she was glad she'd made the effort.

"Oh, Reese, come in. We were just talking about you. Hank," she called to her spouse and led the way for their guest. "Reese is here."

Reese found Mr. Somer in a chair in the parlor, a smile on his face.

"Well, look at you," Reese exclaimed, going to his chair and taking his hand. "You look fit to walk right out that door."

Mr. Somer beamed with pleasure as Reese found a chair.

"We want you to come for dinner sometime, Reese," Mrs. Somer began. "We want to thank you for coming that day."

"I would enjoy that," Reese smilingly agreed. "I hope you'll let me bring something."

"No," Mr. Somer put in. "It's our treat."

"Yes, it is," Mrs. Somer agreed. "Now tell us what's going on in town. We're not out enough these days."

Reese left the Somer house with a smile on her face. It had been great fun to fill them in on her life and to see that Mr. Somer was a new man these days. For the first time in Reese's acquaintance, he was not feeling donsie, as he liked to say, or even unwell. Not a word was said about his back hurting, and Reese had noticed that when Mrs. Somer looked at him, her eyes were alight with love.

Huddling a bit deeper inside her coat, Reese picked up the pace, glad to be going home. She knew the kitchen would be warm and tea would be waiting. Part of her wished that she could be in the garden watching for a certain tall gentleman to wander past, but it was much too cold for that, not to mention that as the weekend neared, Mrs. Greenlowe always grew a bit tired, and Reese knew it was a relief to her landlady to have help with the dishes and cleanup.

Reese let herself into the kitchen, enjoying the warmth that hit her, but she was surprised at how little activity there was. Mrs. Greenlowe was usually waiting, all the aromas of the meal filling the air.

"Reese?" Mrs. Greenlowe called to her in an odd tone of voice, and that woman rushed in the direction of the parlor.

Mrs. Greenlowe was on the floor, her head bleeding and her face pale.

"Did you fall?" Reese asked, running back to the kitchen to grab a towel. She was using it on Mrs. Greenlowe's head when she found her arm gripped.

"He was here," she said, out of breath.

"What?" Reese bent over to hear her.

"He was here. Jenness. He's looking for you."

"Did he do this?" Reese asked, fear shooting through her.

Mrs. Greenlowe nodded and then winced, no fire in her at all.

"He said he was going to the big house, that he could take care of all three of you that way."

"Conner," Reese whispered, but she didn't forget her patient. "Here, sit on the sofa."

"Just help me sit up, and then go for help," Mrs. Greenlowe argued.

"I can't leave you like this."

"I'm all right. He just shoved me, and I banged my head on the table." Some of her fire returned. "Go, Reese!"

Reese hesitated only a moment. She made sure her landlady was able to lean against the chair she'd pulled over, and then shot back out the door. Darkness was falling fast, but Reese didn't go down the green. She ran through the trees and yards that had served as shortcuts for years.

It was her first impulse to go to the front door, but she knew that was foolish. Slowing down when she got to the house, Reese tried to see inside. She thought she might have caught movement in the front parlor but couldn't be sure. Not certain what else to do, Reese swiftly skirted the house and used her key. She let herself in the door that led to the buttery, already telling herself she had to be quiet on the stairs.

∞

"I'm glad you stopped by, Mr. Jenness," Conner said, having invited the man into the parlor when he'd come to the door. "I've been wanting to meet you."

"And I you," Mr. Jenness returned smoothly, his voice quite different than his appearance.

All this time Conner had been picturing a businessman. Victor Jenness looked more like a farmer. Today he was in boots and work pants, with a long flannel shirt for warmth.

"Would you like to sit down?"

"Thank you."

"My business partner isn't here this weekend," Conner said

conversationally after he'd taken a seat. "He'll be sorry to have missed you."

"He's not here?" Mr. Jenness asked sharply, more distressed over this than Conner would have guessed.

"No, I'm sorry. He'll be back on Monday. Could we plan to meet at the bank on that day?"

"Possibly." Mr. Jenness worked to calm himself, and not for the first time, Conner noticed his eyes. They seemed to have trouble centering on him. They would meet Conner's gaze for just moments at a time and then dart away.

"Your wife mentioned that you were away on business," Conner said, hoping to sound ignorant. "Has that gone well?"

"Very." Mr. Jenness' voice turned cold now, and Conner found himself hoping he would not be put into a position of defending himself. He watched as Mr. Jenness got more comfortable in his chair and then realized he was reaching for something. Conner stood when he saw the knife.

"You need to put that knife away, Mr. Jenness. I don't want that unsheathed in my house."

"What *you* want," Mr. Jenness mocked, slipping out of the chair to stand. "It's always what you want. You want your way, you want to be in charge, and you want my bank."

"I would be happy to talk to you about the bank, especially the fine job we've seen in your account books, but you have to put the knife away."

"I don't have to do anything you tell me," Mr. Jenness growled, positioning himself with the knife ready. "All I want to hear from you is that you're going to leave Tucker Mills and never come back. I don't want to hurt you, but I can't have you taking over my bank. It's my bank."

"We can't discuss anything while you're holding that knife," Conner tried again.

"*Don't tell me what to do!*" Mr. Jenness shouted, his eyes alight with rage.

Seeing those eyes, Conner Kingsley fell silent.

From her place in the wide hallway, Reese listened to the awful conversation, fear making her freeze for just a few minutes. He had a knife! Mr. Jenness had a knife, and Conner was in there alone.

The study door suddenly came to mind. If she was hearing right, Mr. Jenness was standing with his back toward the fireplace. Remembering the layout of the house, Reese realized she could enter the large parlor by way of the study. She knew if she slipped through that door, it would bring her in behind Mr. Jenness.

She didn't think about what she would do if she accomplished this, only that she needed to get to that door and somehow help Conner.

Twenty

Having stayed completely calm to this point, Conner felt his heart nearly stop in his chest when he saw the door behind Mr. Jenness open and Reese's face peek in.

"Ah, yes, I see the fear in your face," Mr. Jenness nearly purred with satisfaction. "How does it feel, Mr. Kingsley? What's it like to have something taken from you, the way you're trying to take my bank?"

"I assure you, Mr. Jenness, that was never our intention. In fact," Conner continued, making himself not look at Reese, "my brother was just here, and we're excited about the future of the bank. We'd like to hear your ideas and thoughts."

"Oh, my ideas and thoughts will be heard, but not by you. You have to leave now."

The stunned look on Mr. Jenness' face and the moment of pause when the fireplace shovel hit the back of his head gave Conner just enough time. He covered the distance in two strides and put his fist alongside Mr. Jenness' jaw. That man dropped like a sack of cornmeal, and Conner reached for the knife, placing it on the mantel. He then went to Reese, whose arm he could feel trembling in his hand, and led her away from the crumpled banker's form.

"What were you doing?" Conner asked, barely able to be heard.

"I couldn't let him hurt you," Reese whispered, tears filling her eyes. "I couldn't let him do that."

All Conner wanted to do was crush her in his arms, but he forced himself to be calm. Moving slowly and with a tenderness he didn't feel, he gently took Reese into his arms and held her close.

"Thank you," he spoke in that just-above-a-whisper voice she knew so well.

All Reese could do was shiver in his arms, still afraid for Conner and horrified at what had just happened.

Conner held her for just a little while and then released her, but he kept his hands on her shoulders. He made himself remember the man on the floor.

"Go get Doc MacKay. I'll stay here and make sure he doesn't move."

"He won't hurt you now?" she asked, glancing back at the man.

"No, Reese. He's out cold."

"All right."

Reese left by the front door, ran all the way, and returned with Tucker Mills' doctor. As he checked Mr. Jenness, he heard Conner's story about what had just happened. When Conner got to the part where Reese came in, the doctor's eyes were no longer calm.

"You did what?" he demanded.

"I hit him," she said, tears threatening again.

Seeing them, Doc MacKay only nodded. He didn't have the heart to reprimand her, but the story Conner had just told him scared him half to death. Why Reese didn't go for the sheriff rather than handle things on her own was something he would find out at a later date. The sheriff, however, needed to come now, and as soon as he made sure that Mr. Jenness was all right, Doc MacKay went for him.

"I've got to get home," Reese said to Conner right after the doctor left to get Sheriff Ferndon. "Mr. Jenness was at my house first, and Mrs. Greenlowe was hurt."

"Is she all right?"

"Her head was bleeding, but I think she's going to be fine."

Conner's eyes went to the man on the floor.

"So he was after you."

"All of us, I guess. Troy too."

Reese looked at him for a moment and then turned away. "I'll see you tomorrow."

Conner walked her to the door, never intending to wait until tomorrow to see her but not saying so at the moment. When the doctor and sheriff came back and Mr. Jenness was roused and taken into custody, Conner and Doc MacKay headed to the Greenlowe house together.

ﾍﾌﾋ

"What will happen to Jenness?" Mrs. Greenlowe asked after Doc MacKay insisted that she allow him to examine her.

Her tea forgotten, she submitted to his ministrations but was vocal all the while. The doctor would not answer a single question until he'd seen the wound.

"Well?" Mrs. Greenlowe tried as soon as he stepped away. "What happens to him now?"

"He's not a well man," the doctor explained. "I'm not sure where he'll end up, but it probably won't be Tucker Mills."

"Where is Reese?" Conner finally asked. He had remained quiet throughout the conversation, but when Reese still hadn't made an appearance, he couldn't remain so.

"She's in the parlor. Fell asleep in one corner of the sofa. She told me her story and went right to sleep."

Conner didn't even hesitate but went that way. There was a candle burning on a table nearby, and Conner took the liberty of pulling a chair up close.

"Reese?" he called. "Are you all right?"

When she didn't stir in the least, Conner just sat and looked at her. A thick strand of hair had fallen over one cheek, and Conner gently pushed it back. There was a quilt over her, but it had slipped down her shoulders a bit, so Conner pulled it back in place. After watching her for a few more minutes and thinking she looked very young, he tried waking her a few more times, but she was sound asleep. He was on the verge of heading back to the kitchen when Doc MacKay came in.

"Is she all right?"

"I don't know. I think I finally figured out what wears her down."

The doctor brought the candle closer and checked on her color. He also touched the skin of her face and her wrist.

"Worn out," was the doctor's prognosis before both men went back to the kitchen.

"Thank you, Mrs. Greenlowe," Conner said. "Please tell Reese not to come in the morning if she's not up to it."

"I'll tell her, but you know what's going to happen. She'll come out of that bed like she's never worked a day in her life!"

The men had to smile at her. She just had that effect.

"Go on with you!" Mrs. Greenlowe said as she came to her feet. "Wait a minute." She changed her mind. "I've got some baked goods to send with you. Just bring my baskets back sometime."

They watched as she nearly filled two baskets, but she had more words for Conner when she handed them out.

"I gave the doc more. You've got Reese to cook and bake for you."

The men thanked her, keeping as sober as they could manage when both wanted to laugh out loud.

Had they known it, they could have laughed. As soon as they left, Mrs. Greenlowe did some chuckling of her own. Just thinking about Conner Kingsley falling for her Reese made her want to dance and sing.

❧❧❧

It didn't even take until noon on Saturday for every house and business on the green to know about Mr. Jenness' actions.

The Jenness house was not on the green, but Lillie heard nonetheless. And what was worse, Gerald heard as well. He had come home and confronted his mother, who had already spoken to the sheriff the night before, and she had no choice but to confirm the report.

"Why is he in jail? I don't understand." Gerald sounded as distraught as he looked.

"He went to Mrs. Greenlowe's looking for Reese, and Mrs. Greenlowe ended up hurt. He then went to the big house and threatened Conner Kingsley with a knife."

"He wouldn't hurt Reese. I'm sure of it."

"Gerald," his mother said as she tried to stay calm. "We don't know what your father was thinking. He's not himself right now."

"I heard him," Gerald confessed. "I know he wants his bank back. He's the best banker Tucker Mills has ever had. I heard him tell you."

Lillie's eyes closed for a moment. She had not known about this.

"Listen to me, Gerald. Your father is a good banker, but all of us must understand our place. The bank doesn't belong to him. It never did. And he could have gone on as bank manager if he hadn't panicked and run away."

"But they were trying to take it! Don't you understand?"

"No, Gerald, they weren't!" Lillie said just as sharply. "Everything was fine until your father made that dreadful decision to keep Reese Thackery's papers. If he had just let that go, he would still be bank manager."

Gerald stared at her. "How do you know this?"

"Because I've had several conversations with Mr. Thaden, and they found nothing amiss. They were not trying to take the bank, just rectify this situation with Reese and make sure all else was in order. Your father overreacted."

Gerald sat down slowly. He had been so certain that Conner Kingsley and his partner had been in the wrong. He was ready to forgive Reese for working for them because she'd clearly been duped like everyone else. And here all along it was his father. He had been on the lookout, watching for his father, ready to help in any way he could, and his father was the problem.

Looking at his mother's sober face, he saw what a young fool he had been. It wasn't any wonder that Reese didn't want anything to do with him.

"Gerald," his mother called to him. "When things settle down, we're going to sell the house and move to Boston."

"Sell the house? What about Father? We can't leave him behind."

"He won't be here, Gerald. I'm not sure where he'll end up, but he won't be free to walk the streets for some time."

"He went off the edge, didn't he?" Gerald made himself face the hard truth.

"Yes, he did. I don't think he'll be like that forever, but until he calms down about the bank, he can't be out."

Gerald put his face in his hands, looking younger than ever. She was not a demonstrative person, but Lillie would have given much to hug him right then.

"Can you sell the house without Father?"

"Yes, it's my house, a gift from my parents when we moved here."

Gerald nodded. "Let's move." His voice sounded broken and crushed. "As soon as we can."

Lillie almost broke down then, and Gerald saw this. Not until he came close, sitting on the floor at her feet and putting his head in her lap—something he hadn't done in years—did she let the tears flow.

∞

A lot of color drained from Troy's face when he returned to Tucker Mills on Monday afternoon and heard Conner's account of Friday evening. The older man sat in stunned silence, shaken and alarmed that both Conner and Reese had been in danger.

"If Mrs. Greenlowe heard correctly, he was after all three of us," Conner concluded.

"Do you remember the night you came to my room, Conner, and mentioned this possibility?"

Conner nodded.

"I hadn't dismissed the suggestion, but neither did I know what to do about it. I thought it easily could have been Gerald in the barn and half-expected Jenness to fade away. I felt sorry for his wife and son that they would not know what became of him."

Conner didn't comment. The whole episode kept playing through in his mind. He was weary of thinking about it, but the whole sordid scene wouldn't go away.

"Where is Reese?" Troy asked.

"I'm not sure. Probably the kitchen or buttery. Listen for humming."

Troy left the study to look for her. He found her just across the hall in the kitchen, putting food together for their tea and just about to leave.

"Troy," Reese smiled with pleasure. "Welcome back."

Troy didn't speak but went right to her. With hands on her shoulders, he looked her in the eye.

"I don't want anything to happen to you."

Reese gave him a small smile and then grinned in pleasant surprise when Troy hugged her. Reese hugged him right back, suddenly very glad that he'd come home.

∞

The cold of October did not stop the courtship of a certain couple as they walked on the green each day after dinner. Not a person in town could miss them, both tall and Conner broad as well. With unabashed delight, folks all up and down the green would stop and stare as they passed by, everyone agreeing they made the perfect couple.

Conner had already come to this understanding, but he didn't want to assume where Reese's feelings were concerned, so he was still moving slowly, gaining more information every day.

"I realized something just yesterday after you left," Conner mentioned on their fourth walk.

"What's that?" Reese asked.

"I don't know how old you are."

"I'm 23. How old are you?"

"Twenty-seven. When will you be 24?"

"I just turned 23."

"A few months ago?"

"No, last week."

Conner looked down at her. "Did you celebrate with Mrs. Greenlowe?"

"No."

"Did you celebrate with anyone? Did anyone know?"

"I've never celebrated my birthday. I guess I just didn't think to mention it."

It was happening again. A fierce desire to love and protect her overwhelmed him. At the same time, Conner was thinking who he could ask about this. Both Alison Muldoon and Mrs. Greenlowe came to mind. It would be so simple to have a party and give Reese a long-needed, albeit late, celebration.

This idea was still running through Conner's head when they arrived back at the house. And he probably would have acted on it immediately, but a coach had parked in front of the house. Conner wasn't certain, but he thought it looked like one of his brother's coaches. He held the front door for Reese to go inside and found Troy waiting for him, a letter in hand.

⬦⬦

"Any more word from Conner?" Douglas asked of Troy when he stopped in to the bank. Conner had been gone for almost a week.

"Nothing since he left, but I haven't checked for mail today."

"Might that mean that Jamie is doing better?" Douglas asked.

"I'm hoping that's what it means."

"I wrote to him but just mailed the letter, so he wouldn't have it yet," Douglas mentioned.

"It's hard not to know," Troy confessed. "If Mr. Leffler was comfortable handling things, I would probably head to Linden Heights myself."

Douglas nodded in agreement. This was the moment when trust was tested. This was when a man found out who he really was and whether he truly believed the words that were so easy to quote concerning faith and trusting in God.

"I'll keep praying for all of you," Douglas said finally and rose to leave.

Troy stood to see him off, his handshake warm and word of thanks completely heartfelt.

Linden Heights

"Are you going to wake up and talk to me?"

"Uncle Conner?" Jamie smiled a little, eyes still closed.

"How did you know?"

"I know that whisper."

"Whisper? Couldn't you hear me shouting?"

Jamie's smile widened, and when her too-thin hand moved on the coverlet, Conner reached for it.

The little girl held his hand in return and fell back to sleep. Conner waited a moment longer to let go of her hand, but he didn't move from her side. It looked as though she was out of the woods, but this had been a close one. Conner wanted to be near her as long as he could.

Tucker Mills

"Could I be in love?" Reese asked of Alison. She still wanted to get some things done at the big house this afternoon but could not make herself concentrate.

Alison looked at her guest and told herself not to laugh. She had never seen Reese like this. Reese was levelheaded and hardworking. But since Conner left she'd been slightly distracted, and this was the third time she'd come over in the middle of the day.

Alison believed that everyone needed a break, but Reese usually didn't take one. Able to work through the day, she barely stopped to eat.

"What do you think?" Alison asked, knowing she was skirting the issue a bit.

"I think he could do better than me," Reese surprised Alison by saying.

"What do you mean?" Alison asked, wishing she'd gone a different direction with her questions.

Reese was forming an answer when Martin and Peter shot in the door. Alison had not been expecting them just then, and the noise made Jeffrey cry. In just a matter of seconds, everyone but Douglas was in the kitchen, and before Alison could object, Reese said that she'd talk to her later and slipped through the parlor.

Reese wasn't at all upset about not finishing her conversation with Alison. Indeed she barely noticed. What was on her mind was the fact that she had just realized that Conner Kingsley could do better than Reese Thackery for a wife.

Oh, Reese knew that no one would care for him as much as she did. That wasn't possible, but what did she have to offer? Not a thing. She wasn't even very old in her beliefs and probably could never challenge him the way a more mature believer could.

Reese gave her head a shake. *Snap out of it. What's the matter with you? For all you know he'll never be back in Tucker Mills. And while you're taking all this time thinking about yourself, you could be praying for his niece.*

Reese all but slammed in through the front door, completely

disgusted with herself. Conner needed her prayers right now, not her plans to snag him for a husband or her self-pity when she knew a romance wasn't going to work.

"Conner!" Reese suddenly exclaimed. She'd stormed her way to the kitchen to get back to work and found him there.

"I wondered where you were," he said, smiling at the sight of her and working to control the urge to touch her.

"I just stepped over to see Alison. I'll get right back to work."

Not having a clue what he had missed, Conner watched Reese pick up the broom.

"I feel the need to tell you that I slacked off a bit while you were gone." She said this with her back to Conner, as he watched her sweep like a madwoman. "I'll make it up though. I don't know what came over me," Reese finished, flustered around him for the first time in a long time.

Clearly Reese was upset about something. He thought she would be as glad to see him as he was her, but when he stepped forward to ask that, she was using the broom to get at a place in the corner and suddenly jabbed it backward.

Reese, completely unconscious of what she'd done, noticed only that Conner had slipped from the room without saying a word. Reese came to a complete halt as she heard the front door open and close. Whatever dreams she'd been harboring about a life with Conner Kingsley had clearly been in her mind alone.

∞

"Where's Dooner?" Conner asked of the child that opened the door to him. That little boy had never seen Conner so solemn. He politely stood back, bringing the door with him, and pointed to his father's study.

Conner stopped short of barging in and impatiently knocked. He was told to enter, and still working to breathe, he slipped inside.

"Conner, welcome back."

Conner could only nod.

"What's the matter?"

Conner held a hand up, taking some big gulps of air.

"Is it Jamie? Is she all right?"

Conner nodded and stood, his hand against the wall. Dooner stopped asking questions and waited.

"I tried to talk to Reese," he managed, quieter and more strained than Douglas had ever heard him.

"All right."

"She hit me with the broom."

Had Conner been in any shape to laugh, Douglas' face would have provided the material. Conner shook his head and tried again.

"I was behind her. The end of the broom poked me."

When Douglas' shoulders began to shake, Conner knew he'd been understood, but it didn't make it any easier. The huge man rolled his eyes and lowered himself into a chair.

"You're a big help," he managed, and Douglas laughed out loud.

"I'm sorry, Conner, but I didn't know what to think."

"That's the problem." He was still breathing heavily. "I'm sure Reese is in the same state."

"Just explain," Douglas began and then stopped when Conner looked at him.

"Please go see her," Conner requested, his face looking miserable. "Find a way to make her understand."

"That you wanted to talk to her, but it had to wait a few minutes?"

Conner nodded, weary from the days at home, weary from the train travel, and weary that he and Reese had not been able to pick right up where they'd left off.

Douglas read much of this in his face and wanted nothing more than to help.

"Stay here," the pastor said. "I'll tell Alison where I'll be, and I'll come back to you as soon as I'm done."

Conner thanked him and thought if he could get any more comfortable in the chair, he might fall asleep.

❧

"Hello, Douglas," Reese greeted when she answered the door. "Conner isn't here right now. He left and didn't say where he was going."

"That's why I'm here," Douglas stepped inside, planning to keep this short. Indeed, not wanting to give a wrong impression, Douglas did not even shut the door behind him. "He came to see me," Douglas began delicately. "He planned on talking to you when he got home, and then words just failed him."

Reese frowned a little and then she understood.

"He's sent you to tell me that he's given me the wrong impression, hasn't he?"

"No. He has things he wants to say, but just for a few moments earlier, he couldn't find the words."

Reese nodded, working to understand.

"I didn't give him much of a chance, either," Reese recalled. "I hope he's not upset with me."

"Not at all, but he might just need to take a little time to say what he's thinking. He was so flustered over not having the words that he asked me to speak to you."

Reese smiled at her pastor.

"That was kind of you, Douglas. I know you have better things to do."

"For you and Conner, anything."

Thankful that it went so smoothly, Douglas was gone just seconds later, and Reese made herself keep working. It was, however, halfhearted; she didn't want to make too much noise and miss the sound of the front door opening.

Twenty-One

Reese thought she'd done a good job listening, but it wasn't so. She walked into the study about 30 minutes after Douglas' visit to find Conner at the desk.

"I didn't hear you," Reese said, feeling a little embarrassed.

"I didn't want to disturb you," Conner began, standing to go around the desk toward her. "I shouldn't have taken you by surprise in the kitchen."

"That wasn't your fault."

"Well, we'll debate that another time. Right now, I have something for you. If you want it."

Reese looked surprised by this, and although she was suddenly tempted to start talking, she kept still. As she watched, Conner went to the chair in the corner and picked up a long brown winter coat.

"My niece went through some growth changes this last year," Conner began, the coat over his arm. "She's almost as tall as you are, but in just one year she filled out and can't wear this coat. She wanted you to have it."

"How does she know about me?"

"Dalton."

A silent "oh" formed on Reese's mouth, but no sound was made. Conner held the coat up, and all Reese could do was stare at it. She'd never seen anything like it: The cut and tailoring were perfect. And it had buttons!

"Do you want to try it on?" Conner asked, watching her over the top.

"I've never seen a coat like this," she whispered. "It's beautiful."

"It's also yours."

"Will your niece want it back?"

"No. It's not going to fit her again."

Conner held it in such a way that Reese was able to put her arms into it. He turned her to him and adjusted the collar at her throat. Reese looked up at him.

"Thank you."

"That's what my niece said. She was excited for you to have it."

Conner kept a gentle hold of the collar, and Reese still looked up at him.

"I wasn't able to say this before, but being gone for more than two weeks let me do a lot of thinking."

Reese nodded.

"I want you to know that I'll never play games with your heart, and that our walks and talks on the green are the highlight of my day."

Reese smiled and looked down, suddenly shy.

"I've missed them," she said quietly. "Every day, I've missed them."

The urge to slip his arms around her almost got the best of him. He was rescued by the sound of the front door.

"That'll be Troy."

"Speaking of Troy," Reese suddenly mentioned, "I think they've all plotted against us."

"If you mean Troy and Dalton both, you couldn't be more right."

Reese could not stop looking at him.

"I didn't know you would be here," Conner confessed in the silence that followed. "I came to Tucker Mills to help a woman whose papers were controlled by the bank. No one said anything about her brown eyes or her beautiful red hair. And no one mentioned that she could run a household without a backward glance or that her nose was round like a child's and so adorable that I've had to fight kissing it almost from the first moment we met."

Reese bit her lip, but the smile peeked through. Troy chose that moment to come to the study door.

"What's this?" he asked with satisfaction. "A new coat?"

"Helena couldn't wear it anymore and sent it for Reese."

"Very stylish," Troy approved. "You'll be the envy of the green."

"Always my goal," Reese teased back.

"Did I interrupt something?" Troy asked next, his attempt at innocence not working.

"It would give you way too much pleasure if I said yes," Conner replied.

"Come now, Conner, you know Dalton expects me to report."

Conner had to laugh at this, and Reese took that opportunity to slip away. She went out into the hall where a large mirror hung. She stood in front of it and stared at her reflection without really seeing it. Had it actually just been a few hours ago that she was discouraged, her emotions running away concerning Conner? Seeing him had changed all of that.

Reese finally looked at herself in the glass, noticing that the brown of the coat made her eyes seem darker and more vivid. Reese then remembered what Conner had said about her nose. A smile lit her face as she turned away, unaware that Conner had come to the door to watch her and that his contented smile matched her own.

∞

"All right." Troy had waited only for Reese to leave for the day to find Conner and have a few words. "No teasing, no reporting to Dalton—just talk."

"All right," Conner agreed. "Talk about what?"

"You and Reese," Troy stated plainly. "I can see what's happening between the two of you, and I know you're not talking to anyone, so that begs the question: Is Reese talking to anyone? Much as I think the two of you are perfectly suited for each other, you both need to seek counsel on this."

"You're right, Troy," Conner agreed humbly. "You may ask me anything, and when I see Reese again, I'll make sure she's talking to someone as well."

"I think she would do well with several different people in town, but that's the father in me wanting to take care of her."

"I'll tell her you're available too," Conner said, and Troy could only nod. He wanted so much for these two young people. He wanted their lives to be built in Christ, and around each other and the church family. Suddenly he missed his wife so much that longing filled him.

"Are you all right?" Conner asked.

"Just missing Ivy."

"It would be impossible not to miss her. I wish Reese could have known her."

"She would be pleased to hear you say that, and I know she would have loved Reese."

The men saw that the conversation had taken a turn, a serious one, but they both knew that sometimes such sessions were needed. They never did get back to the topic of Conner and Reese that night, but spent time talking about Troy's late wife and both of their families. Come bedtime, the men were weary.

∞

The long walks, Reese warm in her new coat, continued. Unless it was raining, the townsfolk once again saw their favorite couple walking, sometimes hand in hand, down the green, conversing all the while. At times people would stop them and visit, but for the most part they were left on their own.

One lady, however, came with a purpose. She had something to say to Reese Thackery and wasn't going to leave town until she did.

"Reese," Lillie Jenness called to stop her one day in early November.

"Hello, Mrs. Jenness," Reese greeted, coming to face the other woman.

"You might have heard, but I'm leaving Tucker Mills. My house is sold, and Gerald and I are leaving."

"I did hear," Reese was careful to say, seeing that the lady before her didn't look overly happy.

"I didn't want to leave before I told you that I could have treated you better."

Reese blinked with surprise.

"It wasn't your fault you were sent to my house, and you worked without a word of complaint. You never encouraged my Gerald, who we both know is too young for you."

Reese nodded, not sure what to say.

"I'm sorry, Reese." Lillie's voice dropped a bit. "Victor should never have kept those papers, and since he'll not say the words, I'm saying them for him."

"Thank you, Mrs. Jenness. I appreciate that. Is Mr. Jenness settled in right now?"

"Yes. The doctors at the Massachusetts Mental Health Institute have agreed to accept him. He'll be there for at least a year. Gerald and I will be in Boston, and we can visit."

"Thank you for telling me, Mrs. Jenness. I hope all of you, but especially you and Gerald, will be well."

Mrs. Jenness nodded, looking pleased for the first time, before turning and going on her way.

Reese turned back to Conner, who held an arm out to her. She took it, and he spoke as he started them back down the green.

"That was a pleasant surprise."

"Wasn't it?" Reese still sounded shocked.

"Glad to have it behind you?"

"More than I can say," Reese said quietly, finding it to be very true.

"I want to be able to pray for Maddie's baby," Cathy suddenly confessed to Doyle one morning before he could leave to open the store.

"I can understand that, but there are other things to cover first."

"Like my belief," Cathy said, knowing what he meant.

"Is it getting any clearer?" Doyle asked kindly.

"Some days."

Doyle came back from the door and put his hands on her shoulders.

"I won't ever give up on you. You're too smart not to see what God has done for you, and I'll still be beside you when you realize you have to have His gift."

Cathy put her arms around him and hugged him close. Doyle went out the door a few minutes later than he planned, still praying for his wife's heart.

"Has he asked you to marry him?" Doc MacKay asked Reese when she stopped by his house in mid-December, having taken Troy's advice about meeting with someone. He was like a father to her, and for that reason she had come to him each week.

"No, and I don't want him to until you think I'll be all right."

"What do you think might be missing?"

"He's from a wealthy family and a big city. Right now he might be blinded by his feelings. Down the road, I don't ever want to be an embarrassment to him."

"Dalton didn't seem to think that would be an issue, and neither does Troy, but that's not what I want you to find comfort in.

Your worth is in Christ, and you've let that slip from your mind. You are the delight of this town. It's a rare soul that doesn't think the world of you, so none of us are surprised that Conner has fallen, but that's still not to be your security.

"You are died for, your sins paid for by the very blood of Christ. And you have chosen to take that seriously by listening to others who know more, being a student of the Scripture, and changing because of your fear and humility before God.

"Don't accept peace from any other source, Reese. You know how to keep a house and cook and bake. The new part in your life will be that of being a godly wife, and you're already off to a fine start. Conner's faith is just as real as your own, and between the two of you, you'll help each other to be all God wants you to be."

The weight Reese had been carrying around on this issue lifted. She didn't know where the fear had come from but knew Doc MacKay would have wise words on this topic. And because he'd taken her right back to her salvation and truth based in Scripture, he didn't have to convince her that his opinion was right.

The conversation turned to other topics about marriage during the next hour, before Reese had to get back to work. As always, Doc MacKay gave her a warm hug when she left. Remembering the things he said, and wanting still more changes in her heart and life, Reese was confident that God would bring it to pass.

⚬⚬⚬

Conner was at Shephard Store. He'd gone in for some personal effects but ended up glancing around. That's when he spotted the fabric. It was paisley with a background of dark green, and a brown and gold print. It was elegant fabric, and he was certain it would be beautiful on Reese.

"May I help you, Mr. Kingsley?" Doyle came over to ask.

"Hello, Mr. Shephard. I was noticing this fabric." Conner reached up and touched it, and Doyle brought the bolt down. It was even more beautiful up close.

"How much would you recommend for a woman's dress?"

"A tall woman?" Doyle asked with a smile, wringing one from Conner.

"As a matter of fact, yes—not overly big around, but quite tall."

Doyle did the measuring and cutting, even wrapping it in brown paper because Conner Kingsley was not a man who shopped with a basket. The rest of his needs were also put into brown paper, and Conner settled his bill before he left.

He walked home, trying to figure out how he could best present the fabric to Reese. Anyone who happened to notice his slow progress down the green guessed him to be a man with something on his mind.

∞

"I have a little dilemma," Conner confessed to Reese a few days after Christmas.

"Just a little one?" she teased. "That's good news."

"I don't know about that," he teased back. "You see, I'm in love with you, and I'd like to ask you to marry me, but I have a rule. I can't ask any woman to marry me when I don't know her middle name."

Reese smiled into his eyes but said, "You'll change your mind about asking."

"Try me."

With a roll of those dark brown eyes, Reese admitted, "Valentina."

Conner smiled. "Charisse Valentina. It's a beautiful name. Unusual, but beautiful."

"Now I know you're in love."

"Why is that?"

"You've been robbed of your good sense."

Conner didn't keep his distance any longer. He'd been leaning in the doorway of the small parlor and now came to where Reese stood by the small table she'd been dusting. He took her face in his hands, looked down into her eyes, asked her to marry him, and bent to kiss her.

After a moment, he asked, "Did you answer my question?"

"I don't think I did out loud, but in my heart I said yes."

"Oh, I almost forgot," Conner suddenly said, releasing Reese and going into another room. He returned with a package.

"I found something for you."

Reese's response when she tore back the paper and saw the fabric was priceless to Conner.

"Oh, Conner," she whispered, which was nothing new in Conner's presence, but this time it was out of delight. "I've seen this at the store. It's so pretty."

Conner didn't say anything but continued to watch her.

"I could wear this when we get married," Reese suddenly realized. "I could have a new dress for that day."

Conner was almost too pleased to speak.

"When are we getting married?" she suddenly asked, hoping it wasn't too good to be true.

"How long will it take you to make the dress?"

Laughing in unabashed pleasure, Reese threw her arms around him. Conner hugged her right back, his heart dreaming of the day he could make this woman his wife. They could have stood and hugged all day, but they were too excited for that. They had to find Troy and Doc. This news had to be shared.

❦

"You would think *we* were getting married," Alison confided in her husband as they all made their way to the big house on Sunday afternoon, January 26, 1840. "I'm that excited."

Douglas smiled at her, excited himself. He had talked with both Conner and Reese at length two weeks ago and was extremely pleased by the things they had shared and talked about.

He warned them that marriage was serious but also a one-of-a-kind experience for those who are anchored in Christ. Without a qualm, Douglas had agreed to marry them. Today was the day.

∞

"Thank you for everything," Reese said to Mrs. Greenlowe, hugging her again.

"I didn't do anything," that woman protested, and Reese only smiled at her.

She was the last to leave. Troy was making himself scarce for a few days, and the couple planned to go to Linden Heights the following weekend, but for the first time that day they were alone in the house.

Conner shut the door and turned to find Reese watching him. He walked slowly toward her.

"It was a wonderful wedding," he said.

"Yes, it was. And the ladies cleaned everything up."

"You look amazing in that dress, by the way."

"Do you think so?" Reese teased. "A very handsome, distinguished gentleman picked it out for me."

"Shall I tell you a secret?" he asked as he finished covering the distance between them and slipped his arms around her.

"Yes."

"I love beautifully wrapped presents."

A small laugh escaped Reese just before they kissed. And Conner, living out an image he'd had in his mind since asking Reese to marry him, lifted his wife in his arms and carried her up the stairs to their room.

Epilogue

Reese Kingsley stopped the sleigh in the yard at the Randall farmhouse in mid-February, smiling when Jace came to meet her.

"Congratulations!" Reese cried as she gave Jace a hug.

"Oh, Reese, you should see her. She's so tiny and perfect."

Reese smiled, reached for the gift in the back of the sleigh, and took Jace's arm to make it through the snow and to the kitchen door. She slipped inside, knowing the way upstairs, and went quietly that direction.

"Maddie," she whispered at the bedroom door she found open, but Maddie seemed to be asleep. Reese went quietly into the lovely room, spotting the cradle in the corner, the very one Mr. Zantow had made. It was hung with a beautiful quilt and soft-looking sheeting.

"Oh, Reese." Maddie had woken and spotted her. "Come over and meet our daughter," she invited, holding the baby in the curve of her arm.

"Oh, my," was all Reese could say for the first few minutes. Before her was a rosy-cheeked infant, just three days old. She had a head full of dark hair and hands so tiny and perfect that Reese was afraid to touch her.

"What's her name?"

"Valerie."

Reese laughed with pleasure. "Hello, Valerie. I'm so glad to meet you."

"Do you want to hold her?"

"Yes. She'll be a change after Jeffrey, who's already so big."

While the exchange was being made, Jace had time to join them. The pride and pleasure on his face was contagious. He and Maddie kept smiling at each other and then at their daughter.

"I'm so happy for you," Reese said, staring down into that enchanting, tiny face.

"She's a good eater," Maddie confirmed, "and her cry is so tiny."

"But we hear her," Jace put in dryly. "She makes sure of that."

Reese looked up at them. "It's amazing, isn't it? I mean, such a miracle."

Both Jace and Maddie were still in shock.

"What do Doyle and Cathy think?"

"They can't stop crying," Maddie said. "Both of them are so emotional over her."

"And I wrote my sister," Jace put in. "I'm sure she'll be on the weekend train."

"She's in for a treat," Reese said, her eyes still on the baby in her arms. She was filled with the most unexplainable emotion at that moment, and much as she wanted to stay and hold the baby all day, she was glad it was time to leave after they'd visited for nearly an hour.

The sleigh took her back toward town, and Reese was glad the day was running away fast. She wanted to be with Conner, and she wanted to be near him right now. She let herself back into the house, glad the bank would be closing soon.

∞

"What did they name her?" Troy asked over tea that evening.

"Valerie."

"That's a pretty name. It's nice with Randall."

"And Maddie?" Conner asked. "Is she doing well?"

"She looks wonderful. I think she'll be up and around in no time."

"I don't even have to guess about Jace. He must be pretty excited."

"You should see his face," Reese told them, smiling at the thought.

In fact she was still thinking about it in bed that night. With the Argand lamp burning on the bedside table, Conner looked over to find that his wife had a thoughtful look in her eyes.

"Did you tell Maddie your suspicions?" Conner asked.

"No," she answered, smiling a little. "I didn't want to detract from her news, and we're not sure yet."

Conner gave her that skeptical look that she loved. Reese rolled toward him and looked into his eyes.

"You don't know, Conner . . . not for sure."

Conner kissed her nose.

"You might as well face facts, Reese Kingsley. You're going to have a baby nine months from when we were married. It's just like that for some couples."

"People will think the worst."

"Not people who know us, and that's who really matters. If we had been trying to do something we shouldn't, why did we court on the green, walking in the freezing cold for all the village to see? I didn't make you my wife in that way until after the vows were said, and God knows that."

"I like being your wife," she said as she smiled into his eyes.

Conner didn't say anything.

"You're supposed to return the compliment," she teased him.

But Conner was still quiet, and Reese misunderstood. "Is this one of those times when words come hard?" she asked compassionately.

"What are you talking about?" Conner frowned in confusion.

"Douglas told me. Right after you returned from Linden

Heights, he came and said you wanted to talk to me but couldn't find the words."

Conner began to laugh and could not stop. His wife watched in confusion, a bemused smile on her face. It took some time, but eventually he was able to explain. Reese's mouth opened.

"I did that? I poked you with the broom handle?"

"Yes." Conner was still chuckling. "Our relationship at that time was not to a point of being able to explain it to you."

"I'm sorry, Conner," she said contritely. "I had no idea."

"It was probably for the best."

"Why do you say that?"

Conner had no trouble thinking back. "When I saw you in the kitchen that day, the only thing on my mind was telling you that I was back to marry you, and the sooner the better."

"I wouldn't have minded," Reese confessed, and Conner took that as an invitation. He began to kiss her, but Reese was distracted.

"We'd better start thinking of names for the baby."

"I can't," Conner barely got out, pretending that his voice was going.

"Is that right?" Reese was not fooled.

Conner touched his throat as though it would no longer work, and Reese, always delighted with him, laughed and slipped her arms around his neck. He was right: Names for the baby could wait.

Glossary

This glossary holds reminders from the first book, plus a few new ones. Enjoy!

- **Argand lamps:** I'm sorry this entry didn't make it into the first book. Ami Argand was born in Switzerland in 1755. In 1784, he patented an oil lamp with a circular wick. This wick allowed air to all parts of the flame and made for more efficient burning.

- **bank notes:** coins were hard to come by at this time, so banks printed their own paper notes and folks used them for debts and purchases, treating them like real money.

- **bells:** New England towns had their own system for announcing when someone died—nine bells for a man, six for a woman, and three for a child, and then a bell for each year the person was alive.

- **buttery:** pronounced but'ry, it's a room where dairy goods are worked into various products, cheese and butter making for example.

- **celebrating Christmas:** the influence of the Puritans was still very strong at this time, and they were against the celebration of Christmas.

- **deep in his cups:** drunk.

- **dinner:** the noon meal, always a full-blown affair.

ॐ **donsie:** I've loved this word ever since I heard it on an *I Love Lucy* episode. I'm using it as Lucy did: slightly ill.

ॐ **green:** also called the center or common, it's the middle of town—a grass area where homes and shops sit in a square or rectangle. I know of one in Connecticut that's a mile long.

ॐ **hard cider:** fermented apple juice.

ॐ **laying out:** preparing a body for burial, usually done by family or neighbors.

ॐ **meetinghouse:** a building for public assembly, including the church on Sunday.

ॐ **millpond:** the pond of water that feeds the mill and is fed by spring thaw, or in the case of Tucker Mills, by a huge river that doesn't run dry in summer.

ॐ **parlor** or **sitting room:** where people sat in the evening, entertained visitors, and unless the house was very large, ate their meals. The table in the kitchen was mostly for work and not for eating.

ॐ **pins:** straight pins were often used to hold dresses on. Buttonholes were a lot of work, and women avoided making them.

ॐ **tea:** also called snack—this was the evening meal, which used leftovers from dinner.

ॐ **theocentric** and **theocentricity:** I cover the meaning of this in the book, but this entry is to tell you that technically I shouldn't be using it. My dictionary doesn't list this word until 1886, but I needed it to make my point.

ॐ **tin kitchen:** made of bright tin plate, the tin kitchen is a small roaster that sits by the fireplace and is for meats and poultry.

ॐ **whortleberry:** a European blueberry that's light bluish gray.

About
the Author

LORI WICK is one of the most versatile Christian fiction writers in the market today. Her works include pioneer fiction, two series set in England, and contemporary novels. Lori's books (more than 4 million copies in print) continue to delight readers and top the Christian bestselling fiction list. Lori and her husband, Bob, live in Wisconsin and are the parents of "the three coolest kids in the world."

Books by Lori Wick

A Place Called Home Series
A Place Called Home
A Song for Silas
The Long Road Home
A Gathering of Memories

The Californians
Whatever Tomorrow Brings
As Time Goes By
Sean Donovan
Donovan's Daughter

Kensington Chronicles
The Hawk and the Jewel
Wings of the Morning
Who Brings Forth the Wind
The Knight and the Dove

Rocky Mountain Memories
Where the Wild Rose Blooms
Whispers of Moonlight
To Know Her by Name
Promise Me Tomorrow

The Yellow Rose Trilogy
Every Little Thing About You
A Texas Sky
City Girl

English Garden Series
The Proposal
The Rescue
The Visitor
The Pursuit

The Tucker Mills Trilogy
Moonlight on the Millpond
Just Above a Whisper

Other Fiction
Sophie's Heart
Beyond the Picket Fence
Pretense
The Princess
Bamboo & Lace
Every Storm